Books Can Be Deceiving

"A sparkling setting, lovely characters, books, knitting, and chowder! What more could any reader ask?"
—Lorna Barrett, *New York Times* bestselling author of *Sentenced to Death* and the Booktown Mysteries

"With a remote coastal setting as memorable as Manderley and a kindhearted, loyal librarian as the novel's heroine, *Books Can Be Deceiving* is sure to charm cozy readers everywhere."
—Ellery Adams, author of the Books by the Bay Mysteries

"Fast-paced and fun, *Books Can Be Deceiving* is the first in Jenn McKinlay's appealing new mystery series featuring an endearing protagonist, delightful characters, a lovely New England setting, and a fascinating murder. Don't miss this charming new addition to the world of traditional mysteries."
—Kate Carlisle, author of the Bibliophile Mysteries

PRAISE FOR
JENN MCKINLAY'S CUPCAKE BAKERY MYSTERIES

Buttercream Bump Off

"A charmingly entertaining story paired with a luscious assortment of cupcake recipes that, when combined, made for a deliciously thrilling mystery." —*Fresh Fiction*

"Another tasty entry, complete with cupcake recipes, into what is sure to grow into a perennial favorite series."
—*The Mystery Reader*

"McKinlay's descriptions of the cupcakes in Mel and Angie's shop are guaranteed to make the reader salivate—fortunately, the recipes are included in the back of the book. Engaging characters, hilarious situations, old movie quotes, and, oh yes, a dead body in a hot tub make this a great read." —*RT Book Reviews*

continued . . .

Sprinkle with Murder

"A tender cozy full of warm and likable characters and a refreshingly sympathetic murder victim. Readers will look forward to more of McKinlay's tasty concoctions."

—*Publishers Weekly* (starred review)

"*Sprinkle with Murder* is one of the better recent cozy debuts, and a few cupcake recipes in the back are, well, icing on the cake."
—*The Mystery Reader*

"McKinlay's debut mystery flows as smoothly as Melanie Cooper's buttercream frosting. Her characters are delicious, and the dash of romance is just the icing on the cake."

—Sheila Connolly, author of *Fire Engine Dead*

"Jenn McKinlay delivers all the ingredients for a winning read. Frost me another!"

—Cleo Coyle, national bestselling author of the Coffeehouse Mysteries

"A delicious new series featuring a spirited heroine, luscious cupcakes, and a clever murder. Jenn McKinlay has baked a sweet read." —Krista Davis, author of the Domestic Diva Mysteries

Berkley Prime Crime titles by Jenn McKinlay

Cupcake Bakery Mysteries

SPRINKLE WITH MURDER
BUTTERCREAM BUMP OFF
DEATH BY THE DOZEN

Library Lover's Mysteries

BOOKS CAN BE DECEIVING
DUE OR DIE

DUE OR DIE

Jenn McKinlay

BERKLEY PRIME CRIME, NEW YORK

THE BERKLEY PUBLISHING GROUP
Published by the Penguin Group
Penguin Group (USA) Inc.
375 Hudson Street, New York, New York 10014, USA

Penguin Group (Canada), 90 Eglinton Avenue East, Suite 700, Toronto, Ontario M4P 2Y3, Canada (a division of Pearson Penguin Canada Inc.) • Penguin Books Ltd., 80 Strand, London WC2R 0RL, England • Penguin Group Ireland, 25 St. Stephen's Green, Dublin 2, Ireland (a division of Penguin Books Ltd.) • Penguin Group (Australia), 250 Camberwell Road, Camberwell, Victoria 3124, Australia (a division of Pearson Australia Group Pty. Ltd.) • Penguin Books India Pvt. Ltd., 11 Community Centre, Panchsheel Park, New Delhi—110 017, India • Penguin Group (NZ), 67 Apollo Drive, Rosedale, Auckland 0632, New Zealand (a division of Pearson New Zealand Ltd.) • Penguin Books (South Africa) (Pty.) Ltd., 24 Sturdee Avenue, Rosebank, Johannesburg 2196, South Africa

Penguin Books Ltd., Registered Offices: 80 Strand, London WC2R 0RL, England

This is a work of fiction. Names, characters, places, and incidents either are the product of the author's imagination or are used fictitiously, and any resemblance to actual persons, living or dead, business establishments, events, or locales is entirely coincidental. The publisher does not have any control over and does not assume any responsibility for author or third-party websites or their content.

PUBLISHER'S NOTE: The recipes contained in this book are to be followed exactly as written. The publisher is not responsible for your specific health or allergy needs that may require medical supervision. The publisher is not responsible for any adverse reactions to the recipes contained in this book.

DUE OR DIE

A Berkley Prime Crime Book / published by arrangement with the author

PUBLISHING HISTORY
Berkley Prime Crime mass-market edition / March 2012

ISBN: 978-0-425-24668-9

BERKLEY® PRIME CRIME
Berkley Prime Crime Books are published by The Berkley Publishing Group,
a division of Penguin Group (USA) Inc.,
375 Hudson Street, New York, New York 10014.
BERKLEY® PRIME CRIME and the PRIME CRIME logo are trademarks of
Penguin Group (USA) Inc.

PRINTED IN THE UNITED STATES OF AMERICA

10 9 8 7 6 5 4 3 2 1

ALWAYS LEARNING   PEARSON

For my dudes, Wyatt and Beckett,
I'm so glad I get to be your mom.
I love you to infinity and back.

Acknowledgments

Your library is your paradise.

—DESIDERIUS ERASMUS

Writing is a very solitary venture. Hours are spent alone, hunched over a keyboard, creating a reality that becomes so absolute it's hard to remember that it's actually fiction. To that end, I tend to get lost in my manuscripts while I write them, so I need a talented and reliable crew to help me find my way out. I am fortunate to have such a team in Kate Seaver, my amazing editor; Katherine Pelz, her lovely editorial assistant; and Jessica Faust, my fabulous agent. Thank you, ladies, for always shining the light where I can see it.

Because I do judge books by their covers, I have to give my most awed thanks to Julia Green, the illustrator of this amazing cover, and Rita Frangie, the cover designer. Truly, it is a work of art. Brilliant!

Lastly, I want to acknowledge my family (the McKinlays and the Orfs) and my friends and fans, who have bought the books and shared the books and encouraged me every step of the way. Thank you!

"I could not believe that Lucy agreed to marry Cecil when she was so obviously in love with George," Violet La Rue declared.

Lindsey Norris glanced up from the lace scarf she was attempting to crochet. What had she been thinking when she thought she could do anything with this cobweb-like yarn? It was maddening.

Violet's crochet hook was swooping away, row after row, on a lace pillow cover that she was making for her niece, who was getting married in the spring. Violet was using a perle cotton thread that gave the star pattern a subtle luster when it caught the light just right. It was to be the ring bearer's pillow, and it was sure to be lovely.

"She was expected to marry within her station," Nancy Peyton said.

1

Nancy was Lindsey's landlord and had been teaching her a variety of needlecrafts for almost nine months now. Currently, their crafternoon club was working on crochet projects. It wasn't going well for Lindsey.

As if sensing her annoyance, Nancy put aside the handbag she was working on and took Lindsey's mangled sea foam green mohair and cotton cashmere skeins out of her hands and began to fix them. For that alone, Lindsey was pretty sure Nancy was setting herself up for sainthood.

Both women had about twenty years on Lindsey, and she tried not to take it personally that they could manage to have an in-depth discussion about E. M. Forster's *A Room with a View* and crochet at the same time.

"Don't tell me you've started already," Charlene said as she entered the room. "You always do that."

"That's because you're always late," Violet said.

"No, I'm not," Charlene argued. She took off her coat and hat and hung them on the rack. She glanced at the three women looking at her. "Am I?"

"Uh, yeah, you are," Lindsey said.

Charlene huffed out a breath. She was wearing a stunning red turtleneck sweater, which complemented the rich brown hue of her skin, over tailored black corduroys and black boots.

"Well, as Oscar Wilde said, 'He was always late on principle, his principle being that punctuality is the thief of time,'" Charlene said as she took the cushy seat beside Lindsey.

"Very clever, but you might want to go for 'better never than late,'" Violet said. "George Bernard Shaw."

Lindsey and Nancy glanced between the mother and

daughter. Charlene was the image of her mother, Violet; in other words, she was gorgeous, but even more than that, she shared her mother's formidable intelligence and love of literature.

Violet had been a stage actress in New York in her youth, while Charlene was currently a local newscaster in New Haven, but both women had the ability to command the attention of any room they entered. Lindsey figured it must be in their genetic code.

"Nicely played, Mom." Charlene laughed and Violet bowed her head in acknowledgment. "But I thought we were discussing E. M. Forster today. What have I missed?"

"Not much," Nancy said. Her blue eyes twinkled as she added, "Just Violet being testy because Lucy didn't go off with George right away."

"Not much of a book if Lucy picked the right man at the start," Charlene said. She pulled the ripple afghan she was working on out of her project bag. It was the perfect weather to work on a blanket, and hers was coming together nicely in rows of black, gray and country blue.

The small room boasted cushy chairs and a toasty fire in the gas fireplace. Recently, Lindsey had added a couple of short bookshelves where she kept extra copies of crafting books for the club to peruse during meetings.

The lone large window in the room looked out over the town park and offered a picturesque view of the bay beyond. Today the sea was a deep gray, reflecting the steely cold January skies that loomed above.

The crafternoon club met every Thursday in this small room in the Briar Creek Public Library, of which Lindsey was the director, to work on a craft, discuss their latest book and eat. This week it had been Lindsey's turn to provide the food, so she had baked apple cinnamon muffins, brought a large block of Brie with wheat crackers and made both coffee and tea.

"Who picked the right man at the start?" Beth Stanley asked from the doorway. She was dressed as a giant spider, and the other women watched as she turned sideways to fit her eight limbs, four of which were add-ons suspended by fishing wire from her arms, through the doorway.

"Here let me help you," Mary Murphy offered as she followed Beth into the room and held the back of Beth's story time costume so she could wiggle out of it.

"Thanks. I have a new respect for spiders," Beth said. "I had a heck of a time getting all my legs to go in the right direction while I read *Mrs. Spider's Tea Party* to the kids. I whacked poor Lily Dawson on the bum with one of them."

Lindsey exchanged a smile with Charlene. Beth was the children's librarian and the kids adored her. Mostly because she was a big kid herself. When she did the hokey pokey, her enthusiasm made everyone in the library feel the need to put their left foot in, as it were.

Beth hung her spider outfit on the coat rack by the door, which was already straining under the weight of all their winter coats and hats, and plopped into one of the available seats.

Mary hung up her coat as well, sat beside Beth and pulled out the tea cozy she was working on for her mother. It was white with retro aqua starbursts on it. She thought it would match her mother's vintage 1950s kitchen perfectly.

Mary was a native of Briar Creek and had grown up on one of the Thumb Islands out in the bay. Currently, she ran the Blue Anchor Café with her husband, Ian, and was known for making the best clam chowder in the state.

Her parents still lived out on Bell Island, and Lindsey wished she could see what their vintage kitchen looked like. As she watched the cozy take shape in Mary's skilled hands, Lindsey couldn't help but feel the teensiest bit jealous. She had a feeling if she attempted a tea cozy, it would turn out looking like a muffler for an elephant.

"How far have you gotten in the discussion?" Mary asked.

"Not very. We were talking about how short *A Room with a View* would have been if Lucy had picked the right man from the start," Lindsey said. She glanced at her watch. It was only fifteen minutes past the hour, which gave them plenty of time to finish their discussion. Being employees of the library, both Lindsey and Beth had to confine their crafternoon club time to their lunch hours.

Beth glanced around the group. "Well, I for one am relieved that she picked the clunker first and stayed with him. It made me feel like less of an idiot."

Violet reached over and patted Beth's knee in sympathy. "It happens to all of us, hon."

"Which is why sometimes it is easier to fall in love within the safety of a book," Nancy agreed.

"I hear that," Charlene said.

This was one of the many reasons Lindsey loved her crafternoon friends. They were made up of all different ages, ethnicities and socioeconomic backgrounds, but the one thing they had in common was a deep and abiding love of books. Yeah, basically, they were all nerds.

"Well, the only man I plan to date for a while is Austen's

Mr. Darcy," Beth said. "He always makes such a nice transitional man between boyfriends. Honestly, neither Cecil nor George is really doing it for me."

Beth had recently gotten out of an unfortunate relationship, and Lindsey was sure it had clouded her reading of the novel.

She knew her own recent breakup had changed her take on the story. Her former fiancé, John, had taken up with one of his graduate students while she was in the midst of being downsized from her archivist job. John was a law professor at Yale and he had never seemed the type to be interested in chasing the cute, young coed, but obviously a good education was no buffer against the male midlife crisis.

Lindsey knew she was better off without him, but still it chafed to be tossed aside after five years of thinking she had found the one, especially when her career had been on the skids as well. She shook her head, refusing to dwell in the past. She had a good job in a nice town where she was surrounded by friends. Where was the down?

"Here you are, dear." Nancy handed back Lindsey's scarf, and it was all perfectly tidy with the extra mohair rolled into a neat little ball. How very kind and annoying.

There was a sharp knock on the door frame, and Lindsey turned, expecting to see Ms. Cole, one of her crankier library employees, standing there with her usual scowl of disapproval, but, no, it was Carrie Rushton.

Carrie was a nurse at the local hospital and an über volunteer in the community of Briar Creek. She was on several boards and committees and always seemed to be busy doing something for someone.

"Hi, Lindsey, I hate to interrupt," she said. "But could I talk to you?"

"Absolutely." Happy to put her crochet aside so as to not risk tangling what Nancy had untangled, Lindsey carefully tucked it into her canvas tote bag.

She rose to her feet and crossed the room in a few strides. "What can I do for you?"

"Well." Carrie paused and bit her lip. It looked as if she was trying to decide what to say. "Could you come to our Friends of the Library meeting tonight?"

Carrie was wearing her hospital scrubs under her winter coat, so she was on her way either to or from work. Her long, dark brown hair was knotted at the nape of her neck and fastened into place by a large plastic hair clip. Streaks of gray were just beginning to show at her temples, while a hint of wrinkles had begun to form in the corners of her eyes.

Carrie was on the short side of medium in height, and her figure was gently rounded as if she had been built specifically for giving hugs. She had a maternal softness about her that Lindsey felt sure was one of the reasons she was such a popular nurse.

"Yes, I can make it," Lindsey said. "Any particular reason?"

Carrie let out a worried sigh. "We're having the vote tonight."

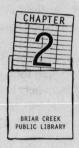

CHAPTER

2

BRIAR CREEK
PUBLIC LIBRARY

66 "Ah," Lindsey said. Now it was all coming into focus. "Bill Sint is still mad that you're running against him?"

"He called me a usurper," Carrie said. She turned her nose up in the air as she said it, and Lindsey could just see Bill saying it in the same snooty way.

"I suppose he could have called you worse," Lindsey said with a chuckle.

"The way he said it, it didn't sound like it could be much worse."

Lindsey patted her shoulder. "I'll be there to keep the peace. I promise. What time?"

"We're meeting in the lecture room at seven," Carrie said.

The library closed at eight, but Lindsey knew that

8

Jessica Gallo, the library assistant for the adult department, was scheduled to work, so the reference desk would be covered and she could attend the meeting.

"I'll see you—"

"Carrie, what is taking you so long?" a whiny voice interrupted. "I've been waiting for hours."

"Markus, we've only been here for five minutes," Carrie said over her shoulder. She turned back to Lindsey and said, "Sorry, he's overtired."

Lindsey raised her eyebrows in surprise. Carrie was apologizing for her husband, Markus Rushton, as if he were a toddler who had missed nap time.

She glanced over Carrie's shoulder and saw a middle-aged man, bundled from his thick boots and puffy purple coat up to his scarf-wrapped head, stomping his feet behind her as if he were contemplating throwing a tantrum.

"No problem, I'll . . ."

"Why do we have to be here anyway?" Markus interrupted her again. "Books are stupid. I mean who wants to waste their time reading when you can watch TV or surf the Net?"

"Excuse me," Lindsey said.

She glanced more closely at Markus and could just make out a beaky nose and a pair of eyes that were too close together. That was all the skin he had exposed. She bit back the suggestion that he take his scarf and go for a full head wrap, but just barely.

"Oh, you're *her*, the new librarian," he said. He looked her up and down. "I thought people said you were hot."

"Markus!" Carrie gasped, obviously horrified.

"What?" he asked. "The way everyone was talking about

her, I expected a little more *Baywatch* Pam Anderson and a little less old Meg Ryan."

Lindsey blinked at him. She had no idea what to say to this. Obviously, Markus found her lacking in the looks department, but she was hard pressed to think of that as a bad thing.

Lindsey pulled her gaze away from him and looked at Carrie. "About tonight, yes, I'll be there."

"Thanks," Carrie said.

"Yippity-do, can we go now?" Markus asked. "Sheesh, if you ask me, they should just sell all these old books and turn this building into someplace fun, like an arcade with mini golf. Now that would be cool."

He turned on his heel and stomped toward the exit as if expecting Carrie to follow on his heels like a faithful puppy.

Lindsey pressed her lips together to keep herself from saying what she was thinking, which would have blistered Markus Rushton even through the layers of his purple puffy coat.

"I'm so sorry," Carrie said. Her face flushed a deep shade of crimson. "He's not much of a reader."

Lindsey forced her lips to curve up. "That's all right, not everyone is a book person."

Carrie squeezed her hand in thanks and turned to go. "I'd better . . . I'll see you later."

"I'll be there," Lindsey said.

The group was silent when she sat back down in her seat. They must have heard. Lindsey blew out a breath, not knowing what to say.

"Mark Rushton is as stupid now as he was as a child," Nancy Peyton finally said. "He went from having his mama take care of him to having his wife take care of him. I hate to say it, but that man is a dreadful waste of space."

"Talk about picking the wrong guy," Charlene said. "Carrie is so nice, how did she hook up with him?"

"For exactly that reason," Mary Murphy said. "She is too nice. We all went to high school together and Mrs. Rushton asked Carrie if she would be Mark's prom date because no one else would go with him. Carrie said yes, and she hasn't been able to shake loose of him ever since."

"I heard he went on disability for a slipped disk in his back a few years ago and doesn't even work now," Violet said with a tsk.

"Two kids in college and poor Carrie has to do it all," Nancy said. "She has a job, does all the cooking, cleaning and upkeep on their house. Do you know last year she re-roofed her house by herself? Markus refused to help because of his back, and she couldn't afford to hire anyone."

"Sully and Ian went over to help," Mary said. "They were surprised to find that Markus could pick up and move his flat-screen TV during Sunday's football game but couldn't apparently hammer down some shingles."

"Now that her kids are grown, why doesn't she leave him?" Lindsey asked.

"It must be the nurse in her," Nancy said.

"She's always taking care of someone," Violet agreed.

"She's just a good person," Beth said.

Lindsey considered herself to be a pretty good person, but she couldn't imagine staying with someone who treated her so badly. She wondered if Carrie ever thought about leaving Markus, but then reminded herself that it was none of her business.

"Let's get back to George and Cecil," she said. She didn't like gossiping about someone she liked. "I don't know about you, but suddenly, Cecil is not looking so bad to me."

There were a few sheepish laughs, and then Mary led the charge into the Brie and crackers and all thought of Markus Rushton was erased by good food and good conversation.

It wasn't until the Friends of the Library meeting that evening that Lindsey thought again about Carrie and her marriage.

She sat on the window seat at the back of the lecture room, which had once been the upstairs study of the sea captain who had originally built the stone building that the library was housed in. Half of the second story of the main building had been knocked out to make vaulted ceilings, but this room, which seated forty people quite comfortably, had been kept for special meetings, such as tonight's Friends of the Library meeting.

Bill Sint, Carrie's competition for the position of president of the Friends of the Library, was dressed in a dark brown corduroy blazer with tan suede elbow patches over a pale blue turtleneck. His jeans were pressed with razor-sharp creases, and his heavy winter boots showed not a trace of the mud and slush that covered the walkways outside. Lindsey wondered how he managed that.

Bill was tall and thin, with jet-black hair that Lindsey suspected was dyed, as he had to be well into his seventies. His most common expression was one of irritation. He always had one eyebrow raised higher than the other, and even when Lindsey said hello to him, she got the feeling he felt interrupted by her good cheer. Not for nothing, but she certainly hoped Carrie was voted in as the new president, because working with Bill had become tiresome. She'd even put up with Carrie's obnoxious husband if she had to.

Although, as she scanned the crowd, she realized that wasn't going to be a problem. Carrie's husband was not in attendance. She didn't imagine he'd be a member of Friends given his feelings about books and all, but still, she would have thought he'd make an appearance to support his wife. Then again, he hadn't really oozed supportive spouse when she'd met him.

As the meeting went through roll call, Lindsey turned in her seat and glanced out over the town park, which was empty. Then she tried to pick out some of the Thumb Islands in the bay, which were visible in the dark evening only as tiny lights on the water. Finally, she glanced at the town pier. The pier was long and wide and had two big pole lights, which kept it illuminated at night to deter vandals from harming or stealing the boats docked in the bay.

At the base of the pier was the Blue Anchor, Mary's restaurant. It was the residents' favorite watering hole, and judging by the light spilling out of its windows, the café was doing a bustling business even on this bitter January evening.

Lindsey caught some movement on the pier and her gaze took in a tall man, his lanky build discernible even under his thick peacoat. He wore a fisherman's knit cap over his mahogany curls, but Lindsey knew it was him, Mike Sullivan, known to the locals and tourists as Captain Sully. She tried to ignore the burst of pleasure she felt at the sight of him and failed miserably.

Sully had become a good friend over the past few months. He shared her love of reading, and she found his quiet presence comforting and intriguing. She told herself she would have felt the same rush of happy if she'd spied Nancy or Violet walking on the pier. Yeah, right.

She watched Sully hunch against the frigid wind that blew in from the water. At the end of the pier, he turned and ducked into the Anchor, probably to see his sister, Mary, and grab some dinner. Lindsey had a sudden longing to be at the Anchor, too.

When she turned back to face the room, she noticed the tension in the lecture room was as thick as a spring fog and much more uncomfortable. Both Carrie and Bill would now address the group, each offering their vision of the future of the Friends of the Library.

Carrie had changed out of her hospital scrubs and looked very professional in a gray wool skirt and matching blazer over a pale pink blouse. She wore thick black stockings, to combat the cold, with a pair of stylish boots.

She looked every inch the efficient person that she was, and her presentation included a PowerPoint that outlined a well-thought-out proposal with realistic expectations to raise funds for the library.

Bill's presentation was technology free and read like a grocery list of things he had accomplished while being president, some of which sounded more fictional than the books on the shelves in the library below.

Finally, they were ready to vote. Lindsey checked out the assembled group. There were about twenty members in attendance. The cold weather had kept most of the elderly Friends home, and much of Briar Creek's summer population was not in residence at the moment, making their turn-out even fewer.

Mimi Seitler, the secretary, asked Carrie and Bill to wait in the hall while the members voted. Lindsey felt sure this was to keep any of the members from being intimidated into voting against their inclination.

Bill yanked the lapels of his blazer with a snap as he surveyed the room with his left eyebrow up in its usual arch. "I trust you'll all make the right decision."

Carrie said nothing. She merely gave a small smile and a wave and followed him out the door. When Bill looked to be lingering in the doorway, Mimi shut it in his face. Lindsey had no doubt about how she would be voting.

"Let's get this over with," Mimi said. She resumed her seat at the front of the room. "All those in favor of Bill Sint remaining president, raise your right hand."

No one moved. Not even a finger fluttered in an upward direction.

"All those in favor of Carrie Rushton becoming our new president, raise your right hand."

All of the hands went up. It was Carrie by a landslide. Not a big surprise.

Mimi opened the door and ushered the two candidates back inside. Carrie looked nervous. Bill looked smug. Oh, dear, Lindsey had a feeling this was not going to go well.

"After all of the votes have been counted, it has been decided by the Friends that Carrie shall be our new president."

Carrie looked surprised and pleased, while Bill opened his mouth and shut his mouth. His left eyebrow arched so high it could practically scratch an itch at his hairline.

"Thank you, all," Carrie said. "I promise to do my very best."

Bill glowered at her and then the group.

"I will not concede!" he said. "I demand a recount."

CHAPTER

3

BRIAR CREEK
PUBLIC LIBRARY

"Oh, no," Mimi said. "You really don't want to do that."

"Yes, I do!" Bill insisted. "In fact, I demand it."

Mimi sighed. She gave Bill an exasperated look like she didn't think he had the sense to look both ways before he crossed the street. "Fine. There is no need to do a recount. It was unanimous. Everyone voted for Carrie."

Bill gasped as if she'd slapped him. "That can't be."

His gaze scoured the room, but everyone avoided eye contact.

"Is this true? Doug?" Bill glowered at an older gentleman sitting in the back row. "Look at me, Doug."

Doug Dowd, wearing a pressed shirt with a string tie, twisted his gloves in his hands and glanced quickly up and over the top of Bill's head.

It was enough. Bill turned to frown at another older and chunkier man in the third row. "Warren?"

Warren was braver than Doug. He raised his hands in a placating gesture and said, "Now don't go taking it all personal, Bill."

"I can assure you, Warren," Bill snapped. "It is personal."

Lindsey would have felt sorry for him if he weren't such a pompous windbag.

"Well, I suppose there's nothing more to be said." He stomped over to his chair and gathered his overcoat and briefcase.

He had trouble tying his scarf around his neck as his hands were shaking. The entire room watched him go; no one offered to help him. Now Lindsey did feel bad for him.

She rose from her window seat and gestured to Mimi that she was going to check on him. Mimi gave her a nod of thanks.

Bill must have been moving at a small run, because Lindsey didn't catch him until he was just stepping out the front door into the cold.

"Mr. Sint, Bill!" she called.

He spun around quickly as if he had been expecting someone to call him back. He looked disappointed to find that it was Lindsey.

"What?" he snapped. "Are you here to gloat about your victory?"

"Excuse me?" she asked. The blast of cold air made her long to step back into the toasty library, but she didn't want to offend him any more than she already had.

"Library directors don't attend Friends' meetings," he

said. "Unless, they're presenting some information. But not you, oh, no, you were there to witness me getting voted out of office. What did I ever do to you?"

"I'm sorry," Lindsey said. "But I had nothing to do with how the vote went."

"Of course you did," he argued. "Everyone wants to impress our new, little library director. Did you tell them all how to vote and then decide to show up to make sure they did?"

"No!"

"Ha!" He scoffed. "Well, now you've got what you wanted. Little Carrie Rushton will run around and do your bidding with no ambitions for the group other than to fund your ridiculous children's programs. I hope you're happy."

Lindsey wanted to tell him that the more he opened his mouth, the more she was delighted with the outcome of the election. But it didn't seem like the most diplomatic way to assuage the ruffled emotions of the former president.

"Your service over the years has been much appreciated," Lindsey said. "We would welcome your advice and input in any capacity you care to share it."

"Get stuffed!" Bill snapped, and he tossed his scarf around his throat and strode off into the night.

As she watched him stomp toward the parking lot, she saw Marjorie Bilson come hurrying up the walk. She was a tiny thing, petite and skinny and full of nervous energy. She reminded Lindsey of a sparrow, hopping about with sharp eyes, a sharp beak and plain brown feathers. She too was a member of the Friends, which Lindsey found odd since Marjorie was not much of a reader.

Marjorie stopped next to Bill and put her hand on his

arm. Lindsey had noticed that the tiny woman looked at Bill with a certain amount of worship in her brown eyes. Lindsey couldn't see why, but who was she to judge.

Bill shrugged her off and said some terse words that were muffled by his scarf. Marjorie emitted a shriek of horror, which even from thirty feet away, Lindsey heard quite clearly. Then she clapped a mittened hand over her mouth and followed Bill out to the parking lot.

This couldn't be good. Marjorie was probably the only person who would have voted for Bill, and obviously, she had missed the vote. Lindsey wondered if Bill would demand a new election based upon that alone.

She stepped back into the warm library with a sigh. She could feel a pair of eyes watching her and she turned to find the indomitable Ms. Cole, who ran their circulation desk, watching her.

"Mr. Tupper never had any problems with Bill as the president of the Friends of the Library," she said. She gave Lindsey a look of disapproval over the upper edge of her reading glasses.

Lindsey sighed. Mr. Tupper, the former director of the Briar Creek Public Library, had been perfect in Ms. Cole's estimation. In the nine months Lindsey had been here, Ms. Cole had never missed an opportunity to make a comment that found Lindsey wanting in comparison to the hallowed Mr. Tupper.

Always a monochromatic dresser, Ms. Cole was usually in shades of gray or beige. Today, she had thrown caution to the wind and she was in varying shades of purple, from her opaque violet stockings and grape lollipop wool skirt to her bulky lavender sweater. Instead of softening her mannish features, however, the pastel colors seemed to wash out the skin tone on her portly person, leaving her looking a bit jaundiced.

"Mr. Tupper was an extraordinary man," Lindsey said. She had discovered that if she praised Mr. Tupper right away, it saved her from having to listen to even more of Ms. Cole's critique of her performance in comparison to her predecessor.

With a curt nod, Ms. Cole glanced back at her computer and the stack of books she was checking in. She was clearly pleased that Lindsey had come to revere the legend that was Mr. Tupper.

The circulation desk was quiet, as was the rest of the library. Lindsey glanced around the room, soaking up the homey atmosphere. The children's area had been picked up, and Beth sat at her desk in the middle of it, cutting out snowflakes for her story time craft the next day.

Jessica was manning the reference desk on the adult side of the library. Two high school students were quizzing her about a list of books they needed for their required reading. They appeared to be asking for the CliffsNotes version, which Jessica was providing but also discouraging.

Two people were on the bank of Internet computers at the end of the room, and one patron had fallen asleep in the cushy chair by the magazines.

Lindsey made her way over there. She wanted to wake the poor guy before Ms. Cole saw him. She had been known to drop the heaviest book she could find beside an unsuspecting snoozer, giving the poor person a small heart attack.

As Lindsey got closer, she recognized the sleeper. It was her friend library board member Milton Duffy. His bald head shone under the overhead lights and his mouth was slightly agape, framed by his silver goatee.

Lindsey gently shook his arm. "Milton, psst, Milton."

He jolted awake and leaned forward with his reading glasses in one hand and his favorite yoga magazine in the other.

He turned, and when his bright green eyes met hers, he grinned. "Lindsey, you're just the person I was looking for. Just give me a moment."

"Certainly."

He rose from his seat and assumed the mountain pose. From here he went into a deep forward bend. Milton was a certified yogi and Lindsey had learned not to rush him when he was in a posture. She waited as he slowly rose to an upright position, vertebra by vertebra.

With a deep breath in and a sharp exhale, he gave her his full attention.

"So, how did the election for the Friends go?" he asked.

As always, Lindsey was surprised by how deeply in the loop Milton was about the library's goings-on. She should be used to it by now. As the chairman of the library board, he generally knew what was happening even before Lindsey did.

"Carrie Rushton won," Lindsey said. "I'm surprised you weren't there, Milton; you're a member of the Friends."

"I felt it might be a conflict of interest, what with me being on the library board and all," he said.

Lindsey just stared at him.

"Okay," he relented. "Bill and I have a history and I

didn't want to do anything that might jeopardize Carrie winning the election."

Lindsey raised her eyebrows. What sort of history could Bill and Milton have? How could he just throw that out there and not tell her any more? She continued to stare at him, unblinking.

"Oh, fine," he said.

Lindsey grinned. The unblinking stare, it worked every time.

"We both dated my Anna in high school, but she chose me and Bill has never gotten over it."

Milton brushed an invisible piece of lint off his navy track suit. He didn't meet Lindsey's gaze and she got the feeling he was embarrassed.

"Why do I think there is more to this story?" she asked.

"Not really," Milton said. Then he sighed. "Bill is a very bitter man. He never got over losing Anna to me and tried to best me at everything I have ever done. I went to Yale, he went to Princeton. I bought the oldest house in town. He inherited his family's estate, which is the biggest house in Briar Creek. I married Anna, he married her cousin. It's ridiculous. You'd think after sixty years the man would get over it."

"I can see why you abstained," Lindsey said. "That was a good call."

Milton opened his mouth to say something, but just then Ms. Cole announced that the library would be closing in ten minutes. Lindsey glanced at her watch in surprise. Where had the evening gone?

She heard the sound of footsteps and saw that the Friends were making their way down the stairs at the end of the room. Ms. Cole heard them, too, and she hushed them as only Ms. Cole could do. It sounded like something between a snake's hiss and the crack of a whip.

The Friends immediately quieted down. Most of them waved and kept on walking out of the building, but Carrie and Mimi stopped by Milton and Lindsey to talk.

Milton pumped Carrie's hand up and down in congratulations and she beamed.

"I'm so excited," Carrie said in a rush. "Mimi and I have a ton of ideas to help get some cash flowing into the Friends' bank account. Warren told me we have some rare books that have been donated to the Friends. If we can't use them in the library, I bet we could sell them in an online auction and make a fortune."

"She's going to be a great president," Mimi said. "No more of Bill's spinning his wheels in indecision. We're going to make some changes."

"That's wond—" Lindsey began but she was interrupted.

"The library is now closed!" Ms. Cole barked from behind the circulation desk and they all jumped.

The others exchanged startled glances and hurried toward the door.

"We'll talk more tomorrow," Milton said to Lindsey. "Ladies, may I escort you to your cars?"

Mimi simpered and Carrie grinned as Milton bundled up and led them out the front door into the brisk January air.

Lindsey helped shut down the building, switching off the computers, copiers and coffeepots and finally setting the alarm. Even after almost a year, she still got tense when she only had fifteen seconds to get out the back door after she activated the system.

Per usual, Ms. Cole set off across the parking lot to her compact sedan without so much as a good night.

"Do you think the lemon is aware of how off-putting her personality is?" Beth asked Jessica and Lindsey as they stood, watching the older woman stride away.

"I think she likes who she is," Jessica said. "The lemon is all about maintaining order, and I think the library gives her a place, her own little corner of the universe, to maintain order within. I think it gives the lemon a purpose."

"That sounds about right," Lindsey said. "And I do think she enjoys her work in her own way."

Ms. Cole had been nicknamed *the lemon* long before Lindsey had come to work in Briar Creek, so she didn't feel it was her place to tell the staff not to call her that. Besides, with Ms. Cole's perpetual pucker of disapproval, it was hard to argue against the name, as it was a dead-accurate description.

"Do either of you want a ride?" Jessica offered. "You're going to freeze biking home in this."

"We're tough," Beth said. As if to prove it, she made a muscle with her right arm, which was completely invisible under her bulky coat.

"Crazy is more like it," Jessica said, and she climbed into her car with a smile and a wave.

Lindsey thought she might be onto something with the crazy comment. When she had moved from New Haven to Briar Creek, Lindsey had committed to a greener lifestyle and sold her car. She hadn't really considered how cold that lifestyle would be, however, when winter came.

"Buck up," Beth said, as if sensing her unhappiness about the bike ride ahead. "Just think how much better your butt looks now that you're biking every day."

"Yeah, and I'm going to need a firm behind to keep people from noticing the toes that go missing due to hypothermia," Lindsey said.

"Are we feeling a little whiny?" Beth asked.

"No, yes, a little," Lindsey said.

"Come on, get moving, you'll warm up and feel better and you can reward yourself with a decadent dessert when you get home."

Beth wrapped her scarf about her head, dumped her purse and book bag in the basket on her bike and set off on her cruiser.

Lindsey watched the blinking light on Beth's bike alerting motorists to her presence, then followed her example, trying to ignore the stinging cold that made her eyes tear up.

What had she been thinking when she sold her car? On Sunday, she was going to look at the classifieds. Surely, there was a small economical and environmental vehicle out there that wouldn't harm the planet and could get her from point A to point B and keep her from feeling like a human Popsicle.

Mercifully, Briar Creek was a small town and she only had about a mile to go to get to her house. She followed Beth to the end of Main Street, where the road forked. Beth went to the left toward her beach house and Lindsey to the right to her top-floor apartment in an old captain's house.

At least the roads were clear now. Last week, after a

snow storm, she'd had to walk for three days until the bicycle path was clear enough to be used again.

With her long, curly blond hair stuffed securely in her helmet as extra insulation, her ears were completely muffled and it took her a second to register the sound of a car engine coming in her direction.

She knew even with her blinky light on, she was not very visible, so she glanced over her shoulder to see where the car was, and her heart stopped in her throat. With its high beams on and its engine revving, the car was headed straight for her.

CHAPTER

4

BRIAR CREEK
PUBLIC LIBRARY

A screech of brakes clawed the stillness of the winter air with a talon's sharp edge. Lindsey jumped off her bike while still in motion, and yanked it with her onto the front lawn of the nearest house.

The driver's side door of the car was shoved open, and Lindsey was sure she'd scared the poor driver as much he'd scared her.

"I'm all right!" she called out.

"Well, that's unfortunate!"

Lindsey reared back as if she'd been slapped. "Excuse me?"

The person was short and tiny, and as she hopped onto the front lawn beside Lindsey, she was immediately recognizable. Marjorie Bilson.

"You heard me," Marjorie snapped. "How dare you run

Bill out of office? He has worked tirelessly all these years with little or no thanks, and then you come along and have him replaced with one of your cronies."

There were so many things wrong with the venom Marjorie was spewing that Lindsey was at a loss as to where to begin in correcting her.

"You're wrong," she said.

"Liar!" Marjorie accused. Her hair was disheveled, her coat wasn't buttoned and she looked as if she were on the brink of having hysterics.

"Marjorie, this really isn't the time or place to have a conversation like this," Lindsey said. "I'm working tomorrow. Why don't you come and see me at the library and we'll talk about it."

"You'd like that, wouldn't you?"

"I . . ."

"Is everything all right out here?"

Lindsey heard a storm door open on the house behind them and turned to see a man chugging down the walk. He was pulling his dressing robe tight around his middle as he hurried toward them.

"We're okay," Lindsey said, realizing she was only speaking in the most general of terms, given that calling Marjorie okay was definitely stretching it.

When Lindsey turned to address the man, Marjorie took the opportunity to hurry back into her car. With the slam of her door and a squeal of wheels on icy blacktop, she was gone.

"Did she hit you?" the man asked. "Are you sure you're all right?"

Lindsey shook her head. "No, she didn't hit me."

"You're shaking," he said.

She looked down, and sure enough, her gloved fingers were trembling and it wasn't from the cold.

"My wife and I were just making some tea, would you care to join us?" he asked. "I'm Tom, by the way, Tom Rubinski."

"Oh, thank you, Tom," she said. "I'm Lindsey. I appreciate the offer, but I live just up the road. I'll be home in less than a minute."

"If you're sure," he said. He looked dubious so Lindsey forced a smile even though it was an effort.

"I'm sure," she said. Then she hesitated. Maybe he could help her with information. "Tell me, do you know Marjorie Bilson?"

"Batty Bilson?" he asked. "Is that who that was?"

"Batty?" Lindsey repeated. She didn't like where this was going.

"Yeah, I went to school with her," he said. "She has issues."

"Is running people over with her car one of her issues?" Lindsey asked.

"Not until tonight," Tom said. "I'd say this is a first, but I can't swear to it."

"Do you suppose one of her issues could be Bill Sint?"

Lindsey went to lift her bike off Tom's lawn. He stepped forward and took it out of her hands and lowered it to the walk for her.

"Thank you," she said.

"Bill Sint? The old guy who lives on the Sint estate on the other side of the bay? The one with the unnaturally black hair and twitchy eyebrow?"

It was a good description and made Lindsey smile. "The same."

"I can't say for sure. I do know that Batty tends to love with her whole heart but not all of her mind, if you know what I mean. If I remember right, she had to go away for a couple of years in high school because she developed an unhealthy crush on our chemistry teacher," he said.

Interesting. Lindsey wondered if she was seeing a pattern here.

"Wow, so Batty has a thing for Bill. Man, he's old enough to be her father, possibly her grandfather."

"Ew," they said together.

"So, why is she coming after you?" Tom asked. "Does she think you're competition for his pruney old heart?"

"Oh, no," Lindsey said with an adamant head shake. "But, she seems to think I had something to do with his being removed as president of the Friends of the Library; I didn't, but she didn't seem overly concerned that she almost ran me down to discuss it."

Tom gave a low whistle and then he peered at her eyes, which were her only visible feature through the layers of scarf and bike helmet she had on her head.

"Oh, hey, Lindsey. I know you," he said. "Or at least, I've heard about you. You're Lindsey Norris, the new librarian."

"Not terribly new," she said. "I've been here almost a year."

"You've turned my buddy Sully into a regular library user," he said. His eyes were teasing and Lindsey was happy that her scarf covered the hot flush that she could feel warming her face.

"He's an avid reader," she said. "He has excellent taste in fiction."

"Yeah, well, I don't think it's the books that have him giving his library card such a workout."

"Tom, what's going on?" A petite woman, also in her bathrobe, came hurrying down the walkway. "Your tea is getting cold."

"Gina, come and meet Lindsey," he said. He turned to Lindsey and said, "This is my wife, Gina."

The corners of his eyes crinkled and his voice dropped a note or two when he said her name. It was obvious that Tom Rubinski was very much in love with his wife.

He looped his arm over his wife's shoulders and said, "Check this out: Batty Bilson has a thing for that old coot Bill Sint, and she nearly ran Lindsey down because Batty thinks she's responsible for his being booted off of the library's Friends group."

Gina stared at her husband and then at Lindsey. "Really? That's mental even for Marjorie. Are you all right? Would you like some tea?"

Lindsey glanced at the small woman and smiled. "No, thank you, really, I'm fine."

She recognized Gina Rubinski immediately. She had been in the library several times over the past few months checking out baby name books. Lindsey wondered if the Rubinskis were expecting, but knowing it was none of her business, she didn't dare ask. That did not stop her from looking at Gina's belly however. If she was pregnant, she wasn't showing.

"You'd better get back inside, Tom; your patient needs you," Gina said.

"Oh, gotta go," he said. "I'm a vet, and we have a golden retriever about to deliver her first litter. It looks to be nine pups. We can't even come up with that many names."

Lindsey smiled. So that explained the baby name books. "Nice to meet you, Tom."

"You, too, Lindsey," he said. Then he grinned and added, "Say 'hi' to Sully for me."

His wife glanced between them with a curious look but didn't comment, for which Lindsey was grateful.

"Good night, Gina," she said.

"Good night."

Lindsey climbed on her bike, and with a wave, she pedaled to the end of the street. She was pleased that she only glanced over her shoulder five times to see if Batty's sedan appeared out of nowhere.

This clinched it. Between the weather and this neardeath experience, she was definitely going to have to look into buying some sort of car. At the very least she could get a motorized scooter, which would still be ecological but would give her enough speed to outrun Batty if she had another episode.

And maybe she'd start carrying a bag of nails with her, too, Lindsey thought grimly as she shut her bike in the stand-alone garage, relieved to be safe at home.

The weather remained unforgivingly windy and bitter for the next week. Interestingly, every time Lindsey and Beth left the library in the evening and started to unchain their bikes, Sully happened by on his way home from the pier.

"It's too cold for that," he shouted out the window. "Hop in and I'll give you a ride."

Lindsey's mama hadn't raised her to be a fool and neither had Beth's. They let Sully load their bikes up into the back of his ancient pickup truck and happily climbed into the toasty warm cab.

For unknown reasons that Lindsey did not dwell upon, Sully always dropped off Beth first, which meant she got to ride in the middle of the bench seat and spend a few minutes alone with him every evening on the ride from Beth's house to her own.

Sully was the original quiet man. He didn't talk much but asked good questions. He listened attentively, as if what she had to say genuinely interested him. Having been engaged to a law professor who quite loved the sound of his own voice, Lindsey wasn't used to being the loquacious one. It was a novel experience, but still, she found herself more and more curious about the boat captain beside her.

"Do you offer many boat tours in the winter?" she asked.

"After December, we're pretty much shut down on tours until the spring. Everyone loves to see the Thumb Islands lit up for the holidays, but after that we're mostly a taxi service for the island residents and their visitors until the end of March."

"Do your parents stay on their island in the winter?" she asked, wondering if it was terribly cold out there.

"Yep," he said. "Mary and I tried to talk them into getting a nice apartment off island but no dice. They're on one of the few islands with electricity and they have a wood-burning stove. I understand why they stay out there. It's over ten acres of peace and quiet. Their island has three houses on it, and their neighbors stay out there, too, so if there was an emergency, there are people around. But they are getting older . . ."

His voice trailed off and he stared out the windshield of the truck toward the islands, which were only visible by their lights reflected on the water.

From what Lindsey had read about the history of the islands, she had learned that the Thumb Islands were an archipelago of seventy to one hundred islands, depending on how you quantified an island. Some people counted the rocks that jutted up out of the water, others felt that there must be some sign of life for it to be a true island. Sully's parents lived on Bell Island, one of the largest and one of the few populated all year round.

Sully parked in the gravel drive beside the house where Lindsey rented an apartment. From their vantage point on the raised cliffs that overlooked Briar Creek Bay and the islands, Lindsey could see Bell Island and noticed that the Sullivans still had their lights on.

She wondered what it would be like to live out there, with the constant sound of the surf as background music and the cries of the seagulls as the days' conversation. After last week's altercation with the screeching Marjorie Bilson, it seemed a nicer option. Which reminded her, she had been meaning to ask Sully about that episode.

"So, how did you find out about Marjorie?" she asked him as he opened his door and circled the truck to open her door for her.

He hadn't said so, but given that he'd been driving her and Beth home every night for a week now, she couldn't believe it was just coincidence.

"Let's talk inside where it's warm," he said.

He gave her a hand down from the truck and then lifted her bike out of the back and walked it to the garage, where she kept it out of the inclement winter weather.

Lindsey followed. She hoped she hadn't put him off by asking about Marjorie. She held the door open for him while he wheeled the bike inside. She closed the door behind him and stepped back.

They were both bundled against the cold, him less than her with his knit cap and peacoat. She had on her puffy coat with a hat and scarf and gloves. Pretty much the only skin she had left exposed was her eyelids.

Sully took her arm and led her across the frozen ground to the walkway. Spots of ice made the walk precarious and she picked her way carefully, aware of his hand at her elbow. If she slipped, Sully was ready to catch her. She found that comforting.

Her landlord and crafternoon buddy, Nancy Peyton, lived on the first floor, and Nancy's nephew, Charlie, lived in between them on the second. He was an aspiring rock star who worked for Sully's tour-boat company. Since winter work was slow, he had packed up his band in his ancient van and migrated south to play some gigs for the month of January. Lindsey liked Charlie, but she had to admit it was nice not to watch her furniture dance across the apartment floor during his weekly band practice.

The front door was never locked and Lindsey opened it and stepped into the vestibule.

The heat from the steam radiator fogged up the window but made the small entryway toasty warm. Lindsey pulled off her hat and unwound her scarf.

"To answer your question, my friend Tom told me that Marjorie tried to run you off the road the other night," he said.

When Lindsey met his gaze, she could see worry in his blue eyes.

"Ah, I thought it was something like that," she said. "I really don't think she'll do it again."

"No, probably not," he said. Although, he didn't sound as sure as she would have liked. "But since I get off work about the same time as you do and it's dark out there, I think we can maintain our current carpool situation for a while, don't you?"

Lindsey nodded. She had to admit it was a bit of a relief to know she could depend upon Sully to get her and Beth home, at least until Marjorie calmed down about the whole Bill Sint thing or she found the time to buy a car.

"Have you seen Marjorie since the incident?" he asked.

"No," she said. "I'm sure, well, mostly sure, that she didn't mean to scare me like that."

"Sure she did," he said.

"Really?"

"Marjorie lacks impulse control," he said. "She always has."

"Has . . . ?" Lindsey began to ask if Marjorie had ever hurt anyone before, but Nancy's door opened and she stuck her head out.

"What are you two doing out here?" she asked as if she'd been waiting for them. "Come on in. I just made some fresh gingerbread and I have some hot cider on the stove."

Lindsey and Sully exchanged a bemused glance before

stepping into her apartment. Nancy was renown in town for her cookie-baking skills. Fresh gingerbread? They didn't need to be asked twice.

Not wanting to worry Nancy, Lindsey changed the conversation to Charlie Peyton and his band. He had been texting Nancy from every city he played in. The messages read like he was an academic exchange student, but even Nancy knew better.

With a laugh, she dug out her phone and read his latest message. "Dear Naners, our gig went well in Charlotte. Lots of college students turned out and we had a great debate on the economics of the pitcher versus the pint. We then took turns driving the big bus in our hotel room. Off to Savannah. Love, Charlie."

Then she translated. "I believe 'driving the big bus' is a euphemism for getting so drunk he threw up in the toilet." Nancy made a big circle of her arms and lowered her head.

Sully and Lindsey laughed over their cider and gingerbread, and Lindsey was grateful for the diversion. She didn't like to acknowledge that the incident with Marjorie had her looking over her shoulder, but there was no denying that she had her guard up, especially when riding her bike.

Mercifully, tomorrow was the first meeting of the Friends of the Library with Carrie as president. Lindsey could only hope that once the first meeting was a done deal, they could start to move forward and put the hurt feelings and hostility behind them, way behind them.

Of course, a lot of that would depend upon whether Marjorie showed up and tried to do anyone an injury or not.

CHAPTER

5

BRIAR CREEK
PUBLIC LIBRARY

Lindsey was working the reference desk on the adult side of the library when the first members of the Friends started to arrive for their meeting. They waved as they passed by and she waved back. She kept an eye out for Bill and Marjorie but didn't see either of them arrive.

She wondered if they had quit the group in protest and figured she could ask Milton after the meeting, as he seemed to be in the know about these things. She thought perhaps it was for the best if they had. Tension in the group couldn't be a good thing.

"Excuse me, can you help me find out when National Pie Day is?"

Lindsey turned away from the hallway to see a young woman standing in front of the reference desk. She looked to be in her mid-twenties. She was carrying a laptop under her arm and looking pretty cranky.

"Sure, is that all you want to know, when National Pie Day is?" Lindsey said.

"No, I have a whole list of events and I need to find out when they are. I'm student teaching at a preschool and they want me to come up with all sorts of activities and stuff."

"Oh, okay," Lindsey said. She rose from the desk and headed for the ready reference bookshelf adjacent to her desk where they kept their favorite reference books.

The young woman let out a put-upon sigh, as if walking five feet and cracking open a book was the equivalent of hard labor. "Can't you just google it?"

"I could," Lindsey said. "But since you have a list of events, using a book is actually going to be faster."

The girl grumbled as she followed her, and Lindsey had to suppress the urge to smile. She reached for her favorite book and placed it on top of the shelf.

"This is *Chase's Calendar of Events*. It should answer all of your questions. There is an index in the back so you can look it up by the type of event. For example, you might want to start with pie. The pages are also broken down by day, so you can look up any day in the calendar year and find out what is special about it."

"Really?" the woman asked, looking suspicious.

"Indeed," Lindsey said. Now she did chuckle. "It's a great book, one of my favorites. And now I'll tell you a secret. When you google things, you have to be able to verify the website. Otherwise Joe Shmoe could put up a web page declaring National Pie Day is October fourth, when everyone knows—and *Chase's* will verify—that National Pie Day is January twenty-third."

The woman looked at her with rounded eyes as if she'd never thought of that. Lindsey smiled and walked away. She loved Google for doing searches as much as the next person, but really, it wasn't *all* that and it certainly didn't verify its sites. It was just one tool out of many in the quest for information.

When she got back to the reference desk, Mimi Seitler was standing there, fretting her lower lip.

"Hi, Mimi," Lindsey said. "Is everything all right?"

"You haven't seen Carrie, have you?" Mimi asked.

"No, not since the last meeting," Lindsey said. "Isn't she here yet?"

Lindsey glanced at the clock on the lower right-hand corner of her computer monitor. It was fourteen minutes past the hour. It wasn't like Carrie to be late, and certainly not to her first meeting as president.

Just then the main glass doors slid open and Carrie rushed in. Her coat was hanging off her shoulders, she didn't have on a hat or gloves and her cheeks were brightly flushed. Lindsey would have thought it was from the cold but she looked agitated.

"Oh, good, she's here," Mimi said.

Carrie was rushing through the main room toward the back and Mimi hurried to join her.

Lindsey thought she heard the words *car trouble* and was relieved that at least it hadn't been Bill or Marjorie causing Carrie grief.

The rest of the evening passed quietly, and Lindsey and

her two remaining staff members were just shutting down the equipment when the Friends adjourned for the night and trooped through the library on their way to the exit.

"So, you must be the notorious Ms. Norris," a voice said from behind her.

Lindsey spun around to see a very handsome man in a long overcoat standing behind her.

"Notorious?" she asked. "I don't know about that."

"According to my uncle Bill, you are quite the femme fatale."

Lindsey sighed. She had a feeling she knew to which Bill he was referring. "You're related to Bill Sint?"

"He's my uncle," the man said and held out his hand. "Edmund Sint at your service."

He was a few inches taller than Lindsey and he had the whole-milk, grain-fed, clean-cut appearance of a model in a Brooks Brothers' ad. With a pang, she realized he reminded her of her former fiancé, John Mayhew, as he had the air of an academic about him with the same ruddy-cheeked good looks and charming manner.

She shook his hand. "I know your uncle is unhappy with me. I'm sorry about that."

"Don't be," he said. "Uncle Bill can be a bit taciturn, but he generally gets over it. He has a horrible cold right now. He sent me as his emissary to make certain no one thought he'd been driven out of the Friends."

He grinned at her, and Lindsey couldn't help but smile back. Whatever Bill Sint lacked in good manners, Edmund made up for by the bucketful.

"Tell me," he said as he leaned close, "is it true he told you to get stuffed?"

He wiggled his eyebrows at her and Lindsey had to laugh. He had the look of someone who did not take life too seriously. She liked that.

"He did," she said. "It was quite shocking." She imitated his eyebrow maneuver and he laughed. It was a good, deep laugh that rumbled up from his chest without restraint. She was glad Ms. Cole wasn't here right now, for she surely would have shushed him.

"Good night, Lindsey," Carrie called as she passed them.

"Good night," Lindsey said.

"Oh, Mrs. Rushton," Edmund called to her. "Won't you join us for a moment?"

Carrie looked uncertain, as if she wasn't sure if Edmund was friend or foe.

He must have sensed her reluctance, because he said, "Don't worry; unlike my uncle, I don't bite."

Carrie smiled with relief and joined them.

"As an apology for my uncle's behavior, I'd like to invite you both to lunch at the house," he said. "It will give us a chance to get better acquainted and encourage my uncle to get over his hurt feelings. I'll even give you a tour of the estate. You can admire all of the family's various collections. What do you say?"

"Well, that's very nice of you." Carrie hedged.

"We'd love to." Lindsey accepted for the both of them. This was just what Carrie and Bill needed to let bygones be bygones.

Carrie gave her a wide-eyed glance while Edmund grinned at her. "Excellent. I'll give Uncle a few days to recover from his cold and then we'll set a date."

Lindsey liked the way his gray eyes darkened when he said the word *date*. Not that she thought it was a date or that he was implying that it was a date. She just liked his eyes, really.

She and Carrie watched him leave with a good-natured wave.

"What was that about?" Carrie asked.

"I'm not sure, but I suspect Edmund wants Bill to get back into the good graces of the Friends and he's trying to facilitate a reconciliation."

"Yeah, or he's warm for your form," Carrie said and gave her a teasing close-lipped smile.

"Why that's just, well, silly," Lindsey spluttered. There was no denying the warmth that heated her cheeks, however. She turned and headed for her office. "I'll call you if I hear from him."

"You mean when you hear from him," Carrie said. She laughed at Lindsey's chagrin and left the building with a wave.

Lindsey ushered her staff out the back door and hurriedly set the alarm. As the large steel door swung shut behind her, she waved good night to her staff. The evening air was bitterly cold, and it felt as if it pierced her lungs on the inhale. As she circled the building to where her bike was kept, she was not at all surprised to find Sully there waiting for her.

"No Beth tonight?" he asked. His pickup truck was parked at the curb, and she wondered if he'd been waiting long.

She had a sudden pang of conscience for agreeing to

lunch with Edmund Sint, which was ridiculous since, as far as she knew, she and Sully were just friends.

"No, she's off today because she's working Saturday," she said.

"Ah," he said and he grinned at her. Dimples bracketed his smile, making him even more handsome than usual, which was impressive, given that Sully could trip up most of the female population without even trying.

Lindsey felt her insides do the flip-flop thing. After her fiancé had cheated on her, she hadn't thought she'd ever feel that kind of sizzle-and-zip attraction for a man, at least not for a very long while. But Sully sure was making her change her mind about that, and suddenly she had no interest in having lunch with Edmund Sint, even if it did include a tour of the Sint estate, which she had been dead curious about since she'd moved to Briar Creek.

She found herself watching Sully as he loaded up her bike. She realized she hadn't bundled up as much as she usually did. Her scarf was loose around her neck and she wore her hat back on her head. She hadn't jammed up all of her hair under it either. She wondered if this had been an unconscious decision because she had hoped she'd be seeing Sully or if she'd just been rushing and forgot.

She decided she really didn't want to know. If anyone asked, she'd been rushing. Yep, that was her story and she was sticking to it.

She glanced away from Sully and noticed a lone car out in the parking lot. Standing beside it was Carrie Rushton. Lindsey remembered she'd been late to the meeting because of car trouble. She wondered if Carrie was stuck.

She told Sully she'd be right back and hurried across the dark lot to make sure her friend was okay.

"Carrie, are you all right?"

Carrie looked at her and then quickly away, wiping at her face with her mitten as she did so, but not before Lindsey saw the trace of tears in the glow of the overhead streetlight on Carrie's face.

"Carrie, what's wrong?" she asked.

Carrie took a long shuddering inhale, and said, "My car won't start."

"Oh, no wonder you're upset." Lindsey glanced over her shoulder to see Sully headed toward them. "Don't worry, we'll help you."

"I keep turning the key, but nothing happens," Carrie said. She gestured at her tears with a mitten. "I'm not normally this much of a baby, but I think the stress of the day is getting to me. I was so stressed about the meeting tonight, frankly, my nerves are shot."

"It's understandable," Lindsey said. "Don't feel bad. Sometimes you just have to let it out. I cried the other day when I realized I'd left my wash in the washing machine for two days and accidentally felted my favorite wool sweater."

"Bummer," Carrie said with a big sniff.

"Big one."

"Carrie, is everything all right?" Sully joined them beside her car.

"Her car won't start," Lindsey said.

"Mind if I have a look?" he asked.

"No, please do," Carrie said, and she moved aside so

Sully could sit in the driver's seat. Lindsey saw him turn the key. Nothing happened. He frowned.

"I'm no expert, but I think it's your starter," he said. "It'll probably need to be towed to Bruce's garage over on Tyler Street."

Carrie closed her eyes and Lindsey was afraid she might cry again, so she said, "Do you want to call your husband?"

"I already did," Carrie said. She opened her eyes, and her face under the parking lot lights looked pale. "He's not answering."

Lindsey wasn't terribly surprised. If he was as lazy as he seemed, he'd probably tell his wife to walk home.

"Don't worry. We can give you a lift," Sully said. "And Bruce can come and collect your car tomorrow."

"See? This will work out," Lindsey said. "Now, is there anything you need to take with you?"

"Well, I have two boxes of donated books that I don't want to leave in the car," Carrie said. "Warren said he'd take them out to Friends' shed at the Drury Street storage facility this weekend."

She opened the trunk, and both Lindsey and Sully took a box and started carrying it to his truck. Carrie locked up her car and followed.

"I really can't thank you enough," she said. "I don't know what I would have done if you two hadn't happened along."

"You'd have managed, but I'm glad we're here to help," Lindsey said.

Sully put his box of books into the back of his truck and then turned to take Lindsey's.

They all piled into the toasty-warm cab of the truck, and Carrie gave Sully directions to her house. She lived a few miles inland in a small development of raised ranch houses built in the seventies with the standard two-car garages and big bay windows.

Carrie's house was at the end of a short cul-de-sac; it was white with black trim and a bright red front door. It looked well kept and cozy, with an outside light on and a yellow glow shining from its main window above.

Carrie hopped out of the truck and fished her keys out of her purse. Sully and Lindsey climbed out of the truck too and retrieved her boxes for her.

"Oh, no, you don't have to," she protested. "I can carry them."

"It's no trouble," Lindsey said as they followed her up the walkway. "Just tell us where you want them."

Carrie unlocked her front door and held it open for them. From the foyer, a short staircase led up while another went down. Carrie pointed to the top of the stairs and said, "Would you mind just putting them in the closet up there? I'm going to check on Markus."

She went down the stairs to the lower half of the house while Sully started up. Lindsey watched him shoulder his box as if it were no heavier than a sack of groceries.

Admirable but also very annoying as she tried not to grunt and groan under the weight of her own box.

The closet door was on the right at the top of the stairs, and Sully put his box on the floor and then turned around to take hers. Lindsey was more than happy to relinquish it.

He had just taken her box when a blood-curdling scream sounded from the basement.

Lindsey met Sully's startled look and then spun around and raced down the stairs. Behind her, she could hear Sully drop the box and pound down the stairs after her. At the bottom of the lower staircase, a hallway led to a couple of bedrooms and a bath in one direction and a large family room in the other. She went toward the family room.

She stepped into the doorway and saw Carrie slumped against the far wall. Her eyes were wide and her face was etched with a look of horror. As Lindsey rushed to her side to see what was wrong, she noticed that Carrie's hands were covered in blood.

CHAPTER

6

BRIAR CREEK
PUBLIC LIBRARY

"Carrie, what's wrong? What's happened?" Lindsey asked as she knelt beside her.

She glanced around the room. A sporting event was on the big-screen TV, and in one of the two recliners facing them was the limp form of Markus Rushton.

At least, Lindsey assumed it was him. Given that she'd only met him once and he'd been bundled from head to toe, it was hard to say for sure, but the circumstances made it likely.

"What happened?" Sully asked as he crossed the room to help Lindsey get Carrie to her feet.

Carrie started to sob; her voice was choked with emotion as she said, "He's dead. Markus . . . he's been shot."

Carrie trembled and Lindsey put an arm around her shoulders, bracing her as Sully turned to examine Markus. He checked his wrist for a pulse and then moved his hand to the spot beneath his jaw. He dropped his hand and Lindsey knew he'd found no sign of a pulse.

"It's a ballistic trauma," Carrie said in nurse speak. "One entry point right through his heart. I thought I could stop the blood loss but I . . . it . . . was too late."

Her knees gave out and Lindsey caught her before she slid to the floor.

"Sully!" she cried, and he rushed forward to scoop Carrie up. She hadn't fainted but she looked on the verge.

"Let's get her upstairs," Lindsey said.

Sully lifted Carrie up and led the way. Lindsey followed, pausing by the recliner. Whatever crazy hope she harbored that both Sully and Carrie had somehow misread the situation and that Markus was not dead quickly dissipated in light of the grim scene before her.

It took her only a second to assess the situation. Markus Rushton had been shot in the heart. A large, dark stain saturated his flannel shirtfront, which covered the chest that no longer rose or fell with breath.

Feeling queasy, Lindsey stumbled after Sully as he went up the stairs to the living room above.

"Sit with her," he said as he set Carrie down on the sofa in the front room. "I'll call the police."

Lindsey went to hold Carrie's hand, but it was icy cold and sticky with blood. She didn't know if there was a protocol that said a person couldn't clean up when they found a dead body, but she wasn't going to let Carrie just sit there with her husband's blood drying on her hands.

She went into the kitchen and dampened a paper towel with warm water. Carrie paid her no mind as she gently wiped the blood off her hands. When she was finished, she left the paper towel on the counter by the sink. If anyone asked, she had no problem saying what she had done.

Silent tears were running down Carrie's face, and Lindsey suspected the shock was just beginning to wear off. She wrapped an arm around her shoulders and rocked her, trying to soothe her.

She heard Sully's footsteps on the stairs before he appeared. He looked grim. "The police should be here in a few minutes."

"I just—I don't . . ." Carrie's voice trailed off.

"There's a hole in the sliding glass door down there," Sully said. "Was that there before?"

Carrie's eyebrows lowered in confusion. "No, why?"

"Well, from what I know of bullets and their trajectory, I'm thinking the shot that got Markus in the chest came through the window."

Carrie turned a sickly shade of green and hunched forward as if she might be sick.

Lindsey rubbed her back. Sully had been in the navy for fifteen years. Lindsey was sure his assessment of the situation was probably right.

But who would have shot Markus Rushton in his own home? And why?

"Do you get any hunters out here in Briar Creek?" she asked, hoping it might all be just a tragic mistake.

"No." Sully shook his head. "It's too residential."

A flashing strobe light sliced through the room in staccato bursts of blue, and Sully rose to let the police in. Lindsey wondered who was on duty tonight. She and Chief Daniels had gotten off to a rocky start the first time they'd met, and they'd never really put it behind them.

Lindsey's first night on the job locking up the library, Ms. Cole had neglected to tell her that the alarm would sound within fifteen seconds, bringing in the local police. Lindsey had stepped out the back door and found herself nose to gun barrel, with the chief on the other end of the gun; it was hard to recover from an introduction like that.

"Hi, Emma, come on in," Sully said at the door.

Lindsey breathed a sigh of relief. It was Officer Emma Plewicki who had answered the call. Lindsey felt certain she would have a better manner with Carrie than Chief Daniels, and she was grateful, given that Carrie was still trembling, the tears still damp on her face.

The attractive brunette followed Sully upstairs into the room. She wore a fleece-lined, navy blue police-issued jacket over her uniform, which was the standard pale blue shirt over navy pants. She took in the sight of Lindsey and Carrie and raised her eyebrows.

"Lindsey and I gave Carrie a ride home from the library because her car wouldn't start," Sully explained. "When we got here, we found Markus."

"Are you all right, Carrie, Mrs. Rushton?" Emma asked.

Carrie nodded and then shook her head and then shrugged. Her distress was palpable.

"Listen, I'm going to go check on your husband and I'll be right back. Can you hang on until then?" Emma asked. Carrie nodded again and Emma turned to Sully and said, "Show me."

Lindsey watched as Emma pulled on a pair of blue latex gloves and disappeared down the stairwell behind Sully.

"They're going to think I did it," Carrie said. Her voice

sounded odd and Lindsey realized her teeth were chattering. She wondered if Carrie was going into shock.

"No, they won't think that," Lindsey said and she pulled a fluffy ecru afghan, crocheted in a pineapple pattern, off the back of the couch and wrapped it around Carrie's shoulders. "You were in a meeting all evening. It couldn't possibly have been you."

Carrie said nothing, but Lindsey noticed her shaking got worse.

Emma must have called for backup, because before she came back upstairs with Sully, Chief Daniels arrived. An abrupt knock announced his presence, but before Lindsey could answer the door, he let himself in.

He huffed and puffed his way up the stairs, hitching up his waistband as he climbed as if afraid his pants were going to make a break for his ankles. Lindsey wondered why he just didn't give in and buy a pair of suspenders, maybe he wasn't ready to admit that his gut now protruded past the point of no return.

"Carrie," he said as he stopped beside her. "Emma called me and told me about Markus. I'm so sorry."

Carrie reached out and he took her hand in his. They stood like that for just a moment, giving each other some unspoken support. Lindsey had never seen this side of the chief before, and she realized that he and Carrie must know one another very well.

"Ms. Norris." Chief Daniels acknowledged her presence with a curt nod. Nope, no warm fuzzies for her. Lindsey got the impression he wasn't happy to find her here.

"Chief, you're going to want to come and take a look at this," Emma said as she entered the room.

Sully had followed her up the stairs, and Lindsey noticed he was frowning.

"I'll be right back," Chief Daniels said to Carrie. "Emma, have you called the medical examiner's office?"

"Yes, they're on their way," she said.

As he lumbered down the stairs after her, Lindsey heard him say, "We get any more dead bodies in this town and they're going to have to open a branch office out here."

Emma said something in return, but Lindsey couldn't make it out.

"What's going to happen now?" Carrie asked.

"At a guess, a whole lot of waiting," Sully said. "It'll be a while before the crime scene personnel get here and then it'll take them several hours to investigate the scene."

"I need to call my kids," Carrie said. Her face crumpled and she sobbed into the corner of the afghan wrapped around her shoulders. "What am I going to say?"

"Where are they now?" Lindsey asked.

"They're at university," Carrie said. "Kyle is a senior at Dartmouth, and Kim is a sophomore at the Rhode Island School of Design."

"It's late," Lindsey said with a glance at the clock on the mantel. "Do you think you should wait until morning?"

Carrie looked confused. "Maybe."

"Is there anyone else we can call for you?"

"My sister is in Florida," Carrie said. "But her husband is very sick. I don't want to bother her."

If not now, when? Lindsey thought, but she didn't say anything. It wasn't her call to make.

They heard Chief Daniels's heavy tread on the stairs before he appeared. His face looked grim, and Lindsey had a feeling Carrie's night was about to get worse, if that was even possible.

"Carrie, I'm going to need you to come down to the station," he said. "I've got some questions for you."

"All right." She rose from her seat on the couch. She looked stoic with her blanket wrapped around her shoulders and her face pale but determined.

"This is in an official capacity," the chief said. "Would you like to call your attorney?"

Lindsey didn't think it was possible for Carrie to get any paler, but she did. Lindsey couldn't stand it. The whole thing was preposterous.

"She was at the library all evening," Lindsey protested. "She's the president of the Friends, and there are plenty of witnesses that can place her there."

Chief Daniels nodded, looking almost relieved to hear it. "Good. So, you were there from what time?"

"Seven," Carrie said. "No, wait, I was running late. I didn't get there until seven fifteen."

An awkward silence filled the room and Carrie glanced around at each of them. "I was having car trouble."

"That's true," Sully said. "I gave her a ride home because her starter is dead."

The chief looked less happy as he glanced at his watch. "It's nine thirty now. That only accounts for the past two hours. I don't know enough about forensics to even hazard a guess at when this might have happened. For your own protection, Carrie, we need to do this by the book."

Lindsey would have laughed at the pun if she wasn't so freaked out that Carrie might find herself in jail for a crime she could not possibly have committed.

"Officer Plewicki is going to escort you to the station, Carrie. Sully, Ms. Norris, we'll need statements about what occurred upon your arrival here. We can take them now or you can give them at the station, too."

"The station," Lindsey said. She turned to Sully. "Is that okay with you?"

"Just fine," he said. He turned to Carrie. "We'll follow you."

She gave them a ghost of a smile. She pulled the afghan off her shoulders and carefully folded it, placing it on the back of the couch. She smoothed it with her hand, as if by tidying up one corner of her shattered life, she might extend order to the rest of it.

Emma appeared on the landing below, and they all trooped out the door with her. There was an awkward moment at the squad car when Emma opened the back door for Carrie. Carrie looked like she wanted to balk, but instead, she gave Emma a nod and climbed into the back.

The small cul-de-sac was filling up with cars. As Lindsey and Sully followed Emma's squad car, they saw the state coroner's van pulling in. She did not envy them their night's work.

Are you sure this is okay?" Carrie asked for the third time.

"More than okay," Lindsey said. "I called Nancy and she said she made up the bed for you."

Sully parked his truck in the short driveway in front of the house where Lindsey rented the third floor. When it had occurred to her that Carrie couldn't go home, she had called Nancy from the police station and they agreed that while Charlie, Nancy's nephew and tenant of the middle apartment, was gone on tour, Carrie could stay in his place.

Nancy had gone through it before they arrived to make sure it didn't reek too much of twenty-something musician man-child. She deemed it okay, and Carrie had gratefully accepted their offer to stay there until she could return home.

After being questioned at the station, Carrie had been allowed to go home to pack some personal items, including a change of clothes and her toothbrush. Sully hauled her overnight bag and Lindsey's bike out of the back of his truck while Lindsey led Carrie up the stairs of the old captain's house.

Sully followed and handed off Carrie's bag in the foyer. "Will you two be all right?"

They both nodded and he said, "Call me if you need anything, either of you."

"Thanks, Sully, for everything," Carrie said.

It was well past midnight now and she looked dead on her feet. Lindsey glanced over her head and she and Sully exchanged a concerned look. Their questioning at the station had been painless, but Carrie's had taken hours and she was looking the worse for wear.

"Go rest," Sully said. "I'll check in on you tomorrow. I'll take care of your car situation."

"Thanks, Sully," Lindsey said.

They watched as he disappeared back into the night.

"He's a good man," Carrie said.

Lindsey had to agree. Parked in the hard plastic chairs at the station for hours, Sully had never once complained or begged off. He had just watched and waited, his solid presence giving the surreal situation an overlying sense of calm. No, there weren't many like Mike Sullivan.

"Hey, you two, get on up here," Nancy Peyton called down as she leaned over the railing on the second-floor landing.

After the grisly discovery at Carrie's house and the stress of the police station, Lindsey was grateful to hit the familiar stairs. Once she got Carrie settled for the night, she planned to toddle right up to her own place. At the moment, she couldn't think of anything she wanted more than to cocoon herself in the softness of her flannel sheets and downy comforter.

She shouldered Carrie's bag and led her up the stairs. Charlie's doors were curtained French doors, probably the original from before the house had been reconfigured into a three-family residence.

Nancy was standing in the open doorway, holding a key. Lindsey could see several candles burning behind her. They were the big pillar kind in a dark burgundy that smelled of cranberries. Probably, Nancy was trying to burn out Charlie's man stink.

"I pushed all of his music equipment to the side in the guest bedroom and made up the bed with my own fresh sheets," Nancy said. "Oh, honey, you look done in."

As soon as the words were out of her mouth, Nancy blanched.

"Oh, I didn't . . ." she began, but if Carrie had noticed the bad word choice, she didn't show it and instead she wrapped Nancy in a big hug.

"Thank you so much," she said. She turned and included Lindsey in the hug. "Thank you both so . . ."

Her voice cracked and she began to sob. Lindsey and Nancy exchanged a look and then hustled her over to the cushy chair by the gas fireplace, which Nancy had already turned on.

While Carrie sobbed, Nancy slipped into the kitchen. Lindsey heard the rattle of glasses, and when she reappeared, Nancy had a tray with three mismatched shot glasses and a bottle of Jack Daniel's.

"The boy is sadly lacking in his brandy supply," Nancy said. "But this will do the trick."

She set the tray down, and while Carrie blew her nose on a tissue and tried to pull herself together, Nancy splashed the whiskey into the glasses. Lindsey took hers up and noted it was filled almost to the rim. Nancy did believe in a generous pour.

"Here's an old Irish blessing: To live in the hearts we leave behind is not to die," Nancy said. "Godspeed, Markus Rushton."

Lindsey took a healthy swallow. It burned on the way down, causing her to grimace, but it also warmed her from the inside out. Carrie took a delicate sip, but Nancy shook her head at her.

"Drink the whole thing," she said. "It's your medicine tonight, and believe me, you're going to need it."

CHAPTER

7

BRIAR CREEK
PUBLIC LIBRARY

"Is it true?" Ms. Cole asked Lindsey the next day.

Lindsey just stared at her. She hadn't slept well and had just stepped into the library when Ms. Cole rumbled toward her from the new-book display. Lindsey couldn't help but feel she'd been lying in wait for her.

"Is what true?"

Lindsey knew full well what she was asking, but she was hoping to avoid the conversation. It was bad enough she hadn't been able to escape the image of Markus's dead body in her dreams. She really didn't want to give voice to the horror she had seen and have it infiltrate her day as well.

"Is it true that Markus Rushton was murdered?" Ms. Cole clarified, looking disapproving, as if Lindsey was holding out on her.

"I really couldn't say," Lindsey said. She had already decided she was not going to gossip about what had happened at the Rushtons' as it would just cause more grief for Carrie.

"But you were there," Ms. Cole protested.

Today was a gray day for Ms. Cole. It was an unfortunate choice, given that her broad frame already lent her the appearance of a large land mammal—the gray just narrowed down the species.

"Who told you that?" Lindsey asked.

Ms. Cole looked nonplussed and then said, "Well, that's not . . . I consider it my civic duty . . ."

"Uh-huh," Lindsey said. "Listening in on the police scanner again, huh?"

"If more people would take an interest in the goings-on of their community, the world would be a safer place," Ms. Cole said.

Lindsey just stared at her. Ms. Cole did not listen to the police scanner because she had some noble desire to help keep Briar Creek safe. Oh, no, she listened because she loved knowing who was getting in trouble and for what. She took great joy in the flaws and foibles of the people around her, and Lindsey had no doubt that it made her feel vastly morally superior.

"I had no idea you were so civic-minded," Lindsey said. "Remind me to have you chair the library's community fund drive this year."

"Oh, but I . . ."

"I'll be in my office," Lindsey said. She moved forward as if Ms. Cole wasn't standing there, blocking her way like a potted ficus.

Given no alternative, Ms. Cole stepped aside and Lindsey shouldered her tote bag and strode into her office. When she shut the door, she hoped it signified clearly enough that the conversation was over.

She hung up her coat and unpacked her bag. She was never sure why she felt the need to bring the same files home every night. She always thought she'd go through them, but she never did. She really needed to break the tote bag habit.

She turned on her computer and checked her voice mail while she waited for her login window to open. There were several messages, mostly from Friends of the Library members who were concerned for Carrie and wanted to know what they could do to help her. Lastly, there was a disturbing message that made the hair on the nape of her neck prickle in alarm.

Lindsey almost erased it, because there was a three-second pause before the voice started, but her finger stalled over the erase button when a whisper-soft voice sounded on the line.

Lindsey wondered if the caller thought that by whispering she was letting Lindsey in on a secret.

"Now that Carrie is going to jail for murdering her husband," the voice said. "You can make sure that Bill Sint becomes the president of the Friends again."

There was a giggle that sounded oddly humorless and then the voice grew harsh, the softness of the whisper was gone. "I'll be watching."

The automated voice mail offered Lindsey the choice to erase or save. She opted to save. Someone else needed to hear this message and reassure her that she wasn't crazy but that Marjorie Bilson most definitely was, because Lindsey was quite positive that the voice on the message belonged to Marjorie.

The call was disturbing on so many levels. First, why was she calling Lindsey? Second, the whispering thing creeped her out. And finally, the woman actually cackled with glee when she mentioned Carrie getting arrested.

Lindsey hung up the receiver. It was apparent that everyone thought Marjorie was a few chapters short of a book, but was she dangerous? The call certainly gave Lindsey the heebie-jeebies, and she had a feeling Emma Plewicki might be interested in hearing it, too.

It was probably crazy for her to even think it, but could Marjorie have shot Markus in a plan to have Carrie arrested for murder? Nah, that made no sense. If she was a murderess and really wanted Carrie gone, she would have just shot Carrie.

Lindsey thought back to the night Marjorie had chased her down with her car. Was she crazy enough to commit murder for Bill?

A knock at the door brought Lindsey's attention up, and she shook her head to clear it. Beth opened the door and stuck her head in. Her black hair was styled in disorderly spikes all around her head, and she had a large plastic bucket of kids' instruments propped on her hip.

"Hey, I heard about what happened," she said. "Is Carrie all right?"

"She's managing," Lindsey said. "Nancy is keeping an eye on her."

"If there's anything I can do . . ." Beth let the sentence dangle.

"I'll let you know," Lindsey promised. "What's with the instruments?"

"Parent-tot music time," Beth said. "I'm planning a parade around the circulation desk when the lemon is on duty."

Lindsey felt the corner of her mouth twitch, but she squashed a full-on smile, thinking she'd best not encourage Beth's shenanigans. "Nice to see you enjoying your work."

Beth grinned. "I have to go Lysol all of these before class. Flu season, you know. See you later?"

Lindsey nodded and turned back to her computer. She had a stuffed inbox of e-mails to deal with and a meeting with the mayor's community liaison officer later that afternoon.

She had answered half of the e-mail when her phone rang. The caller ID listed her landlord's number.

"Hello, Briar Creek Library, Lindsey Norris speaking. How can I help you?"

"Oh, I'm glad I caught you," Nancy said. She sounded winded. "They just took Carrie in for questioning."

"Well, that's pretty standard, right?"

"In handcuffs," Nancy added.

"Meet you at the station in five," Lindsey said and hung up. Now she knew she had to get Emma to listen to the message from Marjorie. It might be the only thing that kept Carrie out of jail.

CHAPTER 8

BRIAR CREEK
PUBLIC LIBRARY

Lindsey shrugged on her coat and was striding to the front door when Ms. Cole moved to stand in front of her.

"You're leaving?" she asked. Although it seemed improbable, her lips puckered even more tightly in disapproval than usual. "It's a little early for lunch, isn't it?"

"It is," Lindsey agreed.

She took a deep breath. She knew if she let Ms. Cole get under her skin, then they were done for in a working capacity. And although the woman drove her nuts with her lack of social skills, she was the institutional memory of the small library, and Lindsey wouldn't want to lose her, not really.

Besides, Ms. Cole couldn't help it if she carried a torch for the former library director, Mr. Tupper, and channeled her disappointment in love into disapproval of Lindsey.

Still, Lindsey was the boss and she did not take orders from Ms. Cole.

"There is an emergency with the Friends of the Library, but no worries. I'll be back in time for my meeting, and Jessica is here to cover the reference desk while I'm gone. If you need me, call my cell phone."

Ms. Cole opened her mouth to protest but Lindsey made a preemptive strike by adding, "I know with your experience and skill, Ms. Cole, you'll be able to handle anything that comes up."

Before the lemon could say a word, Lindsey pulled on her gloves and strode through the front door.

Nancy was just parking her vintage powder blue Mustang behind the police station when Lindsey arrived. Since the library was just a few doors down from the police station, Lindsey was able to get there in just moments. Nancy must have put the stomp on her gas pedal to have gotten here so fast, which made Lindsey even more uneasy about the situation.

Emma Plewicki was manning the front desk when they walked in. She shook her head at the sight of them, as if she should have been expecting this but somehow hadn't.

She was in her standard-issue blue uniform, the winter version with long sleeves. Her thick, shoulder-length hair was cut in a stylish sweep, which framed her heart-shaped face becomingly. She was pretty enough that Lindsey wondered if she ever had a hard time getting criminals to take her seriously. Judging by the hardware she wore on her belt, it would be a mistake a criminal wouldn't make twice.

Lindsey liked Emma. She came into the library a lot and had a great rapport with the teens that congregated in the youth area after school. She knew them all by name and they seemed to like her, too. If a community's safety was built on a foundation of trust between the police and the residents, then Emma was this department's cornerstone.

"Lindsey, Nancy," Emma greeted them. "Carrie's in back talking to Chief Daniels and a state investigator."

"Why the handcuffs, Emma?" Nancy asked. "That's not how we do things around here."

"This is a murder investigation," Emma said. "Everything has to be done according to regulation. It may not seem like it, but it's to protect Carrie."

Lindsey noticed that she dropped her gaze to the countertop when she spoke. Clearly, she wasn't as comfortable with this as she'd have them believe.

"Horse feathers," Nancy snorted. "Since when did you start talking in police speak?"

"It's my job," Emma snapped, looking annoyed.

"The medical examiner gave a time of death, didn't he?" Lindsey asked.

Emma gave her a sharp glance, and Lindsey knew she had reasoned it right. Emma sighed and confirmed, "Mark Rushton was killed between four and eight last night."

"Making Carrie a viable suspect," Nancy said.

Emma didn't say anything. She didn't have to.

"Can we see her?" Nancy asked.

Emma shook her head. "Not while they are questioning her."

"Does she have an attorney?" Lindsey asked.

"She declined," Emma said.

Lindsey swore under her breath. The one thing she had learned while engaged to a law professor who specialized in criminal law was to always have an attorney present when being questioned by police or going in front of a judge. The law was such a labyrinth of legalese that you needed one just to navigate the ins and outs.

"Listen, I got a really unsettling phone call on my office line at the library," Lindsey said. "I'd like for you to hear it."

Emma raised her eyebrows. "Can you retrieve it from any phone?"

"Yes," Lindsey said. Emma turned the desk phone around so that it faced her.

Lindsey quickly dialed the number to hear her voice mail, queued up the message and handed the receiver to Emma.

She watched the officer's face as she listened. A frown formed in between her eyes and she gave Lindsey a searching look.

"Interesting," she said. "Hang on one second, would you?"

She handed Lindsey the receiver and then went to another desk in the back of the room. She opened a drawer and came back to the main desk with a mini tape recorder in her hand.

"Let's play that again," she said. She held up the recorder to the receiver, and when it was done, she clicked it off. "Do me a favor and save that message, okay?"

Lindsey nodded and took the receiver back. When prompted, she saved the voice mail message and then hung up.

Nancy glanced between them, but neither Lindsey nor Emma explained. Lindsey had a feeling Emma wanted to keep it quiet until they talked to Marjorie. To Nancy's credit, she didn't press.

"Can you do us a favor and tell Carrie that we're here?" Nancy asked. "So she doesn't feel so alone."

"Of course," Emma said. She pushed back from the counter and strode toward the back.

"Well, we may as well have a seat," Lindsey said. "There's no telling how long this will take."

"I can wait," Nancy said. "Why don't you head back to the library? You don't want to give Ms. Cole a reason to suggest your termination to the board."

"Do you really think she'd do that?"

"The lemon? Are you kidding?" Nancy asked. "You know she wanted your job, right?"

"No, I didn't," Lindsey said. "Huh. I thought she always gave me a hard time because she was in love with Mr. Tupper."

"What?" Nancy gaped. "The lemon had the hots for Tupper? No way!"

"According to Beth," Lindsey said. "But why didn't she tell me that Ms. Cole wanted my job?"

"She may not have known," Nancy said. "I only know because Milton was on the hiring committee. The committee members were the only ones who got to look over all of the applicants. He asked me, as a resident, what I thought of Ms. Cole's people skills."

"And you said?"

"That although she had her merits, working with people is not her gift."

"She must have been pretty upset," Lindsey said.

"Honestly, it's hard to tell," Nancy said. "She scowls as much as ever."

"But she's been there for thirty years," Lindsey said. "And she has her degree in library science. Don't you think she earned the promotion?"

Nancy sighed. "Can you imagine her running the Briar Creek Library? Just because you have the paper and do the time does not make you the best leader."

They walked across the police station lobby to the line of vacant chairs placed in front of the window. They were hard plastic in a shade of orange usually reserved for bowling alleys and the department of motor vehicles. They did not invite lingering.

Nancy sat down and promptly pulled her crochet out of her tote bag. She had begun a new project, a baby blanket in aqua for her niece who was expecting a boy. It was a super-soft yarn that she was crocheting in a large circle, and she had a fluffy yellow yarn to crochet around the border to give the baby something tactile to grab.

Lindsey watched as she looped the yarn around her hook and pulled one loop and then another in a double crochet. Nancy made it look so easy it was positively annoying.

A glance at the clock and Lindsey knew she had to get back to the library. Ms. Cole would be watching, and it didn't seem that there was anything she could do here.

"Will you call me if I can help?" she asked.

"Absolutely," Nancy said. "I'll keep my ears open and let you know if I pick up anything."

Lindsey stepped back and studied her merry-eyed friend.

Nancy had been widowed young when her captain husband went down with his ship in a bad storm. She had never gotten over it, and during particularly bad storms, she'd been known to climb out onto the widow's walk of her house and look for her husband's ship.

Lindsey wondered if she was feeling a kinship with Carrie because of the dead-husband thing that brought her to this crocheting vigil she was keeping for Carrie. She would have asked, but there was no way to do it without being rude.

"Call me when she's out," Lindsey said.

"Will do," Nancy agreed. "Now shoo."

Lindsey fastened her coat closed and headed out the door. She hadn't known that the lemon wanted her job. Suddenly, Ms. Cole's hostility made so much more sense. It must have been very hard to be passed over for a job she had probably expected as her due. As the wind blew in off the water and yanked at the ends of her coat, causing a wicked draft to slap up inside, Lindsey tried to picture Ms. Cole in charge.

Time clocks and docked pay, no sick time, and vacations denied, that's what it would have been, Lindsey had no doubt. The committee had been right to choose someone else, but Lindsey knew that had to fester like a boil within the lemon's heart.

She needed to call Carole Towles, her mentor, to see if there was a better way to handle Ms. Cole. Along with Milton, Carole was her favorite member of the library board. A former librarian herself, Carole had an understanding of how to motivate staff in a positive way. Although she was presently at her winter home in Arizona, Lindsey knew she could call her and see if she had any ideas for projects to give Ms. Cole that would make her feel important but not give her power over the other staff persons.

Lindsey had never been a supervisor before her position here in Briar Creek. In fact, when she had applied for the job, she was certain her lack of supervision would keep her out of the running. To her surprise, the hiring committee had felt otherwise.

What Lindsey had come to understand over the past nine months was that her staff needed to be invested in the library in order to give it their best. If they felt they had the right to make decisions that best served their patrons and felt empowered to do so, well, their service was exemplary. The only one not embracing the flexible policies was Ms. Cole. Not a big surprise.

Still, there must be a way to utilize Ms. Cole's unique skill set for the good of the library. She just had to figure out what it was.

Feeling marginally better about the situation, Lindsey stepped on the rubber mat in front of the library that activated the automatic doors. As the doors slid open, she stepped inside to find her library in complete chaos.

CHAPTER

9

BRIAR CREEK
PUBLIC LIBRARY

Lindsey felt her mouth slide open as Ms. Cole, brandishing a broom, ran past the open door. On her heels was Beth shouting, "Drop the broom! You're scaring him, you big bully!"

Two pages, teenagers in charge of shelving the books, were racing after them, and Jessica Gallo, the library assistant working the adult reference desk, was looking on with an alarmed stare while Mrs. Holcomb, a patron, stood across from her with her eyes wide and her mouth slightly agape.

Lindsey heard the doors slide shut behind her. For a nanosecond, she considered turning around and going back out, but only for a nanosecond.

"Come here, you little flea-bitten pest," Ms. Cole ordered, and Lindsey saw her broom come down hard on the floor.

"Stop it!" Beth snapped. She snatched the broom out of Ms. Cole's hands and looked like she was considering hitting her with it.

The two teen workers skidded to a halt behind them, and Beth said, "I think he went that way."

Lindsey watched as they hurried toward the children's area, with Ms. Cole in hot pursuit.

"What's happening?" Jessica asked as she came over to stand beside Lindsey.

"No idea."

Several patrons who had been using the Internet had left their desks to check out the ruckus, and Lindsey saw Milton in his usual corner, trying to hurriedly extricate himself from an eagle pose without hurting himself.

She hurried into the children's section to find Beth standing in front of her area with the broom held across her chest like a staff. Ms. Cole was facing her, looking like an ominous thundercloud in her shades-of-gray outfit.

"Back off," Beth snapped. "Or I'll let it bite you."

"That's it," Ms. Cole snapped. "I'm calling animal control and having it put down."

"You can't!" Beth wailed. "He hasn't done anything."

"Watch me!" Ms. Cole retorted.

"Stop it!" Lindsey cried out.

Everyone turned to look at her and she realized she had spoken louder than she'd intended. It was the first time she could remember raising her voice in years.

"Would someone please explain to me what is going on?" she demanded.

Ms. Cole and Beth both started talking at once, and their voices escalated as they tried to out-shout each other in their effort to be heard. Milton had gotten out of his asana and moved to stand beside Lindsey. She was grateful for the support.

"Beth, Ms. Cole." Lindsey tried to interrupt, but now that they were arguing, she was no match for their volume. "Ladies!"

Still, they both kept gesturing and yelling. Lindsey looked at Milton and shrugged.

"Silence!" he bellowed, and both women stammered to a halt.

"Thank you," Lindsey said. She turned to the two teen-age workers who were watching this entire scene with slack jaws and bug eyes. "Perry, Heather, do you think you could fill me in?"

Ms. Cole started to speak, but Lindsey held up her hand and said, "No."

"Well, it started with the dog," Perry said.

"Dog?" Lindsey asked.

"Puppy, really," he said.

"We went to unload the book drop and we found a puppy," Heather clarified. "We told Ms. Cole and she went to grab him and throw him outside."

"But Ms. Stanley said not to because he would freeze or get hit by a car," Perry continued the story. "Then when Ms. Cole went to catch him, he nipped her on the toe and ran."

"Then she grabbed a broom and began to chase him," Heather said. "But then Ms. Stanley tried to stop her."

"And that's when you showed up," Perry finished.

"Are you all right, Ms. Cole?" Lindsey asked.

She gave an indignant sniff. "I'll live. He's probably got rabies, fleas and heartworm. You need to call the pound."

"Perhaps, but I think we need to find him first. Does anyone know where he is?" Lindsey asked.

They all glanced around, completely baffled.

"All right, then, let's find him and then we'll figure out what to do," she said. "What does he look like?"

"Cute," Beth said.

"Mangy," Ms. Cole said.

"I was thinking more of a color," Lindsey said.

"Black," they said together.

"And size?" she asked.

"Large rat," Ms. Cole said.

"Small cat," Beth said.

"All right," Lindsey said. "Everyone fan out. Let's see if we can find him."

Everyone hit the floor except Ms. Cole, who had snatched her broom back from Beth and held it in front of her as if she expected to be attacked.

"He's probably piddling somewhere," she said.

Lindsey sighed and hunkered down on the floor. She looked through the short picture-book aisles and around the children's tables. No sign of a dog.

She rose and walked over to the kids play area. There were several alphabet puzzles laid out on the short tables, and she hunched down to see beneath them, but still there was no sign of anything other than the stray letter *A*.

She glanced around the room. The lid to the treasure chest that Beth used to store puppets and dress-up clothes was open. Lindsey wondered if she were a scared puppy, where would she hide? The trunk seemed like a pretty good bet.

She crossed slowly to the trunk and said, "Here, puppy. Hey, fella, are you in there?"

She didn't want to reach into the trunk and scare him and risk getting bit, so she sat beside it and used her calmest voice.

"It's okay, no one is going to hurt you, I promise."

A low growl followed by a thumping sound came from the trunk. Bingo!

Lindsey peered into the jumble of butterfly puppets and pirate hats. She couldn't see any furry critters, but the growling and thumping could still be heard. She carefully reached in and pushed aside a pair of ladybug wings while she talked. "It's okay. You're safe now."

Growl, growl, *thump, thump, thump.* She smiled when she realized the dog was growling to scare her and thumping his tail to welcome her at the same time; smart dog to cover all his bases.

"Did you find him?" Beth asked.

Lindsey held a finger to her lips and nodded. Everyone went still watching her. She reached farther into the trunk and pushed aside a coned princess hat with a long pink veil.

"It's okay," she said and held her hand up over the trunk, hoping he could smell her.

She waited and there was a shuffling noise from the trunk, a growl, and another series of thumps. Lindsey stayed perfectly still, talking softly until a black nose pushed its way up past a Batman costume to press against her palm.

The nose was cold and wet, but she didn't pull away. The growling stopped and then a pink tongue appeared and took a nervous swipe at her wrist.

"It's okay, buddy," she said. "Come on, I won't hurt you."

A black head with fuzzy eyebrows popped up with a pair of glittery fairy wings hanging haphazardly about its neck. The puppy looked at Lindsey for a second and then wiggled forward, trying to get into her arms. Lindsey blew out a breath and picked him up.

Lindsey held him close and he tucked his head under her chin. The furry, black body let out a soul-deep sigh, and Lindsey felt as if the dog were placing all the trust he possessed in the world right onto her.

Beth was the first one to step forward. "Oh, look, he likes you."

"He probably needs some water," Lindsey said. She untangled the fairy wings from about his neck and carried him toward their break room. It was at the back of the building and had a bathroom, a small kitchenette and a lounging area.

"Shall I call the pound?" Ms. Cole asked.

She looked at the puppy as if she wanted to whack him right out the front door with the broom. Lindsey found herself turning her back to her to protect the wee fellow.

"I'll do it," Lindsey said. "I'd really like to know how he got into the book drop. It's too high for him to have climbed up on his own."

"Someone must have put him in there," Beth said. "You know, like Dewey the library cat in Spencer, Iowa. Vicki Myron, the librarian, has written several books about him."

"Oh, I love Dewey," Jessica said as she joined them. "It broke my heart when he died."

"Maybe it was just a prank gone wrong. I can't believe anyone would harm a puppy," Lindsey said. "Hopefully, his owner will come looking for him."

Perry and Heather, the two teenagers, both came close to pet the dog. From the protection of Lindsey's arms, he wagged and thumped his long tail against her hip while they patted his head.

"He sure is sweet," Heather said. "Look at those eyebrows."

"Yeah, he looks like my uncle Otto, all eyebrows," Perry said. "Man, if we hadn't unloaded the book drop today, he could have frozen to death in there."

As if he understood what they were saying, the dog shuddered in Lindsey's arms and gave her a nervous lick on her chin.

"You're not really going to give him to the pound, are you?" Heather asked. Her face was creased with worry and Lindsey felt a pang of guilt.

She firmly pushed it away. Lindsey did not want a dog. She was a renter. Dogs and renting didn't mix. She would help the little guy out and make sure he found a nice home, but she was not keeping him.

"Uh, I don't know." Lindsey hedged. "Let's just take it one day at a time, unless, of course, Jessica, Beth or Ms. Cole want to take him?"

Ms. Cole gave her a sour look, turned on her heel and walked back to the safety of the circulation desk.

"I'm in grad school," Jessica said. "No time for housebreaking a pup."

Beth shook her head. "I don't think my cats would approve; besides, finders keepers."

"I didn't find him," Lindsey protested. "You all found him first."

Beth just tsked and shook her head. "Deny, deny, deny."

For his part, the dog licked Lindsey's face again. She sighed. She had a meeting to get ready for and she wanted to find out what was going on at the police station with Carrie.

"You really didn't pick a good day for this," she said to the dog. His tail thumped against her hip.

The others left her with her armful, but Milton came and stood by her. Lindsey turned to him with hopeful eyes.

"Alas, no," he said, clearly reading her mind. "I'm horribly allergic." As if to prove it, he sneezed.

"Fine," she said. She strode out the front door with the dog. At the slap of the cold air, he huddled closer to her.

She walked him to the side yard and put him down. He sat on the cold ground, staring up at her with his brown eyes. He thumped his tail.

"Potty," she said encouragingly. "Do you need to go potty?"

He lay down and rested his chin on her loafers. She reached down and patted his head, marveling at how soft his fur was. He really was an engaging little fellow. He was sturdy, with big feet and a long tail. He had a short muzzle that sprouted fuzzy hair, and over his eyes were more tufts of the same. He had the look of a grumpy old man, but she felt sure he was smiling at her.

"It's okay, you know, I won't leave you out here. If you need to go to the bathroom, go," she said. "Believe me, if you go in my office, we'll really be off to a rocky start."

His ears pricked up and he slowly rose to his feet.

"That's right," she said. "Go ahead. I'll wait."

He moved cautiously away from her, as if ready to race back if she made any sudden moves. He lifted his leg on some nearby hedges and then scooted back to her. Lindsey picked him up, happy to have something warm to hold against the bitter wind. *Note to self,* she thought, *next time wear your coat.*

She brought him back inside and found Beth waiting in her office with a bowl of water and a turkey sandwich.

Lindsey put the puppy down and he promptly lapped up the water and scarfed the turkey out of the sandwich.

"He has a really sweet disposition," Beth said. "And he really seems to like you."

Lindsey gave her a flat stare. "Go away."

Beth got up and moved to the door. "Dogs are a woman's best friend, I'm just saying."

"I think you have him mistaken with diamonds," Lindsey said.

"True friends are like diamonds, precious and rare," Beth countered.

"And getting rarer," Lindsey said with a pointed look at the door.

Beth grinned and closed the door behind her. Lindsey checked her cell phone. There were no messages. She wondered if they were still questioning Carrie. She also wondered what they would do with that phone message from Marjorie.

Emma had looked as concerned as she felt when she listened to the message, so she knew it wasn't just her.

Lindsey could only hope they picked up Marjorie and she shed some light on Markus Rushton's shooting.

Lindsey felt a solid weight thump against her foot. She glanced under the top of her desk and saw that the dog had curled up under her desk and pillowed his head on top of her feet.

CHAPTER

10

BRIAR CREEK
PUBLIC LIBRARY

She felt the *aw* bubble up inside of her before she could stop it, then sighed. Dogs required more care than she felt capable of, and he was just a puppy, which meant he'd need even more attention.

She had always considered herself a beta fish sort of person. The relationship, while entertaining, didn't last too long, and it was pretty easy to get a free fish sitter when you wanted to travel. She just didn't think she was ready for more of a commitment at this point in her life.

A soft snore sounded from the floor at her feet. "I'll find you a nice home," she said. "I promise."

When she had to leave for her meeting with the mayor's liaison, she found herself reluctant to leave the puppy. Not because she cared, she told to herself, but because she didn't know what sort of mischief he'd get into. She had read somewhere, probably when helping a patron find a book on dog rearing, that puppies could be soothed by the sound of a clock ticking and something that smelled familiar. She took her coat off the back of her chair, and as she eased her foot out from under the puppy's head, she put her coat in its place so the puppy had something soft to rest on that smelled familiar. She then got her wall clock down and put it near the puppy so he could hear it ticking.

Fortunately, the meeting with the mayor's liaison was being held in the upstairs meeting room of the library. She felt slightly better that she was at least still in the building with the puppy on the off chance that Ms. Cole got crazy with her broom again.

As she gathered her notes and slipped out the door, the only sound she heard was a soft snore. Poor guy was probably tuckered after his ordeal. She figured she'd better take him in to see a veterinarian just to be sure he was okay. Luckily, she now knew the vet on her street, Tom Rubinski. Maybe she could take the puppy to see him after work.

The dog seemed healthy, aside from being hungry and thirsty. She supposed she should probably take his picture and make some flyers to report him found. If someone had taken him and shoved him in the book drop to be mean, well, the owner would probably be frantic. Maybe they would find his owner and all would be well. She wondered why that thought didn't make her feel as happy as she thought it would.

Lindsey had a hard time concentrating on the meeting with the mayor's liaison, Herb Gunderson. It could be because she was worried about the puppy in her office or because she was concerned that Nancy hadn't called to give her an update about Carrie, or it could be the fact that Herb was the single most boring person alive. She tried not to judge, really, but the man could send an insomniac into a well-deserved sleep coma.

She glanced around the table; several of the department heads for the town were in attendance. Herb was giving a fact-laden discourse on the process of work flow and the mayor's desire to improve it.

Jason Meeger, the head of the town sanitation department, had his head bowed as if he was studying his notes. She checked the rise and fall of his chest. Asleep. Candace Collins from the public works department got up for her third cup of coffee, and Lindsey suspected it was a way to keep herself awake.

Lindsey glanced at the clock on the wall behind Herb's head. Five more minutes, they just had five more minutes to go.

"And now the mayor would like me to ask if any of you have any questions about the new work-flow policy?" Herb asked.

No one moved. No one spoke.

"Are you sure?" he asked. "I can go over it again."

"No!" Candace shouted and then cleared her throat. "What I mean is, I'm sure everyone is all clear on how to implement the new work-flow techniques. Right, everyone?"

Lindsey looked at the manic light in Candace's eyes. She was pretty sure Candace would smack anyone who spoke upside the head with the coffeepot.

Herb glanced around the table, looking at each of them over the top of his reading glasses. "All right, then, meeting adjourned."

Like runners in the blocks, everyone made for the door at once. There was a bit of a jam up in the doorway, but Jason Meeger, who had bolted awake, used his former high school football brawn-turned-to-fat to strong-arm his way through the door to freedom. Candace was right on his heels, as were several other department heads.

Lindsey followed them down the stairs, relieved that there wouldn't be another one of these meetings until next month. She waved at the others as they made for the front door.

She turned and headed for her office, wondering what to expect. She eased open the door in case the little guy was asleep. She needn't have bothered. Amid a pile of half-chewed papers, she saw a black furry behind sticking out of her overturned wastebasket.

"Is something wrong?"

Lindsey turned and saw Ms. Cole headed her way.

"Oh, no, it's all good," Lindsey lied and quickly stepped into her office and shut the door behind her.

The snap of the door caused the puppy to back his way out of the wastebasket. When he got a sniff of Lindsey, he went into spasms of delight. He bounded across the office and jumped up on her leg. On his hind legs, he reached just above her knee and wrapped his paws around her leg as if he was hugging her.

"Hi, there, buddy," Lindsey said as she stooped to pet him. "I'm not going to bust you this time, but just so you know, the garbage is off limits."

His tail went into hyper speed, and Lindsey assumed they understood one another. It took her a while to clean up the mess, and she made a note to herself to pick him up some toys on the way home. Just to get him through the night, she told herself.

Lindsey was relieved that it wasn't her night to close the library. Ms. Cole had taken to popping into her office, and Lindsey had the feeling that she was trying to catch the dog misbehaving. And what exactly did she think Lindsey was going to do? Throw him out into the freezing temperatures outside? Not likely.

She called Tom Rubinski and he managed to fit her in at the end of the day. She had to leave work an hour early to catch him before he closed, but that was okay. She had a feeling the sooner she got the dog away from Ms. Cole the better.

When it was time to go, she emptied her tote bag of its usual paperwork and put the dog inside. She wasn't going to be able to bicycle home with him, so she figured she'd hoof it. He was solid, at least ten pounds, but given that she didn't have a leash for him, she didn't want to risk having him run into the road.

As she hefted the bag onto her shoulder, the dog popped his head out. His eyes sparkled under his bushy eyebrows and his pink tongue hung out on one side, making him look like he was enjoying the lift.

Lindsey decided to walk to the police station first to see if Carrie and Nancy were still there. She certainly hoped not. They simply could not have questioned Carrie for a whole day. Then again, she supposed she might have been arrested, but that was just ludicrous. Carrie was not a killer.

She pulled open the glass door that led to the station and saw Emma still at the front desk. No sign of Nancy, however.

"Hi, Lindsey." Emma greeted her. "What have you got there?"

"A library donation," she said.

Emma frowned at her.

"Someone shoved him into the book drop, so I'm taking him home for now. You don't happen to want a dog do you?"

"I have three already," Emma said. She held out her hand for the pup to sniff, and he went all licky-lou on her.

"Aw, he's sweetie," she said. "What are you going to do with him?"

"Put up signs in case his owners are missing him, and then if we can't find them, I suppose I'll take him to the pound."

Emma gave her a nod as if to say she understood, but Lindsey still felt like a heel even using the *p* word. The dog turned and licked her hand and she felt even more rotten.

"I keep lousy hours for having a dog," she said. "It wouldn't be fair to him."

"Hmm, I think he'd find that more fair than being shoved in a book drop," Emma said.

Lindsey sighed because she knew she was right. Still, she didn't want a dog.

"So, I see that Nancy is gone. Does that mean Carrie was released?"

"Yes, just over an hour ago," Emma said.

"So, she wasn't arrested or anything?"

"No, why? Should she be?"

"No!"

"Relax, I'm just messing with you," Emma said.

She winked and Lindsey said, "Funny, really, stop. You're killing me."

"You take it where you can." Emma shrugged. "A word to the wise, though, I played Chief Daniels that message from Marjorie."

"And?"

"He's concerned, and he's planning to pay her a visit," Emma said. "For some reason, she's focused on you, so keep your guard up."

"I will," Lindsey said.

With Emma's warning ringing in her ears, Lindsey headed to the vet's. It wasn't a long walk, but the sun had already set and the streetlights, although helpful, didn't really dispel the shadows that were making Lindsey twitchy. She didn't really think that Marjorie was going to run her down or jump out from behind a trash can, but she couldn't shake the feeling of unease that lingered over her like a stranger's eyes watching her every step.

When she turned onto her street, just a few houses from the vet's, a pair of headlights swung in her direction, catching her in their light. Startled, she felt her heart slam up into her throat like a brick.

CHAPTER

11

BRIAR CREEK
PUBLIC LIBRARY

Lindsey did not want to have another go-round with Batty Bilson. If the chief had questioned her about the voice mail, Lindsey had no doubt that Batty was hunting her down for another little chat.

She should have asked Emma what the plan was so she could be prepared. As it was, she had no intention of engaging in another go-round with a nut burger. She began to jog, hoping her loafers didn't slip on a patch of ice and send her and the puppy sprawling.

She could hear the vehicle behind her coming up fast, and she jumped onto the walkway that led to the Rubinskis'.

"Lindsey, wait! Hey, are you all right?" a deep voice shouted after her.

Lindsey stopped short and spun around to find Sully in

his truck parked against the curb with his window down. She felt her heart resume beating in her chest as the dog wriggled around inside the bag, trying to get a good look at the owner of the deep voice.

She put her hand flat on her chest and sucked in a deep breath. "Oh, jeez, I thought you were Marjorie Bilson."

"Nah, I'm too tall," he said.

A laugh that was mostly relief escaped her. Height was the least of their differences, she thought as she puffed out a breath. She waited while he shut off the engine and stepped out of his truck.

"What have you got there?" he asked as he pointed to the bag.

"A new patient for Dr. Rubinski," she said. "Someone shoved him in the book drop at the library, so I'm bringing him in to make sure he's okay."

"Are you serious?" he asked, looking appalled. "Someone stuck him in that big metal drawer?"

"Sadly, I am," Lindsey said. "Poor guy, we have no idea how long he was stuck in there.

Sully held out his hand, and the fuzzy, black dog sniffed and licked him and then barked in approval. Sully reached up and ruffled his ears. The dog pushed against the bottom of the tote bag, trying to get to him.

"He seems to like you," she said. "Interested?"

"Ah, I'm more of a beta fish kind of guy," he said.

"You can't snuggle a beta fish," she said, using her best sales-pitch voice.

"Sure, you can," he said. "You just hold up their bowl and puff out your cheeks. They love that."

Lindsey rolled her eyes, turned and went up the walkway, following the signs that led to the office. In what she guessed used to be a free-standing garage, the vet practice had been built, complete with cat and dog paw prints leading the way into the entrance.

Sully fell into step beside her, and when she glanced at him, he said, "I just want to get a good look at the little guy."

"Excellent and maybe you know someone who'd like a dog?" she asked. Just then the pup licked her chin and she looked down to see him gazing at her with warm brown eyes.

"Yeah, I think he's already found his person," Sully said.

"I work too much," Lindsey protested. "And I don't know how Nancy feels about dogs. She may not even let me keep him through the night."

"Sure she will," he said. "Nancy's a softie. She lets Charlie live there, doesn't she?"

"He's housebroken," she said.

"Barely," he teased.

They entered the building and she approached the reception area. A young woman in scrubs greeted her and handed Lindsey a clipboard.

"Hi, Ms. Norris," she said. "This is a form for new-patient information."

"Here, I'll watch him," Sully said as he took the tote bag off her shoulder and let the puppy out.

"Thanks," Lindsey said, and she sat down on the lone couch to fill out the forms. Given that she knew nothing about the dog, it went fairly quickly.

Sully and the puppy played on the floor while they waited. Lindsey noticed that Sully's large square hands dwarfed the dog and yet he played with an innate gentleness that she found endearing.

"Ms. Norris," the young woman called her. "We're ready for you."

Lindsey rose from her spot on the couch and Sully scooped the puppy up from the floor and followed her into the exam room.

Tom, Dr. Rubinski, was already there, and he took in the sight of the two of them with the dog with a large grin.

"Lindsey, we meet again," he said. He held out his hand and they shook. "At least I'm wearing clothes this time."

Sully raised his brows and looked in between them. Lindsey felt her face grow hot and she said, "He was in his pajamas the last time we met."

"Oh, really?" Sully asked.

"As was his wife," she added. "It was the night of the Batty incident."

"Oh." Sully smiled and shook hands with his friend. "I hope it wasn't those embarrassing SpongeBob ones that you own."

Tom laughed. "You'll never forget those."

"They're burned on my retinas," Sully agreed. He turned to Lindsey to explain. "We were on an overnight fishing trip on my boat, and when we decided to do some night fishing, he showed up on deck in these neon yellow pajamas. I'm pretty sure he scared all of the fish away."

They both chuckled and Lindsey smiled. She could see there was a strong friendship between them. They looked to be about the same age, but where Tom's blond hair was thinning at the top and his middle was developing a decided paunch, Sully's thick chestnut curls barely showed any gray and he had the build of a man much younger than he was. She supposed that working outside kept him trim. Not that she thought about him or where he worked or his physique . . . much.

Thankfully, the puppy was not to be ignored, however, and he wriggled out of Sully's arms to check out the newcomer.

Tom crouched down on the floor so as to be level with the puppy and held out his hand. The dog sniffed and licked and wriggled closer to the good doctor.

Tom ran his hands over him and listened to his heart and lungs with his stethoscope. He took the puppy's temperature, apologizing for having to be so rude. The puppy had a hard time staying still, but Tom talked to him in a soothing voice, and Lindsey could swear the puppy was trying his hardest to be good.

When he finished the exam, the dog stood up on his hind legs and licked Tom's face, and he simply said, "Oh, thank you, buddy. You're a good dog, aren't you?"

The puppy wagged and barked in agreement. Tom's way with animals was amazing, and Lindsey knew if she were a dog, she'd probably try to get him to adopt her.

"You're not looking for a dog by any chance, are you?" she asked.

"Thanks but, no," he said with a grin. "With that litter of nine we just delivered, I doubt we'll be taking in any strays any time soon. Gina and I are pretty sure having a baby will be a snap after this."

"Oh?" Sully asked.

"Not that we're having a baby just yet," Tom said. He looked embarrassed and both Sully and Lindsey grinned at him.

"So, I heard this guy was dumped at the library?" Tom asked, obviously hoping to change the subject.

"Shoved in the book drop," Lindsey confirmed. "How did you hear?"

"News travels pretty fast in Briar Creek," he said. "Well, that and Mrs. Holcomb was in the library when he made his appearance and she brought her dachshund in this afternoon."

"Tinkerbelle?" Sully asked.

"That's the one," Tom said. "I keep telling her that she can't dress her up in a pink tutu or Tinkerbelle's going to get depressed, but she doesn't listen."

"Really, she would be so much happier in purple," Sully joked.

"I keep saying that," Tom returned. Then he turned to Lindsey and asked, "So, what are you going to name him?"

"I'm not naming him," she said. "That will be up to his new owners."

"Any takers yet?" Tom asked.

"No, but there will be." She hoped she sounded more confident than she felt.

Tom gave her a dubious look.

"What?" Lindsey asked.

"Well, I'm thinking what you've got here is a mutt," he said. "A lot of people won't take mutts."

"But he's so sweet."

As if he knew she was talking about him, the puppy wiggled his way across the exam room to her and sat on her foot. Lindsey tried to ignore the way he gazed up at her, but still she felt the need to scratch his ears in reassurance.

"Well, there's one other problem," Tom said. "He looks to be a mix of a pit bull and a schnauzer. Pit bulls, even half breeds, have a pretty bad reputation, and they're hard to find good homes for because people either want them for the wrong reasons, to be aggressive, or they are afraid of them."

"But that's ridiculous. Who could be afraid of him?" Lindsey asked, kneeling down beside the dog, who licked her face and thumped his tail. "He has the nicest disposition."

"Well, he's a puppy," Tom said. "At a guess, since he still has his puppy teeth, I'd put him between three and four months. He's going to get bigger and stronger and harder to find a home for."

"No worries," Lindsey said stubbornly. "He'll also get cuter and more loyal. I'll find a great home for him. You'll see."

Tom smiled at her. She glanced over her shoulder and noticed that Sully was smiling, too.

"Oh, quit it," she said. "I'm not keeping him."

To their credit, both men refrained from comment.

"I'll keep my ears open. If I hear about anyone looking for a pup, I'll let them know you've got a good one," Tom said.

"Thanks," Lindsey said and shook his hand. "Come on, little fella, let's show you your temporary home."

Lindsey wasn't positive but she was pretty sure he waggled his eyebrows at her. She plopped him in the tote bag and handed it to Sully so she could pay the bill.

Sully and the dog waited for her by the door, and they all stepped out into the cold night air together.

"Can I give you a lift?" he asked as they headed down the walk toward his truck.

"Thanks, but I'd feel silly taking a ride for just a few houses."

He nodded and an awkward silence fell between them.

At the risk of making an uncomfortable moment worse, Lindsey shifted the tote bag on her shoulder and said, "So, what brought you out here tonight?"

"You," he said.

CHAPTER

12

BRIAR CREEK
PUBLIC LIBRARY

Whatever she had been expecting, that had not been it. Instead of asking an open-ended follow-up question like any good librarian, Lindsey had merely gulped and stuttered and shouldered the tote bag with the wiggling puppy, and with an awkward wave that must have had all the grace of a pimply twelve-year-old, she set off down the street toward her apartment.

She had seen Sully's slow smile as she departed, red-faced and stammering, and she knew he was amused by her.

Good grief, how would she ever face the man again?

Her reaction had been so, well, lame. What if he had just been being neighborly and he meant he'd been checking on her because he knew she biked home and she'd left her bike at the library tonight? He might not have meant *you* as in he was interested.

Lindsey looked down into the bag where the puppy was trying to stand and groaned. "I am so embarrassed."

As if he completely understood because it happened all the time, the puppy licked her hot face and Lindsey laughed. "Make an ass of yourself frequently, do you?"

She felt the puppy's tail thump against her hip and she felt immediately better.

"Come on, you're going to need to work some charm on my landlady so she'll let you stay. And here's a tip, don't piddle in the house."

A short yip was his only reply as they stepped into the foyer. The house was quiet. Lindsey wondered if Carrie was holed up with Nancy. If so, she didn't want to disturb them. Oh, who was she kidding? She wanted to sneak the dog upstairs and then come tell Nancy he was here. Sort of give her a few minutes to digest the situation before she was confronted with his furriness.

She crept up both flights of stairs and fumbled for her key. At the door, the puppy began to try to jump out of the bag as if he sensed they were home.

"Don't get so excited, this is temporary."

He didn't appear to be listening. As soon as she opened the door, he bolted into the main room, nose to the ground, sniffing and running faster than his big paws could carry him.

"Surprise!" a shout erupted from the couch, and Lindsey jumped with a small shriek of alarm.

The puppy stopped in mid-sniff and looked at her as if to see if she was okay. With her hand on her chest, she staggered into the room. One more fright tonight and she'd probably keel over.

The entire crafternoon club—Beth, Nancy, Violet, Charlene and Mary, plus Carrie—were there with a spread of food and an assortment of gift bags.

"I'm sorry," Lindsey said as she approached, hugging each woman in turn. "But I'm pretty sure my birthday is in May."

"This isn't for you," Violet said. She crouched down and waggled her fingers until the puppy approached, wagging his whole behind in greeting. "It's for this poor little guy. Would you look at those eyebrows?"

"He certainly does have some dark, brooding good looks," Mary said. She handed Lindsey a gift bag and plopped down next to Violet.

Lindsey warily peeked inside the bag. Inside was a collar and a leash in a bright shade of blue.

"Mine next," Nancy ordered and she hefted a large bag into Lindsey's arms. Puppy food and two dishes.

"But, Nancy, it's your house; do you really want a puppy in here?" Lindsey asked.

"Are you kidding? I love dogs."

"Let's feed him," Beth said. "The poor guy is probably starving."

"This was your doing, wasn't it?" Lindsey asked.

"I know you don't want a dog," Beth said as she walked over to the kitchenette and filled a bowl with water. "But even if you're just going to foster him for a while, you need dog stuff. So, I'm assuming Sully was able to catch up to you and stall you?"

Lindsey closed her eyes. So, that was why he'd shown up at the vet's. It was his part of this mission to stall her.

Fabulous, and just when she thought she couldn't be any more embarrassed, wow, there was a whole new level of red-faced mortification to wallow in.

Lindsey watched as her friends oohed and aahed over the boy. He was going to get a swelled head if this kept up.

They had put out a lovely spread of people food on the kitchen counter, so she filled a plate with lasagna and salad while the dog dug into his chow and the ladies began to debate names for him.

"No names," Lindsey protested, taking a seat on the couch.

"I like George," Charlene said, ignoring her. "It's a good dog's name."

"No, Marley is a good dog's name," Beth said.

"That *Marley and Me* book made me cry," Lindsey said. "He can't be a Marley."

"He should have a literary name," Nancy said. "After all, he was found in the library."

Lindsey glanced over at Carrie, who was looking on the scene with some bemusement.

"Yes, they're always like this."

Carrie gave her a small smile. "It's nice."

Lindsey blew out a feigned exasperated breath. She refused to admit that she was more than a little touched by her friends' thoughtfulness.

Violet wandered over to the bookshelves. She scanned Lindsey's titles until she found what she was looking for. When she rejoined the group, she said, "I have it. Listen."

The room went silent as, in her best Broadway stage actress's voice, Violet read aloud from a brown leather volume in Lindsey's collection.

"'A ray fell on his features; the cheeks were sallow, and half covered with black whiskers; the brows lowering, the eyes deep-set and singular. I remembered the eyes.'"

She looked down at the puppy as she read. He was still eating.

"I give you Heathcliff," Violet said. She snapped shut Lindsey's volume of Emily Brontë's famous tome *Wuthering Heights*.

The room went silent. It was a treat to see Violet use her gifts, even if it was just a short paragraph. All eyes turned to the puppy, who lifted his head from his bowl and gave a mighty belch.

He looked so proud of himself, Lindsey couldn't help but laugh. The other ladies joined in and Mary said, "I think that means he approves."

"Heathcliff it is," Charlene said.

On that note, the ladies rose to go. Carrie and Nancy stayed behind to help clean up while Heathcliff sniffed around the apartment.

"So, how did it go at the police station?" Lindsey asked as she wrapped up the lasagna.

Carrie shrugged and sighed. "About as good as can be expected since I'm suspect number one."

"What? Why you?" Lindsey asked.

"She's the spouse," Nancy said. "They always look at the family first."

"Well, they didn't arrest you, that's something, right?"

"I don't know," Carrie said. She unclipped her long brown hair and shook it out. Then she scraped it back with her fingers and refastened it in a knot at the back of her head. "I have a feeling it's only a matter of time."

Lindsey could tell by the quaver in her voice that she was afraid. She couldn't blame her.

"Listen, I have the name of a criminal defense attorney that was recommended to me when a friend looked like she might need him," Lindsey said. She crossed the large room from the kitchenette to the small writing desk in the corner. It was a built-in desk and blended right into the wainscoting. It was one of the many reasons she had fallen in love with this apartment.

She pulled out the fold-out top and searched through her address book until she found the name she was looking for. She wrote the information on a Post-it and handed it to Carrie.

"If they call you in again, or even just to ease your mind, you need to call this man," she said.

"Is he expensive?" Carrie asked. "The kids' tuitions have pretty much destroyed any retirement or savings that I had, and now with Markus, ugh, it sounds callus to even say, but without his disability check, I'll probably lose the house."

She pressed her lips in a firm line as if she could clamp down the panic that was obviously consuming her.

Lindsey put an arm around her shoulders, and Nancy leaned forward and patted her hand.

"It's going to be all right," Lindsey said, afraid that she might be lying.

"Of course it is," Nancy said. But when she met Lindsey's gaze, Lindsey could see the doubt dimming the usual sparkly blue irises.

"It won't hurt you to call at any rate," Lindsey said.

"I suppose not," Carrie agreed. She gave them both a brave smile. "I can't thank you enough for all that you've done. I feel safe here, and that is pretty amazing given that there is a killer out there somewhere."

"That reminds me." Nancy dug into her jeans pocket and fished out two keys. "I had Ian Murphy put a new dead bolt on the front door. Here is a key for each of you. I know we usually leave the front door unlocked, but until this is resolved, I think we'd better get into the habit of keeping it locked. Agreed?"

Lindsey and Carrie nodded as they each took a key.

"Carrie, are you ready?" Nancy asked. "I'll walk you down."

Carrie nodded and Lindsey gave each of them a hug. One look at the dog—she was not going to start calling him Heathcliff—and she could tell he needed to go out. She dug through his pile of puppy gifts until she found the blue collar and leash.

As if anticipating what was to come, the dog sat very still while she fitted the collar around his neck and then began to bounce on his large puppy feet while she tried to clip the leash on.

"Sit, boy," Lindsey said. "Sit."

He managed it for a second, but then excitement overtook him. Lindsey sighed. "We're going to have to work on that. No, I mean, whoever your forever person is, they'll have to work on that."

He thumped his tail and gazed at her with his dark eyes, and Lindsey pulled on her jacket, scarf and mittens, trying to harden her heart against his funny little face.

It was a brisk walk outside to take care of business. Nancy's backyard was a long one that ended in a cliff that overlooked the bay and the islands beyond. Lindsey took the opportunity to enjoy the smell of the sea—it was strong, signaling that the tide was coming in—and admire the stars that twinkled in the sky above.

People had been muttering about a bad storm blowing in, but it was hard to imagine on this clear and quiet night.

Once inside, Lindsey prepared for bed. She wasn't sure what to do about the puppy. She didn't know where he normally slept or where he would want to sleep. Mary had given her a flat fleecy dog bed. Lindsey figured she'd better put it in her bedroom, so he didn't go chewing up her apartment during the night.

"Okay, buddy," she said as she draped a fluffy throw over the fleece bed, "you sleep here."

She patted the bed with her hand and he trotted over to sniff it. He seemed to get the idea as he climbed into it and did the circling thing that dogs do.

"Good night, little fella," she said as she climbed into bed.

Lindsey had shut out the light and was just drifting off when she felt the foot of the bed sag. She figured she had two options, either turn on the light and get the boy back in his bed or ignore him. The poor guy had had a rough day and it was bitterly cold. Even with the heat on, the apartment wasn't getting much warmer than sixty-two degrees.

Her bed was big enough, he would make it warmer, and besides, it wasn't as if he was staying. Bed training him would be someone else's problem. She burrowed into her flannel sheets and tried not to think about why that made her sad.

CHAPTER

13

BRIAR CREEK
PUBLIC LIBRARY

The feel of hot breath across her chest woke Lindsey the next morning. Heathcliff, or rather the puppy, was dead asleep with his head on her shoulder. She felt her mouth curve up in a smile. He was a snuggler. How cute was that?

She glanced down and his fuzzy head tickled her chin. He was lying pressed close beside her, and she wondered if he had been cold or scared during the night and had sought comfort in closeness. Either way, she knew she was going to have to find a home for him and fast. He was too charming for his own good, and despite what Tom the vet had said about pit bulls or pit bull mixes being put down just because they had pit bull bloodlines, she knew she'd be able to find someone to take this sweet young dog.

With that in mind, she got them both suited up to go outside. She was standing in the backyard with him when

Nancy poked her head out of the back door and called her over.

"What are you going to do with Heathcliff while you're at work today?"

"I don't know. I hadn't really figured it out yet," Lindsey answered. Nancy was holding out a steaming cup of coffee to her, and Lindsey took it with a grateful smile.

"Leave him with me," Nancy said. "I'll puppy sit for you."

"Are you sure?"

"Absolutely. Honestly, it'll make me feel safer to have a barker around."

Lindsey glanced across the yard. All of the houses on this street were old and big and sat on very large lots. She had never noticed before how isolated they all were, probably because when Charlie was in residence, the horde of musicians that came and went were nonstop, making the place feel as busy as the New Haven train station. Until now, the quiet had been a nice reprieve. Now it was just creepy.

"He's all yours," Lindsey said. "I took a picture of him this morning. I'm going to put up some flyers and see if anyone is missing him. Hopefully, he'll be reunited with his people soon."

Nancy pursed her lips but said nothing. As the puppy trotted into Nancy's first-floor apartment, to be spoiled rotten no doubt, Lindsey raced upstairs to get ready for work, dropping off Heathcliff's essentials with Nancy on the way out.

Things were quiet at the library. Maybe it was just the hullabaloo of the day before, or perhaps the crazy events of the week, but Lindsey found herself relieved to be answering normal questions on the reference desk and writing up her weekly report for the mayor's office.

It was midafternoon and she had just called Nancy to make sure the puppy was behaving—he was—when she heard two women talking over by the new-book area.

She recognized one as being on the high school PTA, but the other woman was a new face, not a regular library user. They both appeared to be in their late forties, with the requisite rounded figures and hair dyed improbable shades of blond to hide the gray.

"Well, I heard that she was having an affair," the PTA woman whispered to the other.

"Really?" the woman asked.

"Marjorie didn't say, but I got the feeling it was an inappropriate liaison," the PTA woman said. "I'll bet she was sleeping with a married man, probably one of the doctors at the hospital where she works. You know, she always works the night shift."

The woman's voice was sly, as if working nights was proof of anything.

"Do you think poor Markus knew?"

"I doubt it," the other woman said. "He trusted her so completely, besides the poor man never left his house. He was disabled, you know."

"I didn't," the other woman clucked. "Do you think she shot him so that she could be with her doctor?"

"I don't know. I mean, if her doctor is married, he'd have to leave his wife, wouldn't he?"

"Oh, I just had a horrid thought," the other woman said. "If Carrie shot Markus to be free of him, would she shoot her doctor if he refused to be with her or would she shoot his wife?"

"Oh, dear," the PTA woman said. "We could have a serial killer on our hands."

Lindsey felt her teeth set. She didn't like gossip as a rule, especially malicious gossip about a friend. Since one of the women had mentioned Marjorie's name, she got the feeling Batty Bilson was the one planting the seeds of the malicious talk.

Knowing that it was none of her business, Lindsey rose from her seat anyway and approached the two women.

"Good afternoon," she said. "Was there anything you needed help finding?"

The two women looked startled at her approach, sort of like kids caught pilfering cookies out of the cookie jar when they've already been told it's too close to dinner.

"Uh, no, I'm good," the PTA woman said. She held up a current bestseller.

"Well, there's a young adult series called *Gossip Girl* that is quite the gripping read, if you're interested," Lindsey said.

The PTA woman had the grace to blush while the other one gave Lindsey an irritated look and said in a rather snotty tone, "I'm fine, but thanks so much for your concern."

"Anytime," Lindsey smiled. Okay, it was really more a showing of teeth, but she figured she should get points for trying.

She turned and headed back to the reference desk. A glance at the circulation desk and she saw Ann Marie give her a sly thumbs-up from behind her computer.

So, Ann Marie had heard their conversation, too.

Lindsey shook her head. How could anyone believe that Carrie would cheat on her husband and kill him? Truly, it mystified, especially if Batty Bilson was the source of the gossip. Everyone knew the woman was a few slices short of a loaf; how could they listen to her?

She was not surprised to see the two women leave the library shortly thereafter. When the doors slid open again a few minutes later, she glanced up and had to smile as Edmund Sint made his way into the building, looking as if the drafty bitter air from outside was chasing him into the library's welcoming warmth.

He unwrapped the plaid scarf from about his neck and pulled off his leather gloves as he approached the desk.

"Hi, Edmund," Lindsey said. "What brings you in this afternoon?"

"This freezing weather has put me in the mood for a noir mystery," he said. "Who can you recommend?"

"That depends. Are you looking for old-school Mickey Spillane or modern Ian Rankin?"

"Hmm, let's go modern," Edmund said.

"Follow me," Lindsey said.

She walked him over to the fiction shelves.

"I'm surprised to find the library still open," he said.

"Oh? Why's that?" she asked as she crouched to find the selection of Rankin titles.

"The weatherman said a nor'easter is coming," he said. "That's why I need to stock up on reading material in case the power goes out. Uncle Bill's library is a dead bore. I need something to keep me entertained if we get snowed in, otherwise I'll be stir-crazy within hours."

"A nor'easter?" Lindsey frowned. She had heard there was a snow storm in the forecast but nothing as dramatic as a nor'easter, which typically brought hurricane-force winds and arctic cold.

"If you'll excuse me," she said. "I'd better go check on this."

"Absolutely," he said. "It's already started snowing."

Sure enough, now that she stood close to him, she could see the damp spots on his jacket where the snowflakes had already melted.

Lindsey hurried back to her desk. A glance at the window and she could see the swirling snow falling outside. She hadn't really paid it much attention before. She quickly brought up the weather website on her computer and typed in the zip code for Briar Creek.

The forecast was not good: bitterly cold temperatures, gale-force winds and lots of snow. They were supposed to be open for a few more hours, but if this was just the start of it, she didn't want her staff to have to drive home in this weather.

She quickly called the town hall to see if the mayor was available. She would close the library whether he approved or not, but she thought it wise to get his okay.

"Mayor Henson's office, this is Judy," his secretary answered.

"Hi, Judy, it's Lindsey Norris at the library; is the mayor in?"

"Yes, he's just debating whether to close the town offices for the day. Horrible storm coming, you know."

"I do; in fact, I was just calling to ask if I could close the library."

"Hold one moment," Judy said.

"Sure," Lindsey said. No sooner were the words out than Muzak began to play in her ear. It was a slicked-out version of the Beatles' "Let It Be," and in her opinion, they should have.

"Hi, Lindsey," Judy came back on the line. "The mayor says go ahead. Whiteout conditions are predicted, and he says it's not worth anyone getting stranded in this."

"Thanks," Lindsey said. She hung up the phone and went over to the circulation desk. Ann Marie glanced up from the cart of books she was fine sorting.

"We're going to close early," Lindsey said. "There's a nor'easter coming."

Ann Marie gave her a wide-eyed look. "Oh, no, the last time we got hit with a storm like that, the power went out and I had to keep all of my perishables out in the snow. Never did find my whole fryer chicken until the thaw hit a few weeks later."

Lindsey blew out a breath. She turned to assess the library. Other than Edmund, there was a mother with two children in the kids' area, two computer users and a couple of teens looking over the DVD collection.

Lindsey cleared her throat and raised her voice to be heard throughout the room. "Due to the weather, the library will be closing in fifteen minutes. If you need to call for a ride, please come and use the phone. If you'd like to check out materials, please do so in the next few minutes."

She saw Edmund appear from the stacks carrying several novels. He strode purposefully to the circulation desk, and Lindsey was glad he'd been able to find something.

"I'm so glad you came in today," she said. "I didn't realize it was going to be this bad and I'm not sure the mayor's office would have remembered to call us."

"I think this storm snuck up on us all," he said. "No one expected a tropical cyclone and an Arctic cold front to collide, but they have."

"It can't be worse than the blizzard of '78," Lindsey said. "I was only a year old, but my parents still talk about how ice coated the trees and the snow drifts were higher than the house."

"Yeah, and people got stranded in their cars for two days," Edmund said. Then he wiggled his eyebrows and added, "And the baby rate boomed nine months later."

"I have two cousins who arrived nine months later," Lindsey said with a laugh.

"You know, this storm is going to put a crimp in our lunch date," he said.

Lindsey felt her face get warm at the word *date*, which was ridiculous. He'd invited both Carrie and her. It wasn't as if he was asking her out.

"That's all right," she said. She tried to make her voice sound casual, but it still seemed to come out a bit higher than normal. "I don't think Carrie will be able to make it for a while."

He handed his books and card to Ann Marie for checkout and gave Lindsey an understanding nod. "I heard about what happened with her husband. Is she okay?"

"She's getting through it," Lindsey said.

"Do the police have any leads?"

"I really don't know," she said.

She glanced at Edmund. He reminded her so much of her former fiancé, back before he turned into a two-timing jackass. Edmund was smart and charming, and she felt an immediate kinship with him, probably because she had spent her entire life around academic types and he definitely had the Ivy League stamp upon him.

A thought occurred to her and she couldn't pass up the opportunity to ask. "Listen, do you know Marjorie Bilson?"

Edmund took his books back from Ann Marie and began to wrap his scarf about his neck again. Lindsey thought she saw his jaw tighten, but when he spoke, his voice was neutral. "She seems quite taken with my uncle."

Lindsey nodded as they walked toward the front doors. Good, then her erratic behavior might not be such a surprise.

"Has she done anything—how can I put this?"

"Crazy?" Edmund offered.

Lindsey bit her lip and nodded.

They paused before the doors, causing the remaining patrons to go around them on their way out into the whirling scene of white.

"I can't say there's been anything specific," he said. "But I do know that she calls and texts him all day long. So far, he hasn't complained, but I do wonder if he tried to put a stop to it, if she would turn on him."

"Yikes."

"I'm hoping it doesn't come to that," he said. "Maybe if we do get snowed in with a power outage, she won't be able to charge her phone and she'll have to stop calling."

"So, she'll chill?" Lindsey offered, unable to resist the pun.

Edmund broke into a wide grin and said, "In a word."

They stood smiling at one another and then Lindsey

said, "Well, I'd better help close up. Thanks again for coming in. Your timing was excellent."

"No problem," he said. The doors whooshed open behind him, but he ignored them as he said, "I've noticed you usually ride a bike to work, do you need a ride home today? I'd be happy to wait."

"She has a ride home," a voice said from behind him.

Lindsey glanced over Edmund's shoulder to see Sully standing there in his thick navy coat, looking as bland as the blankets of snow beginning to cover the cars in the parking lot.

CHAPTER

14

BRIAR CREEK
PUBLIC LIBRARY

Edmund spun and glanced at Sully. "Oh, well, very good, then."

Sully held out his right hand. "Mike Sullivan."

Edmund clasped his hand briefly. "Edmund Sint."

Neither of them smiled, and Lindsey got the distinct feeling they were measuring one another like two dogs trying to decide if the bone was worth the fight. Utterly ridiculous.

"Are you about ready?" Sully asked her.

"Almost, I just need to get my things and set the alarm," she said.

"No, problem I'll wait," he said.

"Thank you," she said.

Edmund glanced between them and then gave her a

small smile. "Be safe in the storm and we'll have to reschedule our lunch date for when the roads are clear."

"Sounds good," she said. She could feel Sully watching her, and she knew her face had just flamed hot.

Edmund gave her a mischievous grin and left the building, whistling into the snow.

"I'll meet you out back," Sully said. He turned and followed Edmund out.

Lindsey stood there staring for a second, wondering whether she should be flattered or offended. Finally, she decided that she was relieved that when she had seen Sully again, she hadn't keeled over with embarrassment. She supposed she could thank Edmund for that. He had provided a nice buffer.

"Hey, boss, you coming?" Ann Marie called from the workroom.

Lindsey shook her head and went to gather her things.

Ann Marie met her at the back door with a knowing smile.

"So, it looks like you have two admirers," she said.

"No, no." Lindsey shook her head. "Sully is just a friend and Edmund is very nice, but I don't know that he's interested in me as anything more than a librarian."

Ann Marie rolled her eyes. "Oh, puleeze, I saw their faces. They both looked like Cupid came down and shot them in the butt."

"I'm so not talking about this," Lindsey said. "And don't say anything to Beth or she'll start matchmaking and you know how that goes."

Ann Marie grinned. "What? You didn't like that sad

parade of guys she trotted in front of you when you first moved here?"

"I know she meant well, but I wasn't even ready to think about dating," Lindsey said.

"And a guy who still lives with his mother and is obsessed with alien abductions didn't work for you?" Ann Marie tsked. "Imagine that."

It was true. When she first moved here, Beth had so wanted her to like Briar Creek that she brought forth every single male she could find in a parade of losers that still lived in infamy to all who worked in the library and had been witness to the freak show.

"How about that guy who smelled like rancid olive loaf?" Ann Marie said. "He was a keeper."

"You can stop now," Lindsey said.

"Or how about the one who wanted you to be a mother to his twelve-year-old daughter?" she added. "With his receding hairline and potbelly, now he was a catch!"

Lindsey tapped in the alarm code and led the way out the back door.

"Or that middle-aged pizza delivery guy," Ann Marie said as they stepped into the cold. "Free pizza for life. Really, you should have at least given him a chance."

"The one with fifteen cats?" Lindsey clarified.

"I think he only has twelve."

Lindsey groaned and glanced up at the falling snow. "Drive home safely. If this is as bad as they say, I doubt we'll be opening tomorrow, but I'll call everyone and let them know for sure."

Sully was waiting at the curb; the hot exhaust from his

pickup puffed out the back like a steam engine. Lindsey unlocked her bike and hurried toward the warm cab of his truck, feeling very grateful that she hadn't embarrassed herself so much that he no longer gave her a lift.

He hopped out and opened the door for her, and she scooted in while he put her bike in back. She felt the snow that covered her head and shoulders start to melt immediately.

He climbed back in on his side and they waited while Ann Marie started her car and drove out ahead of them with a wave.

"Thank you," she said. "You've really been a life saver this past week."

"No worries," he said as he slipped the gear on the steering wheel into drive and set off on the road. "I was in the Blue Anchor helping Ian storm proof the place when Jason Meeger and Candace Collins came in and said the town offices were closing. I figured that meant you, too, and that you might need a lift. In these conditions, you don't want to be walking or bicycling."

"Do you think it's going to get as bad as they say?"

Sully was quiet for a moment. She noticed his eyes strayed toward the islands in the bay, and she wondered if he was worried about his parents.

"It feels like it's going to get bad," he said. "I was stationed on a warship in the Barents Sea when I was in the service. We saw a lot of blizzard conditions and this has the same feel."

"The Barents Sea? That's near the Arctic Circle, isn't it?"

Sully looked impressed. "Yeah, we were just off the

island Svalbard, which is Norwegian. Not many people know where the Barents Sea is."

"My older brother, Jack, is quite the globe-trotter," she said. "He's the adventurous one of the two of us. I spend a lot of time studying maps to figure out where he is. He was in Hammerfest, Norway, for a summer, and I remember seeing the Barents Sea on the map."

"Beautiful area," Sully said.

"Do you miss it?" Lindsey asked. "The traveling?"

"Sometimes," Sully admitted. "But then I think about it being fifteen degrees below zero in the Arctic or one hundred and six degrees above zero while stationed in the Persian Gulf, and I'm okay with Connecticut."

They turned onto Lindsey's street and a gust of wind buffeted the truck and the snow took on a ferocity that resembled ice bullets and not the whirly twirly flakes that had been falling just minutes before.

"Looks like you closed just in time," he said. He pulled up in front of the house, and Lindsey fished her new key out of her bag.

They put her bike in the garage and he walked her to the porch and waited while she unlocked the door.

"Thanks again," she said.

"Anytime," he said. "If you need me, just call the Blue Anchor."

Another gust of wind whipped around the side of the house and almost knocked Lindsey to her knees, but Sully caught her by the elbow. She stared up at him and saw snowflakes coating his eyelashes and the dimples that bracketed his mouth when he smiled like he was now. She felt that same zip she always did when he was around, and she just couldn't resist. She leaned up and gave him a quick hug.

Without hesitation, he hugged her back, and when they separated, she noticed his smile had deepened.

Then he leaned close and said, "You know, I think I'm glad this storm hit."

"Why's that?" she asked.

"Because it's keeping you from dating the wrong man," he said.

With a wink, he spun her toward the door and gently pushed her inside, closing the door behind her.

Lindsey leaned against the door and tried to slow the pounding inside her chest. *Did he really say that? Did he mean that?* Did he mean it like she thought he meant it?

It was a good thing she was leaning against the door, trying to get her mental faculties to function, because Nancy's door opened and a wriggling black ball of fur came at her as if she'd been gone for weeks instead of hours.

He stood on his back legs and wrapped his paws around Lindsey's leg as if he was determined not to let her go now that she had come back.

Lindsey leaned down and ruffled his ears. He licked her hand and she glanced up to see Nancy enter the foyer.

"He has been looking out the window for you for the past hour," she said. "I swear it's like he knew you'd be home early. I heard the town is shutting down."

"Yeah, they're saying it's going to be a bad one."

"Well, I went out to the grocery store this morning and stocked up. I had to throw a few elbows in the soup aisle to get the good stuff, but I should have enough supplies to get all three of us through this storm."

"How is Carrie holding up?"

"Better today. Her son called. He and his sister have been really good about calling her every few hours since she telephoned them and told them the news yesterday. He was on his way down from New Hampshire, stopping in Rhode Island to get his sister, but I think they're going to have to wait out the storm at her place. There's no sense in them getting stranded in a whiteout somewhere."

"Have the police been by today?"

"No," Carrie said as she came out of Nancy's apartment and joined them. "I think they may actually have run out of questions for me."

She was dressed in a thick turtleneck sweater and jeans over fleece-lined slippers. She was pale and looked as if she hadn't slept, but still, she looked better than she had two days ago when they'd found Markus dead.

"Well, come on in." Nancy pulled Lindsey into her apartment. "We've got hot chocolate and fresh macaroons and the fire is crackling. If we're in for a blizzard, we may as well settle in."

"Heathcliff missed you," Carrie said as they followed Nancy inside with the puppy dancing between them.

"I doubt if it's me he missed," she said.

"Oh, it's definitely you," Nancy said. "He gets the same moony look as Sully when he's around you."

"Sully does not look at me that way," Lindsey said as she unwrapped her scarf and took off her coat and hung them on a hook in the hall.

"I hate to disagree, but, yes, he does," Carrie said.

"Oh, don't you start," Lindsey said. She sat on the ottoman by the fire and Heathcliff—rather, the puppy—sat with her, resting his head on her feet. If there was an award to be given for cuteness, she was pretty sure he'd win it paws down.

Nancy brought in a tray laden with mugs of cocoa and a plate full of macaroons. If this was blizzard survival, Lindsey felt like she could manage this no problem.

Then the power went out. Lindsey was in her own apartment, reading in bed, when the lights blinked the first time. The wind had become a steady ferocious roar, and when she looked out the window into the darkness of the night, she felt the nor'easter pressing against the fragile window panes like a peeper trying to get a look-see.

The puppy had come upstairs with her and had sprawled himself next to her with his head on the neighboring pillow. Lindsey settled back in bed, turned the page of her book and her reading lamp went out.

Thinking it might be the bulb, Lindsey reluctantly left the cozy warmth of her bed and stumbled across the room to the light switch that controlled the overhead lamp. She flicked it on. Nothing. She tried the bathroom switch. Nothing.

A feeling of vulnerability swept over her much as she tried to ignore it. She took a deep breath. There was no need to panic. The power would be back shortly; all she had to do was wait it out.

She thought about lighting a candle but figured she may as well just go to sleep. It was early, but it had been an intense few days and probably she could use the shut-eye.

She took one step toward the bed when a high-pitched

scream out-shrieked the howl of the wind, making Lindsey jump and Heathcliff bark. Snatching up her bathrobe, she pulled it on and rushed to the door. She knew it had to be either Carrie or Nancy who had screamed. She hoped no one had fallen in the dark.

She had no idea how she could get someone to the hospital in this weather. Then again, Carrie was a nurse, so they were in good hands, unless it was her and she was unconscious.

The hallway was black. With the power off, it was impossible to make out the stairs. Lindsey reached out with her hands, trying to find the banister. She inched forward slowly, not wanting to slam into it.

Finally, she felt the wood beneath her fingers. She could feel the dog pressing close to her side, and she was grateful for the contact. The relentless darkness spooked her more than she would have thought. Why hadn't she grabbed her flashlight?

She inched her way toward the stairs, feeling the floor with her sock-clad feet. When she felt the edge of the first step, she eased her way down the steps.

A beam of light shot up from below, and she could just make out the rest of the steps. She moved more quickly now.

"Nancy, is that you?"

There was a beat of silence and Lindsey felt her heart hammer in her chest.

"Yes, it's me." Nancy's voice echoed up the hallway. "Did you hear that scream?"

"Yes, have you seen Carrie?"

"I'm on my way there now," Nancy said.

"I'll meet you there," Lindsey said.

Together they arrived on the second-floor landing. Nancy knocked on the door, but there was no response.

"Carrie, it's us, open up," Lindsey shouted.

There was no answer and Heathcliff started to whimper.

"Do you have a key?" Lindsey asked.

"I think so," Nancy said. "Here, hold the flashlight."

Lindsey trained the meager light onto Nancy's hands. They shook with cold or agitation as she flipped through her key ring until she found what she was looking for.

"Are you sure this is all right?"

"We have to make sure she's okay," Lindsey said.

"You're right." Nancy turned and banged on the door again. "Carrie, we're coming in."

No answer.

She unlocked the door and they hurried into the room. Lindsey wasn't sure where to shine the light so she swept it across the room like a searchlight. It bounced off pictures and furniture, and as they followed it farther into the room, Lindsey felt a bitterly cold draft sweep over her. She could hear Heathcliff sniffing the floor, and he left her to follow the cold air.

The beam of the flashlight picked out a figure framed in an open window. Gusts of wind and pelting snow swirled in around it, but the body didn't move.

"She's not going to jump, is she?" Nancy asked. Her voice was filled with horror.

Lindsey wasn't about to wait to find out. She dashed forward and grabbed Carrie by the elbow, hauling her back into the room.

"Shut the window," she ordered, and Nancy hurried forward, slamming the window shut with a bang.

Lindsey set the flashlight on its end so that its beam illuminated the part of the main room in which they stood. She snatched an afghan off the back of the couch and wrapped Carrie in it. Her flannel pajamas were icy cold and damp. The snow on her head was beginning to melt and her teeth were chattering.

"Carrie, are you all right?" Lindsey asked. She rubbed Carrie's arms through the blanket, hoping to get some warmth coursing through her.

"It was him," she said.

The flashlight illuminated Carrie's eyes from below. The whites circled the irises like big saucers. Her brown hair was mussed from the wind and snow. She was shivering and looked as if she was going into shock.

"Him who?" Lindsey asked.

"Markus."

"What? Where?" Nancy asked.

"I saw his ghost," Carrie said. "Outside the window."

"There are no such things as ghosts," Lindsey said. "And even if there were, they don't hang outside windows."

"I'm sure it was him," Carrie said. "He's haunting me. I know it. He wants me to find his killer, or maybe, maybe he wants to kill me."

CHAPTER

15

BRIAR CREEK
PUBLIC LIBRARY

"I think she's in shock," Lindsey said.

"Let's get her down to my place," Nancy said. "She can spend the night there. In fact, we'll all sleep there. This storm is officially terrifying me."

Lindsey understood. A nor'easter was one thing, but a storm like this without power was nothing to mess with, and the thought of staying up on the third floor during hurricane-force winds wasn't really working for her.

"My fireplace has a standing pilot ignition system, so it can switch on without electricity. I had it installed for just this sort of situation," Nancy said. "We'll light a fire and camp out in the living room."

"Sounds like an excellent plan," Lindsey agreed.

They half carried, half dragged Carrie down the stairs to Nancy's apartment. The old house ran on an oil furnace,

but with the extreme cold, it was having a hard time com-
bating the bitter wind that seemed determined to infiltrate
the house through any crack or crevice. And now with the
power out, the remaining warmth was going to disappear
in a matter of hours.

Nancy lit several candles around the living room, and
their fragile glow seemed to force back the creepy shadows
to the corners of the room. Lindsey switched on the gas
fireplace while Nancy went to make some food.

Still wrapped in her blanket, Carrie knelt beside the
hearth.

"I know I must sound like I'm crazy," she said.

"No, you sound like you had a very bad dream, and with
all that you've been through and this vicious storm, it's
small wonder," Lindsey said.

Carrie was silent and Lindsey had the feeling she hadn't
heard a word she'd said.

As she turned the knob higher to increase the gas flow,
the fire in the fireplace leapt up, wrapping the faux ceramic
logs in its hot hungry mouth.

Carrie turned her back to the fire, letting the heat dry
out her clothes. Lindsey wished she had some words of
comfort for her.

Nancy bustled in with a tray laden with crusty bread,
Havarti cheese, sweet pickles and a pitcher of milk. Perfect.
Lindsey was beginning to think of Nancy as always com-
ing to the rescue with a tray of goodies.

Nancy silently handed them each a plate. Lindsey loaded
a thick slice of bread with a couple of pieces of cheese and
several pickle slices. Carrie and Nancy did the same.

After a few minutes of listening to the wind claw at the

side of the house while they ate, Carrie said, "I'm sorry I woke you both."

"No worries," Nancy said. "Nightmares happen."

"No, there was a man," Carrie said. "I saw him standing on the ledge outside my window."

Nancy and Lindsey exchanged a look but said nothing. Heathcliff began to pace the room, as if on patrol, and Lindsey found it sweetly comforting.

"It must have been a shadow," Nancy said. She poured them each a glass of milk and took a sip of her own. In a most pragmatic voice, she added, "I mean, who would be fool enough to be out in this weather?"

"I don't think it was a who," Carrie said. "I think it was a what."

"A ghost?" Lindsey clarified. "Really?"

Carrie looked at her with huge eyes, and maybe it was the shadows being cast by the fire, but she noticed that the dark circles beneath Carrie's eyes stood out against the pallor of her skin, and Lindsey surmised she hadn't really slept in days, which was not a big surprise but would explain why she had hallucinated a man looking into her window.

"He wants me to solve his murder," Carrie said. Her voice was whisper soft and sent a shiver down Lindsey's spine. "He won't rest until I find out who shot him."

There was a beat of silence and then Nancy said, "Well, that does sound like Markus."

Her tone was wry and managed to reach out and tickle Lindsey's funny bone. She had to muffle her chuckle in her glass of milk, but it fooled no one, and after a second, Carrie chuckled, too.

"It does sound like him, doesn't it?"

Whether it was from nerves or lack of sleep, Lindsey couldn't tell, but suddenly the three of them started to laugh.

Heathcliff jogged over from the door as if he wanted in on the joke and jumped into Lindsey's lap, almost sending her glass crashing to the ground. She hugged him close and he licked her face as if delighted to be included.

Boom. Boom. Boom.

The blows against the front door to the house were unmistakable. Someone was out there. Someone who wanted in. Heathcliff barked and raced to the apartment door. He scratched at the door, eager to be let out to investigate whoever was out there.

Nancy rose first, looking startled.

Carrie jumped up, too, and grabbed her arm. Her hands were trembling and she looked terrified.

"Don't answer it," she said. "It's him. I know it."

Nancy patted her arm, but even Lindsey could see that the older lady looked frightened, and she realized that this must bring back bad memories for her, memories of another bad storm where officers came to tell her that her husband had gone down with his ship.

"You two stay here," she said. "Lock the door behind me. Heathcliff and I will check it out."

"No!" Carrie argued.

"I don't think . . ." Nancy began, but Lindsey interrupted.

"It could be someone in trouble. We have to answer it."

Before they could argue, Lindsey picked up one of the candles and strode across the room. With a bracing breath, she stepped through the door with the dog at her side.

The candle had been a poor choice she realized as soon as she stepped into the foyer. It didn't cast enough light and it just made all of the shadows in her peripheral vision dance, making her more skittish than she already was, which was saying something since she felt as nervous as a cat in a room full of rocking chairs.

A growl sounded from beside her, and she glanced down to see the fur on Heathcliff's shoulder bristling. His already low brow seemed to lower, and the gleam of his puppy teeth showed that he had curled his lip back in a ferocious sneer. If she didn't already know he was a complete goofball, she would have been afraid. His bravery in facing the unknown made her stiffen her spine and approach the front door.

The glass pane in the door was frosted, making it impossible to see outside. Lindsey had no choice but to open the door if she wanted to see who or what had made the banging noise.

She unlatched the shiny new dead bolt and pulled the door open. A gust of freezing cold air blasted her and snuffed her candle, but before the light went out she saw a gloved hand reaching out of the darkness for her, and despite her best intentions to be brave, she screamed like a little girl.

With a roar, Heathcliff launched himself at the figure in the darkness. The door to Nancy's apartment banged open, and the body on the porch, unprepared for a flying dog, went down in a heap with a thump and a yelp.

Nancy came out of her apartment with her flashlight in one hand and a cast iron frying pan in the other.

"Who is it? What is it?" she demanded. She shone a

beam of light on a puffy blue coat lying under a sitting dog that looked intent on licking every snowflake off the newcomer.

A young male voice said, "Call him off, Naners, before he licks me to death."

"Charlie, is that you?" Nancy asked.

"Heck, yeah," he said.

"You know this man?" Carrie asked.

"He's my nephew," Nancy said.

"Heathcliff, come," Lindsey ordered, and the dog leapt off Charlie, looking quite pleased with himself.

Lindsey reached out and grabbed Charlie's gloved hand and pulled him to his feet.

"What the heck are you doing out here in weather like this?" Nancy demanded. "Did you drive in this? Are you crazy?"

"I didn't know what I was in for until I was halfway here," Charlie said. "Then it was too late to turn around."

Nancy hustled him into the house, pushing him into the apartment. "You could have been killed in an accident or frozen to death. You idiot!"

"It's good to see you, too, Naners," he said with a grin as he unwrapped his scarf and unzipped his coat. "And you might have mentioned that you added a dead bolt to the front door. I couldn't get in, so I tried to get into my apartment from the porch roof, but the window I usually leave unlatched for those times when I lock myself out was locked."

"It was you!" Carrie said as she made him a sandwich from the bread and cheese. "You're the man I saw peering in my window."

"Charlie, that was twenty minutes ago," Lindsey interrupted. "Why didn't you knock on the door earlier?"

Charlie gave her a sheepish look. "Well, when I slid off the roof, I clipped my head on the porch and sort of knocked myself out. The snow woke me up, good thing, or I might have frozen out there."

"Let me see your head," Nancy ordered. "Oh, for heaven's sake."

She tugged off his hat and pushed back his hair, and sure enough, a knot the size of a chicken egg had formed above his temple.

"I'll go get some ice," she said.

Carrie handed him the plate and he looked blissful as he sat by the fire and let the warmth wrap around him. Charlie was a tall, skinny kid with stringy black musician hair, which, without his hat, stood on end, fully charged with static.

"I'm sorry," Carrie said. "I locked the window. It didn't occur to me . . ."

"Of course it didn't occur to you," Nancy said, returning with a cloth full of ice that she held to Charlie's head. "Normal people don't have to access their apartments from the porch because they've locked themselves out—again. As for you," she said to Charlie, "I was planning to tell you when you came home from your tour next week. Why are you back early anyway?"

Charlie heaved a sigh and stared gloomily at his plate. "The band broke up. Our keyboard player dumped our bass player for our drummer, and the two of them got into a fist fight on stage in Panama City. I've been driving for three days in a van full of people who are not speaking to each other. This is why some bands don't allow girls."

As if sensing his utter defeat, Heathcliff sidled up to Charlie and licked his face.

Charlie grinned. "So, who's the new addition?"

"Lindsey's dog," Carrie and Nancy said together.

"No, he isn't," Lindsey said, feeling a sharp stab of guilt when Heathcliff looked at her. "I'm simply fostering him until I can find him a good home."

"We call him Heathcliff," Nancy said.

"Good name," Charlie said, demolishing his sandwich in three bites.

"Oh, and this is Carrie Rushton," Nancy said, obviously just remembering that Charlie and Carrie had not been introduced. "Carrie has been staying in your apartment while you've been gone."

"That's cool," Charlie said with a shrug. He looked longingly at the tray, so Lindsey slapped together another sandwich for him.

"See? I told you he wouldn't mind," Nancy said to Carrie.

"Thanks for letting me stay there," she said to Charlie.

"Sure, what happened? Did you lose your crib?"

They all stared at him until his meaning finally registered.

"Not exactly," Carrie said. "My husband was murdered."

She caught Charlie on an inhale and he started to choke. Lindsey thumped his back a few times and Nancy handed him a glass of milk.

"Wow, not what I expected," he said.

"For me either," Carrie agreed.

"I'm sorry," he said. "You can stay in my place. I can bunk with Naners."

"Oh, I don't want to be a bother," Carrie said. "I should probably move back to my own house now anyway."

"No, really, you can stay in my apartment," he insisted.

"You're a good boy," Nancy said to him. "But I never really could get the man stink out of your place. Carrie will stay with me. That's final."

Lindsey turned to Carrie and said, "I hope you didn't really think you had a say in the matter."

Carrie gave a small smile and said, "Thank you. Thank you all."

"Don't be silly," Nancy said. "We're your friends and this is what friends do."

Lindsey fell asleep in one recliner of Nancy's while Charlie crashed in the other. She didn't think she'd actually sleep, but the warmth of the fire soon lulled her into a lethargic state, and the thought of climbing two flights of stairs to her cold apartment above did not appeal. Somehow Heathcliff managed to wedge himself against her in the chair, and she was grateful for his furry warmth.

At some point in the late hours, Nancy draped a heavy comforter on top of her and another on Charlie. She and Carrie took to their beds. When they awoke in the morning, they found that the power was still out, the fire had been turned low so it was just a flicker of blue flame and it was still snowing.

Lindsey brought a portable radio down from her

apartment and put fresh batteries in it. She dialed into the local New Haven news station to get the weather. It had been snowing for twenty hours with no sign of stopping. The gale-force winds had diminished, but it was still blustery outside. Along the shoreline, over twenty thousand people were without power.

Knowing that they may not get power back anytime soon, Charlie went up to his apartment and dug out his propane cookstove from his camping gear. They set it on the kitchen counter, opening the window behind it to let out any fumes it gave off.

Charlie then whipped up some coffee and scrambled eggs. Lindsey didn't know if it was the bone-chilling cold or the fact that a hot meal had seemed impossible, but she was sure these were the best eggs she'd ever eaten.

Feeling better with some food in her belly, she ran up to her apartment to change her clothes and get her cell phone. She had left it charging last night before the power went out. She had enough of a charge to check in with all of her staff today. She called each one, letting them know that they would not be opening the library.

The only one who didn't answer was Beth. Lindsey tried not to get anxious, but Beth lived alone in a small beach house close to the shore. If the waves had gotten high, she could be in trouble.

She paced Nancy's living room, debating what to do.

"Well, how about I teach you how to crochet, Carrie?" Nancy offered. "You're not going to be able to go home for a while, so you may as well keep your mind and your fingers busy."

"All right," Carrie said. She looked relieved to have

something to do. Lindsey was about to go retrieve her own crochet project when the sound of a motor broke through the quiet morning. They all hurried to the window to see a snowmobile zip across the snow-buried yard.

CHAPTER

16

BRIAR CREEK
PUBLIC LIBRARY

It only took Lindsey a second to recognize the hot pink ski suit. She had been skiing with that snowsuit before, and it served as an excellent visual marker against the relentless white of the slopes.

"It's Beth," she announced. She expelled a huge sigh of relief and hurried to the front door to let her friend in.

"Excellent," Nancy said. "I hope she has news."

Beth came in on a blast of arctic air. It took both her and Lindsey to shut the door against the incoming wind.

As Beth unwrapped her head, she took the cup of coffee Charlie offered with a grateful smile. "Hot coffee? It's a miracle!"

"Where have you been? Why haven't you answered your phone? Is your place okay? Where did you get that ride?" Lindsey peppered her with questions.

Beth held up her hand and took a long sip of the hot java. "Okay, I think I can feel my feet again. Let's see, to start with, I've been mostly at home, but I just took a quick tour of town, the battery on my phone is dead, my house is fine, so far, and the snowmobile is my neighbor's, but he's too old to ride it so he lent it to me."

"Is it totally fun?" Charlie asked.

"Totally," she assured him. They pounded knuckles and Lindsey rolled her eyes. There were times she was pretty sure Beth was a twelve-year-old boy trapped in a thirty-two-year-old woman's body.

"So, tell us," Nancy said as she pulled Beth into her apartment and pushed her into a chair by the fire. "What's it look like out there?"

Beth sobered immediately. "It's bad. The drifts are already six feet high and getting higher. You can't even tell what's buried under them. The waves crested with the high tide, and Jeanette Palmer's Beachfront Bed and Breakfast took a pounding. I think the only thing that saved her from losing her back porch to the sea was Ian Murphy and Sully spent most of last night hauling in sandbags from the highway department."

"Is Jeanette okay?" Nancy asked.

"She's fine," Beth said. "The B and B was open today for business, and she was out sweeping her front steps when I stopped to check on her. She says this storm is nothing compared to the ones in '52 and '78."

"It's not over yet," Nancy said, looking out the large bay window where the snow continued to fall.

"Which reminds me," Charlie said. "I'm going to get out there and start shoveling before it gets too deep."

"I'll just call a snow plow," Nancy said. "You don't have to go out in this."

Beth shook her head. "There isn't a plow available. They've all been called out to do the roads. They're hoping to get them at least partially dug out before the second half of the blizzard hits."

"Is the library okay?" Lindsey asked.

Beth smiled at her. "That's the first place I checked. The drifts are halfway up to the front door, but otherwise the building looks fine."

Lindsey felt her shoulders lower in relief. She hadn't realized she was so worried until Beth assured her that all was well.

"Can you give me a lift over there?" Lindsey asked. "I think I'd better start digging the building out. The town's maintenance crew has enough to do and I don't want it to get even worse."

Nancy looked as if she would protest, but Lindsey held up her hand. "Unless you're going to offer to loan me a snow shovel, don't bother."

Nancy blew out her lips in an exasperated puff. "They're in the garage. Help yourself. But if the weather turns, get back here immediately, and take your cell phone with you."

"I can . . ." Carrie began but Nancy cut her off.

"Oh, no, you don't," she said. "You can't fit more than two people on that contraption, and besides, I need to teach you how to crochet. It will give me something to do besides fret."

"Thanks anyway," Lindsey said to Carrie, who shrugged.

Lindsey was glad Nancy had put the kibosh on Carrie going out in this weather. Carrie looked as pale as the snow drifts that surrounded the house, and Lindsey really didn't think she had the stamina to be out in the cold.

"I'll just go suit up," Lindsey said and she darted up the stairs to her apartment. Heathcliff wanted to come with her, but she distracted him by throwing his chew toy to Beth, who began to play tug-of-war with him.

She didn't want the young puppy out in this weather. There was no knowing when the storm would turn, and the thought of losing him in one of the drifts made her positively queasy.

Lindsey bounded back downstairs wearing her blue ski suit. It was not quite the neon pink of Beth's, but at least she wouldn't be confused with a snow drift either.

Charlie was already digging out the front porch and the driveway. He was as bundled as the Michelin tire man, leaving only his eyes visible above the scarf he'd wrapped around his face.

Lindsey borrowed two shovels and tucked them under one arm. When she climbed onto the snowmobile behind Beth, she looped her free arm about Beth's waist. They both wore their ski goggles, and despite the bitter wind and pelting snow, Lindsey felt fairly warm with all of her gear on.

Beth revved the engine and they shot out over the snow and headed toward town. It took all of Lindsey's coordination to hang on to the shovels and Beth. Although, she was driving carefully, not knowing what lay under the drifts, it was still a bouncy ride as she swerved to avoid dangerous bumps, and the visibility was poor as the snow continued to fall, and the sun's light was a hazy gray at best as it tried to burn its way through the clouds.

Lindsey glanced up when they got closer to town. Roofs

had several feet of snow on them, the trees bowed to the ground under the weight of the snow on their branches, cars were abandoned all over the road and the eerie sight of absolutely no one moving about town gave Lindsey a creepy chill up her spine.

Beth pulled onto the side lot of the library and cut the engine. They both climbed off and Lindsey had to straighten out the cramps in her knees. She hadn't realized she'd been clenching them so tightly around the seat.

"Where should we start?" Beth asked. Her voice was muffled because of her scarf.

"Let's start at the front," Lindsey said. "We can dig the back door out later if we have time."

She handed Beth a shovel, and together they began to attack the four-foot drift of snow that pressed against the glass doors to the library. Lindsey wondered how much snow it would take to bust open the doors. She was hoping she didn't find out.

It was excruciatingly boring work. Because the walkway was so full of snow, they had to start at the curb and work their way toward the stairs to the doors. Lindsey had intended to dig out the entire building, but after an hour and a half, they had just finished the steps and were beginning to get to the drift against the doors, and she realized once they were done with that, she was done.

She was pushing her shovel into the meaty part of the drift when she felt someone tap her on the shoulder. Beth pointed with her glove at a person coming their way. The person was unrecognizable as they, too, wore a snowsuit. They had snowshoes on their feet and were making good time as they came toward the library.

"Who is it?" she asked Beth.

Beth shook her head.

As the person got near, they went right past Lindsey and Beth to the book drop. It was then that Lindsey noticed the backpack that they wore. The person swung the backpack off their shoulders and opened the book drop and began unloading a pile of books into the drop.

"Really?" Beth asked Lindsey. "A nor'easter is happening and this person snowshoed to the library?"

The person turned around and lowered their scarf. It was then that Lindsey recognized Javier Ramirez. He was a middle-aged man, married, with kids, who worked in a neighboring town as a teacher. He was a big fan of Clive Cussler and Tom Clancy.

"There," he said. "My books were due today and I returned them today."

"Thank you, but that really wasn't necessary, Mr. Ramirez," Lindsey said. "The library is closed."

He waved his hand at her as if to say that was incidental. "You two are my witnesses. You tell that mean old Ms. Cole that Javier Ramirez returned his books on time. I don't want to get any fines from that one. Last time she made my wife cry."

Lindsey sighed. The lemon had obviously struck again.

"If Ms. Cole ever treats you or your family in a way that is unprofessional again, please tell me," Lindsey said. "You're a good patron and I won't have that."

"I am a good patron," he said. "I returned my stuff on time. Remember that."

With that, he set off back across the drifts toward home. Lindsey and Beth exchanged a look. Then Lindsey started to laugh and so did Beth. It may have been a fit of giggles or a small bout of hysterics due to the stress of the storm, it was hard to say. But Lindsey felt better afterward, and digging out the rest of the drift seemed to go faster.

Lindsey was eyeballing the last pile. It was pushed up against the door like a sleepy cat that had no intention of being moved from its favorite chair. Lindsey could feel the ache in her shoulders beginning to throb all the way down her arms.

She glanced at Beth. She was moving slower, too, and her breath was coming out in exhausted white puffs.

"I've heard about dedicated employees, but this is above and beyond the call of duty."

Lindsey glanced around to see a person on cross-country skis approaching.

She recognized the plaid scarf immediately. It was Edmund. He used his poles to stop beside her.

"Fancy seeing you here," she said.

"Indeed," he agreed. "I came out to survey the damage and pick up a few things for my uncle."

Lindsey took in his puffy jacket. It must have been quite a trek because his jacket was showing serious signs of distress. She had never seen either Bill or Edmund look less than impeccable, so it was a surprise to see a tear and several streaks of dirt mar his appearance.

He must have seen her look, because he brushed at the dirt and said, "I had a heck of a time getting these skis out of the storage shed. Even though we knew it was coming, we weren't quite prepared for a storm like this."

He used the tip of his pole to pop the latch on his ski and took out first one foot and then the other.

"I know what you mean," Lindsey said. She glanced around the town buried in the white stuff. "I don't think anyone saw this coming."

Edmund propped his poles and skis against the wall and approached Beth. He took the shovel from her hands and gestured for her to go stand with Lindsey. He then began to dig out the last of the huge drift.

When Lindsey went to help him, he waved her away.

"No, I've got it," he insisted. "You catch your breath."

Lindsey was too tired to argue.

"Isn't he nice?" Beth asked as Edmund shoveled twice as fast as they'd be able to.

"He really is," Lindsey agreed. "He must take after his mother's side."

Beth laughed. "He's certainly a refreshing change from surly Uncle Bill."

Edmund finished in just minutes and joined them by the curb. He handed Lindsey the shovel.

"Thank you," she said. "Your timing was perfect."

"Yeah, I think my arms were about to give out," Beth said.

He grinned at them and then popped his skis back on.

"Well, I'd better get back to Uncle Bill before he gets testy," he said. "He doesn't like to be alone in this weather. I think it makes him feel vulnerable."

"Yeah, we should get back, too," Lindsey said.

There was an awkward pause. Beth glanced between them and then took the shovels and headed for the snow-mobile.

The sparkle left Edmund's eyes as he studied Lindsey

with a frown. "I don't like the thought of you out in this storm; promise me you'll be careful."

"I promise," she said. "You, too."

"Oh, I will," he said. Then he grinned as if pleased with her concern. "I have a lunch date that I'm looking forward to."

Lindsey waved as he pushed off into the snow. When she joined Beth, her friend looked at her and asked, "Okay, now what?"

Lindsey glanced around the snow-blanketed town. The only place showing any sort of life was the Blue Anchor. Several plow trucks were parked in front of it, and a plume of smoke was rising from its chimney.

"How about a hot toddy at the Anchor?" she asked. "My treat."

"Get on," Beth said. "And you'll notice I'm not even teasing you about Edmund and his obvious crush on you."

"We're in our thirties; we don't have crushes," Lindsey said.

"Speak for yourself," Beth argued. "And you're full of baloney; otherwise, why does your face get red every time you see Sully?"

"It does not!"

"Oh, please, you're a regular hothouse tomato when he comes around."

"Just drive!" Lindsey assumed her previous position and Beth shot them across the street, through the park and into the semiplowed lot of the local watering hole.

Not wanting to lose Nancy's shovels, Lindsey handed one to Beth and gestured that they were to take them into the restaurant with them.

As they lumbered into the room, Ian Murphy, the owner, piped up, "Lindsey and Beth, is that you? Are you here to fatten up your skinny dates with some shepherd's pie?"

All the heads in the bar swiveled in their direction, and chuckles broke up the room as the two women hugged their shovels close in a mock embrace before leaning them against the wall by the door.

Lindsey pulled off her goggles and scarf and teased in return, "Eh, I'm afraid I'm going to have to dump him. His personality is too wooden."

Always appreciative of a good pun, Ian slapped down his bar rag and laughed. "Get in here, you two, and sit down. We don't have any power, but I can offer you a nice shot of brandy to warm you up, and we've got the wood-stove doing triple-time over there. Mary's cooking up ham and potatoes on it."

Lindsey glanced over to the corner of the room, where the woodstove, which was used more often as a decoration than a stove, was in full use. Ian's wife, Mary, a member of their crafternoon club, was standing over the stove and stirring something in a cast iron pot that made Lindsey's mouth begin to water.

"I'm in," Beth said, and she hurried over to the warmth of the stove. Lindsey was right behind her.

"You look frozen," Mary said when she saw them.

Several of the men who had been sitting by the stove rose to offer them their seats.

"Oh, no, we're fine," Lindsey said. She had a feeling these men had been working all night to plow the town out. They had to be exhausted and she didn't want to take their seats.

"We're headed back out," one of them said. "We're trying to dig out some of the harder-hit areas before the storm worsens." He downed the remainder of his coffee and started to pull his heavy coveralls back on.

He gave Mary a smacking kiss on the cheek and yelled at Ian, "You married above yourself, Ian Murphy!"

"Don't I know it," Ian called back. "She reminds me every day."

"I do," Mary said to Lindsey and Beth. "That's the first thing I say to him every morning. You traded up when you married me. Don't forget it."

Lindsey grinned. Mary and Ian were her favorite couple ever. Ian was short and bald and wore glasses, but he was so charming that within five minutes of meeting him you forgot he wasn't much to look at. And Mary, well, she looked like her older brother, Sully. With mahogany curls that reached past her shoulders and bright blue eyes, she was a beauty, but she was also smart and funny. They simply adored one another and it made them delightful to be around.

"So, what are you two doing out in this?" Mary asked.

"Digging out the library," Beth said. "We only got the front done."

"Good thing," Mary said. "Sully just called in and he thinks the storm is going to take a turn for the worse within the hour."

Mary put a chunk of soda bread and heaping ladle full of ham and potatoes on each of their plates. She then came back with two steaming cups of coffee supercharged with brandy.

"We're trying to keep the food going for the road crews,"

Mary said. "Sully and Ian were out with them last night, but I forbid Ian to go back out until he slept a bit. He just woke up so I expect he'll be leaving me shortly."

Lindsey could hear the worry in her voice and she nodded. She didn't much like the idea of Sully being out there all night either, not that it was any of her business.

"Has Sully gotten any rest?" she asked, trying to sound casually inquiring and failing miserably.

Mary gave her a knowing smile. "He came in for coffee and I hid his keys this morning. He got about two hours of sleep. Don't worry. His naval training has put him in better shape than most for this sort of thing."

"Is it just me or is this the best food you've ever eaten?" Beth asked through a mouthful.

Obviously, shoveling snow had given the woman an appetite; her plate was almost clean. Then Lindsey glanced down at her own plate. Where had all the food gone?

Mary laughed at both of them and dished up some more of the ham and potatoes and bread. They ate hurriedly, and when her belly was full, Lindsey was sure that if she lay down on the table she'd sleep for a week.

"I don't want to chase off the only pretty customers we've had," Ian said as he approached the table, "but the wind is picking up and the snow is falling harder. You'd better get while the getting is good."

"Be careful," Mary said as she hugged them both.

Beth and Lindsey bundled back up. Stepping out into the biting wind and thick snow was almost more than Lindsey could stand. She grabbed the shovels and held on to Beth as they zipped back to Nancy's house.

The porch and path to the front door had been cleared, but the snow was beginning to pile up again.

"Why don't you stay here?" she asked Beth. "It might be safer if the storm gets really nasty."

"I can't leave Slinky and Skippy John," Beth said.

Lindsey wanted to argue, but she knew how much Beth loved her two kitties.

"Besides, I have to get this snowmobile back to Mr. Chester so he doesn't worry."

"Be safe," Lindsey said.

"I will," Beth promised. "Mr. Chester has a cell phone. I'll call and let you know I made it."

"All right," Lindsey said. "Don't forget."

Beth nodded and revved the engine. Lindsey watched her hop over the drifts with a nervous flutter in her chest. She glanced up at the sky. The snow pelted down onto her goggles, melting against the flesh-warmed plastic until all she could see was spots.

CHAPTER

17

BRIAR CREEK
PUBLIC LIBRARY

Heathcliff danced a doggy dance of delight when Lindsey stepped through the door. She smiled, almost tempted to match his happy dance. There was something about coming home to a being that had no compunction about showing how much he had missed her that made Lindsey's mood lighten even as the storm beat down on the eaves with a hammering that was relentless.

Although they had not discussed it, they all gathered in Nancy's living room to while away the rest of the afternoon and evening. They cooked spaghetti on Charlie's stove while Nancy whipped up a salad and Lindsey ran up to her apartment to bring down a fresh loaf of olive bread.

They ate in candlelight, and conversation moved from Charlie's tour and the uncertain future of the band to what Lindsey had seen while she was digging out the library.

Carrie offered to help Lindsey with the dishes. Since she was bone weary from shoveling the snow, Lindsey was grateful for the assist.

The window over the kitchen sink looked out over the side yard, and Lindsey noticed that Carrie scanned the yard every time her gaze strayed to the window.

"Are you looking for your kids?" she asked. "Are they on their way?"

"No." Carrie shook her head. "I told them to wait until the roads were passable. Our family has suffered enough tragedy for the time being."

Lindsey was silent for a moment, not sure if she should say more, but she wanted Carrie to know that she could talk to her.

"What is it, then?" she asked. She figured it was better to offer Carrie the opportunity to talk even if Carrie gave her the brush-off. "It's obvious something is on your mind."

"I just"—Carrie hesitated—"I just can't help wondering if Markus was the intended target of the shooter."

"What do you mean?" Lindsey handed her the last of the dripping plates.

"I mean, and I know this sounds nuts, but what if the killer was looking for me?"

"Is there a reason you think this?"

"Well, I know Markus wasn't very well liked," Carrie said. "But I don't think anyone hated him enough to shoot him. He rarely left the house. He never left his zip code. Who could have wanted him dead?"

"The police don't think it was an accident, do they?"

"They haven't said for sure."

"But?"

"But I don't see how they could," Carrie said. "Both of my neighbors have called me to see how I'm doing, and when we talked about what happened, neither of them could remember hearing anything like a shot being fired in the evening. No matter what the medical examiner says, I know he was shot after seven o'clock, because when I left the house, he was fine."

"It's nice of your neighbors to check on you," Lindsey said.

"Well, we've all lived there for twenty-five years. Marcia lives on one side and Cindy on the other," Carrie said. "Our kids ran in and out of each other's houses for years. I know them almost as well as I know myself."

She stacked the dried plate on top of the pile, and Lindsey put the stack up in the cupboard.

"But if what you say is true, then you're saying someone would want to shoot you. You're very well liked in the community," Lindsey said. "I can't imagine that anyone would want to harm you."

Carrie carefully folded her dish towel and placed it on the counter. When she looked up again, her brown eyes were troubled.

"There's one person," she said. "But I hate to name names. I mean, what if I'm wrong? That would be slander."

Lindsey studied her. She thought about who in town might have a grudge against Carrie. One name leapt forward and she said, "How about if I guess?"

Carrie raised her brows and nodded.

"Marjorie Bilson, aka Batty Bilson, who apparently has a passion for Bill Sint?" Lindsey asked and Carrie gasped.

"How did you know that was who I was thinking?"

"Because she's off her rocker," Lindsey said. "She came after me when you took over Bill's role as president of the Friends."

"Really?"

Lindsey nodded. A draft of cold air circled around her and she shivered. "Come on, let's talk by the fire."

They rejoined Charlie and Nancy in the living room. The two of them were engrossed in a game of chess. Judging by the accumulated pieces by each of them, Charlie was winning.

Lindsey and Carrie sat down on the hearth and let the fire's heat wash over their backs. Soon it would be too hot to sit this close, but for the moment it felt good. Heathcliff lay down beside Lindsey and rested his chin on her feet. She reached down and gently rubbed his ears.

"The day after Markus was shot, I got a weird and very creepy phone call from Marjorie Bilson," Lindsey said. "I didn't mention it to you because I felt you had enough going on, but I did play it for Officer Plewicki and she recorded it."

"What did it say?" Carrie asked.

"Basically, that now that you were going to jail for murdering your husband, she wanted to know when Bill would be reinstated as the president of the Friends."

Both Charlie and Nancy turned their attention from the game to listen.

"Is that the message you played for Emma at the police station?" Nancy asked. "I heard her tell the chief about it. I got the feeling she was going to bring Marjorie in, but I wonder if the storm has shifted their priorities."

"It would have to," Charlie said. "They can't chase down a murderer when half the town is out of power and buried under snow."

They were all silent for a moment or two. The house, still without power, creaked and groaned under the onslaught of wind and ice. Even huddled together in the cozy living room, it was impossible not to feel vulnerable.

Heathcliff rose to his feet and did a quick survey of the doors and windows. To Lindsey, it looked as if he were checking the perimeter. He was just a puppy, but she found it incredibly comforting to have him finish his circuit and sit back down at her feet as if assured that all was well.

"If your neighbors didn't hear a shot, and assuming it wasn't an accident, then that means it was someone who knows how to use a gun," Lindsey said. "Does Marjorie have a history with firearms?"

Carrie, Nancy and Charlie all looked at one another. Charlie was the first to raise his hands in defeat.

"I don't know," he said. "I mean everyone knows her elevator doesn't reach the top floor, but it's not like she's Dale Wilcox."

"True," Nancy said. "Now there's one you don't turn your back on."

"Who's Dale Wilcox?" Lindsey asked.

"He's a local fisherman," Charlie said. "You see him down at the pier a lot. He runs a charter operation, but he's as mean as a hornet, and when he's drunk, he's mean and crazy. He did time for assault and battery a few years back, and if I remember right, he had a weapon on him at the time of his arrest."

Carrie fretted her lip. "It wasn't Dale. I know he has a

bad reputation, but he wasn't always like that. I don't believe he'd harm anyone."

"He went to jail for assault!" Charlie argued. "Rumor has it he was going to shoot that guy."

"As you say, rumors not facts," Carrie said.

"Wait a minute," Nancy said. "I just remembered! I was at the grocery store, and I saw Dale and Markus get into a road-rage incident a few weeks ago. Dale thought Markus had cut him off to steal his parking spot, and when he yelled at Markus about it, Markus threatened to call the police. Dale got so mad at that he threatened to back over him."

"Did Markus call the police?" Lindsey asked. This would be excellent, as it would give the police yet another lead.

"No, Milton Duffy happened by and tried to talk them both into doing some sort of yoga thing together," Nancy said. "Markus refused because of his back, and Dale just stalked off toward the package store."

"I never heard about this," Carrie said, and she began to fret her lower lip with her teeth. "I wonder why no one told me."

"Probably, so you wouldn't worry," Charlie said. "Dale drunk is flat-out scary. Sully won't even let him on the pier if he smells booze on him."

An icicle snapped off the side of the house and fell with a thump. They all jumped. Lindsey's back was hot now, so she scooted off the hearth and sat on the floor beside Heathcliff, who obligingly rolled onto his back to have his belly rubbed.

"Well, this does give us a new direction to look in,"

Lindsey said. "Was there anyone else Markus had an altercation with recently?"

"Define altercation," Carrie said. "He had a row with our handyman, Clyde Perkins, over the tile we hired him to put in our bathroom. Markus refused to pay him when he was done because he said he didn't like the way the tiles felt under his feet. He thought they were too spongy."

Nancy shook her head and Charlie blew a breath out between his lips.

"What happened?" Lindsey asked.

"I had to pay Clyde on the sly," Carrie said. "But, oh, he was so mad at Markus. Apparently, Markus said he did shoddy work and he was going to report him to the Better Business Bureau."

"Then what happened?"

"I believe Clyde threatened to use his tile cutter on him."

Nancy clucked. "Clyde is one of the best handymen in town."

"I know," Carrie said. "Markus also got into a tiff with Della Navarro, his physical therapist. He said she was nothing more than a gym teacher and should have her therapist license revoked. He was going to file a complaint against her."

"Della is a big girl," Charlie said. "I don't think I'd sass her."

"Didn't she rehab Cooper Highsmith after his car accident?" Nancy asked.

"Yes," Carrie said. "She got him walking again when they said he never would."

"Wow, I'm surprised she didn't snap your husband like a twig," Charlie said.

Carrie sighed. "My husband was not an easy person."

Nancy and Lindsey glanced swiftly at one another and then away. Not fast enough, however.

"What was that look for?" Carrie asked.

"What look?" Nancy asked.

Lindsey gave her props for sounding so innocent, but she knew they were busted.

"That look that says you think I'm mental," Carrie said.

"No, that's not it," Charlie said. He moved his leg right before the toe of Nancy's sneaker would have connected with his shin in an attempt to shut him up.

"Oh?" Carrie looked at him. "What is it, then?"

"It's just that no one in town has ever been able to figure out how such a nice lady like you ended up with such an old, well, stinker," Charlie said.

"Charlie!" Nancy reprimanded him, but Carrie held up her hand to indicate that it was okay.

"He wasn't always like that," she said.

Nancy looked at her with one eyebrow raised in disbelief.

"Oh, all right, he was always like that," Carrie said with a sigh. "He really thought the world owed him."

"You think?" Nancy asked. "I mean, I didn't know him well, but even I knew that he spent his days cooking up one crazy, get-rich-quick scheme after another."

"Yeah," Charlie snorted. "He wanted Sully to buy some boat parts from him. He'd gotten them from some guy at the dump and they were crap."

Carrie nodded, looking pained. "I remember that."

"He was so mad when Sully said, no, thank you." Charlie shook his head. "He really thought he was going to make a fortune."

159

"Oh, and remember when he wanted the Blue Anchor to carry his signature cookies?" Nancy asked. "Turns out he was buying the nearly expired throw-out cookies from the bakery and palming them off as his own."

Nancy tsked. Lindsey could tell that this left Nancy with a particularly bad taste in her mouth, not surprising since she was known for baking the best cookies in town.

"He said he always figured he'd be rich and living in a mansion like the Sint estate by the water on the bay," Carrie said. "But he never wanted to work for it."

"So, why did you stay with him?" Lindsey asked. She couldn't imagine what Carrie had seen in such a lazy scam artist.

"I just, well, I made a vow. And when you make a vow, you have to stick to it."

"Oh." Charlie nodded. "So, when you made your wedding vows before God, you took them to heart. I get it. That's really admirable."

"No, you don't understand," Carrie said.

They all looked at her. A wry smile parted her lips.

"I know God would have forgiven me for leaving Markus. He was a miserable person and tended to bring everyone around him right down into the muck with him. Truly, he is . . . was a complete downer."

"Then why did you stay?" Lindsey asked.

"His mother, on her deathbed, she made me swear I'd never leave him," Carrie said. "She was dying. I couldn't refuse."

"So you kept your vow to a dying woman," Charlie said as if it all made sense now. "Wow, that's amazing."

"No, it wasn't," Carrie said. Then she snorted. "The

truth is, I was afraid the old bat would haunt me if I broke my promise. The only person more high maintenance than Markus was his mother. God rest her soul."

"I think you were wise. If there was a woman who could haunt you, it would be Jane Rushton," Nancy said. "You were right to be afraid."

The two women looked at each other with sheepish grins. Charlie looked at them like they were both loony, which made them laugh.

He looked at Lindsey for backup, but she had started to crack up as well. Probably, it was exhaustion creeping up on her, but she couldn't stop the indelicate snort that escaped through her nose.

Surprised, Charlie laughed at her, and Heathcliff hopped to his feet to lick any face he could reach.

A deep, repeated banging broke through their laughter.

"What was that?" Nancy asked.

They all went silent, listening. Then the banging started again.

CHAPTER

18

BRIAR CREEK
PUBLIC LIBRARY

For a crazy second, Lindsey thought it was Jane Rushton coming to haunt them for being so callous as to laugh at her.

Heathcliff, the bravest of them all, charged the door, barking a warning.

"It sounds like someone knocking on the front door," Charlie said. He rose slowly to his feet. "Who would be insane enough to come out in this weather?"

"Well, you did," Lindsey said.

She stood, too, feeling more nervous than she wanted to let on. At least Charlie lived here. It wasn't so odd that he'd tried to get in during the storm. But now that all of the residents were accounted for, there was no reason for anyone to be knocking.

"Well, we won't know until we answer it," Charlie said. He picked up a flashlight and led the way, leaving Lindsey and the others to follow him. He opened Nancy's apartment door and peered out into the darkness.

"Hello?" he called.

There was no response.

Heathcliff began to growl low in his throat. Lindsey reached down and stroked his head. The fur between his shoulder blades bristled, and Lindsey tried to soothe him with whispered words of comfort. Heathcliff wasn't having any of it.

"Stay back," Charlie said. "I'll answer it."

"No, don't," Carrie said. "It could be the murderer."

"We have to," Nancy said. "It could be someone in trouble."

"Nancy's right," Lindsey said. "You two stay back. Nancy, get your cell phone ready. If it is someone bad, shut yourselves in a back room and call nine-one-one."

Nancy opened her mouth to say something, but the pounding on the front door resumed and they all jumped.

"Go now," Charlie ordered.

As the two women stepped back into the apartment, Charlie and Lindsey stepped forward. She held Heathcliff's collar to keep him from jumping.

Charlie unlocked the door and pulled it open just a crack. "Who's there?"

"It's Sully, and I'm freezing."

Charlie yanked the door open. "What are you doing out in this weather, boss?"

"Looking for Lindsey," he said. He had to shout because

Heathcliff started barking an enthusiastic greeting and launched himself at Sully, obviously recognizing him.

"You found me," Lindsey said with a wave.

Sully knelt down and let Heathcliff lick his face. "How are you doing, boy?"

Heathcliff wiggled even closer to Sully, and Lindsey had to smile. There was a definite mutual-admiration-society thing happening there.

"Come on in," Lindsey said. "We have a fire and I'm sure Nancy has some hot tea."

"Sounds nice," he said.

They stepped toward the door and Lindsey realized Charlie wasn't following.

"Are you coming?" she asked him.

"In a minute," he said. He started up the stairs. "I need my guitar. 'Looking for Lindsey' sounds like a top-ten hit to me."

Lindsey and Sully exchanged a look and then a shrug. Charlie was always looking for his one-hit wonder.

Nancy was already making Sully's tea when they returned to the living room.

"Michael Sullivan, what are you thinking?" Nancy asked. "What could bring you out in this?"

Lindsey glanced at Carrie. She was looking at Sully with scared eyes, as if she had expected something much more malevolent and couldn't quite process the large quiet man before her.

"Bad news, actually," he said.

He had their attention now. Lindsey mentally ran through a panicked list of people who could be in trouble. Was it

Beth? Or Jessica? How about Ann Marie? Her boys? Surely, nothing had happened to them. Was it one of her crafternoon buddies? Or Milton? What about Milton? Yes, he was fitter than men half his age, but he was still in his eighties and he lived alone.

Sully took a sip of his tea and then glanced up. Lindsey realized that the others must have looked as nervous as she did, because he frowned and said, "No one is hurt."

"You might want to lead with that next time," Nancy said, and she swatted him with the dish towel she'd been fretting in her hands.

"Sorry," he said. To his credit, he really did look remorseful.

"What's the bad news, then?" Lindsey asked. She gestured to a seat by the fire, and Sully gratefully sank down into it.

Heathcliff took the opportunity to wriggle into Sully's lap, even though he was by no means a lap dog. Sully grinned and let him try to curl up on his legs while he held his tea out of tail-knocking range and steadied the puppy with his other hand.

Lindsey glanced at his face and realized he must have been working all day and well into the night. His skin looked stretched and his eyes had a heavy-lidded weariness that bespoke someone who hadn't slept in a few days.

"The heavy snowfall caused the roof to collapse on the Drury Street storage facility," he said.

"Oh, no," Carrie said. "Are you sure no one was hurt?"

"Luckily, because of the weather, no one was out there, but the damage to the goods inside is going to be severe."

Carrie nodded. Then she turned to Lindsey and said,

"That's where the Friends store all of their donated books for the annual book sale."

Lindsey thought the name sounded familiar. "That's the one on the edge of town that's owned by Owen Pullman, isn't it?" she asked.

"Yes," Nancy confirmed. "Was the whole place destroyed or just a few of the sheds?"

"About half," Sully said. "Owen called me a few hours ago. I use a shed out there to store old paperwork and boating equipment. Owen was pretty distraught, so I told him I'd get word to the other owners if he gave me a list."

"I hope he was insured," Lindsey said.

"I think the physical structures will be covered, but I don't know if the contents will be," Sully said.

"I'll call Mimi Seitler tomorrow and see if we can get a list of what we had in the shed," Carrie said. "I know we had some rare books donated a while back. I hope they weren't just boxed and put out there. That could be disastrous."

"Do you want me to call Bill Sint?" Lindsey asked. "He may be more forthcoming, talking to me."

Carrie thought about it for a moment. "I appreciate that, but he's going to have to start talking to me sometime. It might as well be now. I'll call him in the morning, too."

Lindsey noticed that Carrie had a little color in her cheeks and her eyes had lost some of their grief-stricken haze. She was a doer; maybe having a cause like the warehouse collapse would help her through this stressful time.

Sully finished his tea and Nancy reached out to take his mug.

"Thanks," he said. "That hit the spot. If you all don't mind, I'm going to get some shut-eye. The storm is supposed to blow over by morning, but I have a feeling the digging out may take a few days."

Lindsey felt the sore muscles in her shoulders bunch in protest at the thought of more digging, and she winced.

"Care to walk me out?" Sully asked her.

Lindsey was about to answer when Nancy said, "Of course she will."

Lindsey turned to look at her. Subtle, Nancy was not.

"What?" Nancy asked, the picture of innocence. "Someone has to lock the door behind him."

Sully grinned at Lindsey as he rose from his seat. He picked up a candle and stopped before her chair and held out his free hand to help her up. Lindsey let him pull her out of the chair. To her surprise, he didn't let go of her hand as they walked toward the door.

Lindsey felt her pulse kick up a notch. As if he knew, Sully looked down at her and grinned. His dimples bracketed his mouth and his smile almost outshone the candle he held in his other hand.

The strains of Charlie's guitar could be heard up above, and Lindsey noticed that Heathcliff hadn't followed them to the door. When she glanced back, he was getting a treat that looked suspiciously like bacon from Nancy.

She closed the door behind them. The foyer was cold and she shivered. Sully set the candle down on the windowsill above the radiator. Their shadows flickered against the wall as a small draft from the window made the candle dance.

"I had an ulterior motive for getting you out here," he said.

So much for the cold; Lindsey felt her whole body flash hot with anticipation.

"Really?" she asked. "So you were trying to get me alone?"

Sully's grin deepened and Lindsey was mortified to hear that her voice held a decidedly flirty tone. It was too late to retract the words, and she felt her face heat up in embarrassment.

"What I meant to say was—" she began, but he interrupted her by pulling her close.

"You're shivering," he said. He opened his coat and hugged her close.

The proximity to his warmth made her dizzy, and she was relieved that he was holding her up or she might have toppled over from the contact.

His voice was close to her ear, and when he spoke, his words were little more than a whisper.

"I didn't want to say anything to Carrie," he said. "But I don't think the warehouse roof collapsed because of the snow."

"What?" She pulled back and discovered her face was just inches from his.

In the candlelight, his normally bright blue eyes had darkened to a deep navy, and she was momentarily distracted by the heady scent of him, a masculine bay-rum sort of smell, and she lost the thread of the conversation.

"About ten sheds were demolished," he said. "From what I could tell, a small explosive was used to do the damage. I think whoever did it was counting on the blizzard being blamed."

"But why?"

Sully shrugged and Lindsey felt his hands slide up and down her back at the movement. She swallowed hard, trying to clear her head.

"The target could be any one of them, but the Friends shed was in the center of the rubble, leading me to think it's the one that was the object of the break-in."

Lindsey blinked and tried to focus on his words. Someone had deliberately broken into the storage shed.

"Do the police know?" she asked.

"I haven't said anything yet. Owen thinks it was the storm and until the police have a chance to check it out, nothing is for sure."

"We need to find out what was in that shed," she said.

She glanced up to see if he agreed and found him studying her. His gaze traced her features, and he looked as if he was contemplating kissing her. Lindsey felt her breath stall in her lungs.

In an instant, she knew that she would welcome it, and that she could no longer deny that she had a case of the scorching hots for Mike Sullivan.

He leaned down; she leaned up. They were a breath apart when a door slammed above them, followed by the pounding sound of Converse sneakers bounding down the stairs in their direction.

Lindsey and Sully broke apart. She cupped the back of her neck with a hand and tried to appear casual as Charlie popped into the foyer with them.

"Leaving already?" Charlie asked.

Sully glared at him, looking like he wanted to pick him up and toss him out into the snow. For some reason this made Lindsey feel unaccountably better. She didn't want to be the only one feeling denied, and she was quite pleased that Sully looked as frustrated as she felt.

Sully looked over at her and said, "Lock the door behind me."

She gave him a snappy salute, and his mouth curved up in one corner. He opened the door and gave her a scorching look. "We'll revisit this conversation later."

CHAPTER

19

BRIAR CREEK
PUBLIC LIBRARY

The door shut behind him and Lindsey stood staring at it until Charlie nudged her.

"Your candle blew out," he said.

Lindsey couldn't have disagreed more, but she picked up the smoking wax stub from the windowsill and followed him back into the main room.

Nancy and Carrie were huddled by the fire. No one said as much, but they all started to assume their sleep positions. Somehow, while the storm raged outside, it felt as if there was strength, or at least warmth, in numbers.

Charlie stretched out in his recliner while Lindsey took the other. Heathcliff climbed up with her and Lindsey snuggled him close.

Carrie and Nancy departed to their rooms, and a silence

fell over the house, broken only by the whistling wind and the occasional hiss from the gas fire, which Nancy had turned down to blue flicker.

Even though it warmed her from the toes on up, Lindsey decided not to think about Sully or what might have happened in the foyer if Charlie had been just a few minutes later. She wasn't sure if he had been planning to kiss her or if it was just her own temporary insanity at being that close to an attractive man.

It had been almost a year since she'd left John, and she wasn't sure she could even read a signal from a man anymore. She had the horrible feeling that she was going to embarrass herself by leaning in to kiss Sully when he was merely trying to tell her she had spinach in her teeth.

She decided to think about what Sully had told her about the warehouse instead. He thought the damage had been deliberate. But why?

The books donated to the Friends were everything from a lifetime collection of *National Geographic* to an oily repair manual for a Yugo. Why would anyone want to bust into their shed?

Having no answers, her mind wandered back to Markus Rushton's murder. A rifle shot through a sliding glass door that no one heard; there were so many things wrong with this scenario it was hard to tell where to begin.

Could it have been one of the men he'd recently had an altercation with? It seemed unlikely, but any newspaper in the country reported stories of murder for even less. It was a mystery. One she intended to solve before Carrie became the winner of the most-likely-to-have-shot-him award.

* * *

A light awoke Lindsey first thing in the morning. She blinked against the intrusion, and it took her a moment to realize it wasn't just any light but the lamp beside the chair where she was sleeping. They had electricity!

"Charlie!" she shouted as she bolted upright. "Wake up. We have light!"

"Hunh, what?" Charlie grunted.

"Light and power!" Lindsey repeated.

Nancy and Carrie stumbled from their rooms, looking bewildered.

"What's happening?" Carrie asked.

"Behold," Lindsey said. "Light."

She flicked on all of the nearby light switches, and Nancy clapped her hands together and jumped up and down.

"I'll start the coffeepot," she said.

"Shower," Lindsey said. "I'm going to take a hot shower, plug in my cell phone and reprogram my clocks. I'll be back."

She bolted up the stairs with Heathcliff at her heels. It was such a relief to go back into her apartment and be able to turn on the lights, play the radio and know that she wasn't limited by battery life.

She was towel drying her long blond hair when her phone rang. She was so happy to have her cordless working again that she didn't bother checking the caller ID.

"Hello," she answered.

"I'll be watching you," the voice on the line said.

"Excuse me," Lindsey said. She clutched the phone to her ear, concentrating on the caller's words.

173

"You heard me. I'll be watching you, and if you know what's good for you, you'll do the right thing."

The caller hung up. The bubble of joy Lindsey had been feeling at listening to NPR popped like a soap bubble.

She knew that voice. She was unlikely to forget that shrill tone anytime soon. It was Batty Bilson.

She settled the receiver in its cradle. Should she call the police? It seemed trivial given all that they had going on. Marjorie hadn't threatened her exactly, although it sort of felt that way.

No, she wasn't going to cause a stir over this. She would call her staff and get the library back open, then she would deal with Marjorie Bilson and her cryptic message.

I t took Lindsey and Beth the better part of the morning to shovel out the building. Once the walkways were clear and Lindsey felt that patrons and staff could navigate the stairs and enter the building without risking a broken limb, she opened the library. It was a few hours later than usual, but at least they were open.

The book drop was full. When they opened the door to the small room, a tidal wave of books slid into the main room. Lindsey stooped down to pick them up and put them on a cart. The covers were icy-cold to the touch.

Ms. Cole was logging in to her computer at the check-in desk, getting ready to deal with the deluge of books. Once she and Beth had filled a cart, Lindsey wheeled it over to Ms. Cole. She glanced at the check-in screen on Ms. Cole's monitor and frowned.

"Ms. Cole, you have today's date as the check-in date," she said.

"We *are* checking them in today," Ms. Cole said.

Lindsey could almost hear the unspoken *duh* at the end of her sentence.

"Yes, but the library was closed for two and a half days. We need to go back three days, so that people who returned their books on time don't get fined unfairly."

Ms. Cole looked outraged. "But what about people whose materials were due three days ago, who just returned them today?"

"They get amnesty," Lindsey said with a shrug.

"Well, I just . . . that's just . . ."

"It's just what?"

"It's setting a horrible precedent," Ms. Cole said. Her bosom heaved with her agitation. "I mean, people might expect . . . they might demand . . ."

"Good customer service?" Lindsey supplied.

"Exactly!" Ms. Cole said. "They might think that we'll always bend the rules just for them. I'm telling you, you're inviting anarchy."

"I'm afraid I'm going to have to risk it," Lindsey said.

When Ms. Cole looked like she might continue her protest, Lindsey held up her hand, indicating the conversation was over.

"I'm sorry, but this is how we're going to do it," Lindsey said. She leaned over Ms. Cole's chair, took her computer mouse and clicked the check-in date back three days. She saved the change and then went back to the book drop to load another cart, leaving the lemon sputtering behind her.

"How very unlike Mr. Tupper you are," Beth said with a teasing smile. She handed Lindsey a stack of books.

"He wouldn't have rolled back the check-in date?" Lindsey arranged the books on the truck.

"He would have let Ms. Cole decide," Beth said.

"Oh, I don't think that's wise," Lindsey said.

"It wasn't," Beth agreed. "But between you and me, I think he was afraid of her."

Lindsey glanced over her shoulder to where Ms. Cole was muttering while the check-in machine beeped with each item. She was in shades of brown today. Not her best color.

"Maybe that's why he retired to Florida," Lindsey said.

Once the drop was empty, Beth went to man her desk in children's while Lindsey wheeled the cart over to Ann Marie to assist Ms. Cole with the check-in. She'd called in their teen shelvers for an extra afternoon shift later in the day to help get them on track, and all was slowly getting back to normal in the quiet little library.

Lindsey walked over to the big windows that looked over the town. Huge drifts of snow still covered the park, but the roads had been sanded and salted and were just becoming passable.

She glanced over at the pier. She wondered if Sully was around. She noticed that several of the boat owners were out checking their rigs, including the charter boat that Dale Wilcox owned.

She could just make out a man in a navy blue hooded sweatshirt, unzipped, with a knit cap on his head and yellow waders. He was stomping around the end of the pier, looking ornery. She knew without being told that this was Dale Wilcox.

She glanced over her shoulder at the library. It was quiet. Most people were home digging out from the blizzard or they were back at their first day of work.

The clock on the wall showed it was fifteen minutes until her lunch hour. Good enough. She turned away from the window and headed toward her office.

If she dragged it out, getting suited up to go out into the cold could take at least five minutes. She slipped off her favorite loafers and slipped on her storm chaser boots from L.L.Bean. Scarf, hat, jacket and mittens were next and she was ready.

She strode out of her office and stopped in the children's area.

Beth glanced up in surprise. "Going somewhere?"

"I'm going to get some soup at the Blue Anchor," she said. If she actually did pick up soup, then it wasn't a total lie. "Can I bring you some?"

"Are you kidding? If you bring me some of Mary's chowder, I'll be your best friend," Beth said.

"You already are." Lindsey laughed. "Back in a few."

She stopped by the circulation desk and offered to bring Ann Marie and Ms. Cole some chowder as well. Ann Marie was game but Ms. Cole declined with a sniff. Lindsey suspected she was still miffy about the backdated check-in. Ah well, she'd just have to get over it.

Lindsey stepped on the rubber mat and the doors slid open. A blast of frosty air smacked her face and she sucked in a breath.

Ducking her head, she hurried out into the cold and headed for the pier. The packed snow on the road had melted just enough to freeze again after the abrupt temperature drop from the second half of the storm and had formed a nice sheen of ice.

Lindsey stepped carefully but still managed to half slide across the road as she navigated the treacherous conditions.

The parking lot of the Anchor was surprisingly clear, but then again, because it had become a meeting place for the plows, it had gotten the most use over the past few days.

She strode past the Anchor, keeping the man in the yellow waders in sight. She wasn't sure exactly how she was going to broach the subject of Markus Rushton with him, but she'd worry about that when she got there.

The pier, made of thick solid planks, hadn't been shoveled, and the snow had drifted over to one side of it while the footprints of the many boat owners had stomped the deep snow into matted patches.

Lindsey approached the boat, noting that the name *Pilar* was written in a forest green script across the stern. Interesting.

Dale was up on his boat sweeping the snow off the bow. Huge chunks fell over into the water with a splash.

Lindsey could hear him muttering while he swept. She wasn't positive, but it sounded like a nice string of profanity he had going. She hated to interrupt.

For the first time, she debated the wisdom of approaching a man known to be volatile when he was irked.

But she was only going to ask him some questions; it wasn't like she was going to accuse him of murder or anything.

"Hello?" she called out.

The boat went silent and then a knitted hat appeared over the side. Unshaven, with a jailhouse tattoo on his neck of what looked like a dragon or maybe a mermaid on steroids, and sporting a gold incisor that sparkled in the morning sun when he sneered, Dale Wilcox looked like he ate small children for breakfast.

CHAPTER

20

BRIAR CREEK
PUBLIC LIBRARY

Lindsey swallowed. She briefly wondered if her storm chaser boots could get her out of here before the man on the boat jumped over the side and whacked her with his broom.

"What do you want?" the man growled, glaring at her. "Can't you see I'm busy?"

"Sorry," Lindsey said. She was pleased that her voice didn't betray how nervous she felt. "You know, the original *Pilar* was custom built in 1934 in Brooklyn."

"By Wheeler Shipyards," he said.

"Oh, so you did know." Lindsey smiled.

"That's not surprising," he said. His scowl relaxed into a wary look. "I'm a fisherman. What is surprising is that you know."

"Not really." Lindsey shook her head. "I'm a librarian."

"Ah, then you also know, 'a man is never lost at sea,'" he said.

"*The Old Man and the Sea*," she said. "Brilliant book."

"Hemingway was a brilliant writer," he said. He looked her up and down. Not in an insolent way, but as if trying to get the measure of her. "I read all of his works when I was in prison."

"I think he would have liked that," Lindsey said.

Dale indicated the ladder with a shrug. "Feel free to climb aboard."

Lindsey had a feeling he was testing her, to see if she was brave enough to be on the boat with the big, bad ex-convict. For some reason, she wanted to pass his test and show him that she wasn't afraid.

She stepped forward and pulled herself up the short ladder. Dale continued sweeping, completely ignoring her. At a loss, Lindsey saw a second broom propped in the corner, so she picked it up and began to sweep the snow off the side. Dale paused to watch her for a moment and then set back to work.

They worked silently for a while. There wasn't much snow left to sweep, but the stuff she managed to push off the starboard side fell into the water with a satisfying splash. When they were done, she handed the broom back to Dale.

"You know, if you like Hemingway, there are other authors I could hook you up with," she said. "Library cards are free."

"Is that why you're here?" he asked. "To drum up business for the library? Things must be slow."

"No, actually, I came by to find out if you killed Markus Rushton," she said.

Dale's mouth opened in a small O and he blinked. "I didn't see that coming."

"Sorry, I didn't mean to blurt it out like that," she said. "Right now the police are focusing on his wife, but everyone knows you had an altercation with him a few weeks ago over a parking space."

Dale's brow lowered, bringing his knit cap with it so it rested just over his eyes. "So, naturally, because I am an ex-convict, you think I couldn't control my anger and I went and shot him over a stupid parking space. You know, it's assumptions like that that made Hemingway hate women."

"No, I think it was more due to his domineering mother and a crushing heartbreak from his relationship with his nurse while he was recuperating after being injured in the war," Lindsey said.

Dale grunted and looked out at the sea. "I should know better than to debate a librarian."

Lindsey lowered her head and smiled. People were wrong about Dale. He had a certain grouchy charm.

"For your information, the police have already been by to question me. I don't own a gun and I have an alibi. I was visiting my mother in Madison. She's in an assisted-care facility over there, and the place has the sign-in log to prove how long I was there. Satisfied?"

Lindsey sighed. "I've offended you."

"You think?" he asked. "You can't accuse a guy of murder and not expect him to get a little testy."

"Fair enough," Lindsey said. "I'm sorry. I'm just trying to help out a friend."

"I know," Dale said. He glanced away, and Lindsey was

surprised by the sudden softening of his features. "Carrie is a good woman. She was always nice to me even when we were kids. She never judged me because my family was poor. If I hadn't gotten sent to jail . . . well, you can't go back."

"What do you mean?" Lindsey asked.

Dale shrugged. "It doesn't matter. She deserved better than that mealymouthed whiner. I don't know who shot him, but they did her a favor."

His words were harsh, but Lindsey knew he was only saying what everyone else seemed to think of Markus Rushton. She glanced at her watch and realized she was pushing it if she was going to get back to the library with food within the hour.

"Thanks for talking to me," she said. She held out her hand.

Dale hesitated and then clasped her gloved hand. His grip was firm but not punishing.

"Maybe I'll stop by and see what you've got in that library of yours," he said.

"I'd like that," Lindsey said. She climbed down the ladder and waved as Dale stood and watched her go with a thoughtful expression on his face.

"So, I know that Mary's clam chowder could cause a person to walk a mile on shards of glass sans shoes, but I have a sneaky suspicion that there was something else motivating you to go for soup," Beth said.

Lindsey dipped her clam fritter into her chowder and took a bite. It was rude to talk with your mouth full, after all.

Beth thumped her spoon on the table. "Seriously? You're not talking? But I'm your best friend!"

Lindsey swallowed. "There's nothing to say."

Truly, her conversation with Dale was a bust. He had a solid alibi and she had discovered that the man had layers. She didn't really think he was as bad as people said. In fact, she wondered if he cultivated the bad-boy image just to keep people at a distance.

"Really?" Beth asked. "Are you trying to tell me that there is nothing going on between you and Sully? That you didn't go over to the pier today to see him?"

Lindsey choked on a bit of clam and had to cough into her napkin before she could respond. "Are you saying I went over there to see Sully?"

"Yes!"

"Well, I didn't, and as far as I know, there is nothing going on between us," Lindsey said.

"Oh, please." Beth scoffed. "Everyone knows you two like each other."

Lindsey glanced around the small break room where they sat eating their lunch. Thankfully, no one else was on break right now.

She leaned over the table and whispered, "If you must know, I went to the pier to see Dale Wilcox."

"The ex-convict?" Beth gasped. "Have you lost your mind?"

"Nancy said he had a road-rage incident with Markus Rushton just a few weeks ago."

"And you questioned him about it?" Beth's eyes went wide. "Lindsey! Don't you know the amateur sleuth is never supposed to go off on her own? This isn't an Agatha

Christie novel and you're not Miss Marple. You could have gotten yourself into a heap of trouble."

"Well, given that I pretty much accused him of murdering Rushton," she said, "I concede your point. But I didn't go off alone. I happened to be going for lunch and saw Dale Wilcox on his boat. I was simply being neighborly."

Beth slapped her hand to her forehead in exasperation. "You're lucky you're still alive!"

"Nah, I don't think Dale is as bad as everyone says," she said. "He reads Hemingway."

"Didn't Hemingway hate women?" Beth asked.

"I don't know if I would say *hate* exactly," Lindsey said. "But, yes, he had misogynistic tendencies."

"So, Ernest had issues," Beth said. "And you decided that it was a good idea to question a fan of his about committing murder. Yeah, this all makes perfect sense."

"I did discover one thing," Lindsey said. Then she paused, wondering if she should voice her speculation. "Don't say anything, but I think Dale had feelings for Carrie when they were younger."

"How so?"

"I think he only talked to me today because he knew I was asking questions to help out Carrie. And he got this look on his face, like, well, like he was very fond of her."

"Interesting. You don't think that fondness would have caused him to kill her husband, do you?"

"No, his alibi must be airtight or the police would have taken him in by now," Lindsey said.

"So what's next?" Beth asked.

"Well, Carrie has asked us all to meet her out by the storage shed this evening so we can try to move the Friends items to an undamaged shed. I imagine we're going to have to toss a lot of the ruined books."

"I'm in," Beth said. "My house is already dug out, so I'm happy to pitch in."

"Thanks," Lindsey said. "The more hands the better."

She did not mention that she planned to have a chat with the other two people Markus had offended recently, Clyde Perkins and Della Navarro. Since she didn't know if it would lead to anything significant, she figured she'd keep it to herself. Unlike the warehouse, the fewer people involved in this the better.

"Last call for hot chocolate and donuts!" Mimi Seitler shouted as she headed into the storage facility office, where she had a huge pot of hot chocolate plugged into the wall. Carrie had brought a big orange and pink box full of donuts, which was in there as well.

After hauling twenty-five boxes of books from the old shed to the new one, Lindsey felt like the hot chocolate was the only thing that might bring back the feeling in her toes. She trotted into the office and filled a foam cup before heading back out into the cold.

They'd been here for a couple of hours now. Carrie had picked up her and Beth after work, and she'd brought Heathcliff with her because he had been cooped up all day and needed the exercise. He had been overjoyed to see Lindsey and had been chasing the snowballs that Lindsey and the others threw for him for the past half hour.

Lindsey stamped her feet on the ground. It was a great turnout and the work was going quickly. There had to be at least fifteen people here, including both Edmund and Bill Sint. Mercifully, there was no sign of Marjorie Bilson.

A car turned into the small parking lot, its headlights sweeping over the area. Then again, maybe Marjorie had decided to show after all. Lindsey stood up straighter, bracing herself for a possible confrontation.

Before the car had even stopped, the passenger door flew open and out jumped a young woman. She had long, dark hair and was yanking on her winter coat as her eyes scanned the people in front of her.

"Mom!" she cried.

CHAPTER

21

BRIAR CREEK
PUBLIC LIBRARY

Carrie popped out of the new shed and cried, "Kim! Kyle!" Then she broke into a run.

The driver shut off the car and got out, too. He was a tall young man with the same dark hair as his mother and his sister. In fact, the three of them had the exact same face, with big brown eyes, delicate noses and strong jaws.

Carrie opened her arms wide as she ran, and the three of them tumbled into a group hug in the middle of the parking lot. Lindsey turned away to give them some privacy.

"Her kids?" Beth asked as she joined Lindsey.

"I'm assuming."

"Good. She could use the support."

It was several minutes later when Carrie brought her grown children over to meet Lindsey and the others.

"Kyle, Kim, this is Lindsey Norris, the director of the library, and Beth Stanley you already know."

"I remember the parties you used to throw for the teens every time a new Harry Potter book came out," Kim said.

"And I remember that you did the best artwork for my programs," Beth said and gave the girl a hug. "I still have some of those posters. How are you enjoying RISD?"

"I love it," she said.

"Welcome to Briar Creek," Kyle said to Lindsey and extended his hand.

Lindsey took his gloved hand in hers. He had a good handshake.

"Thank you. It's a lovely town," she said. She paused and then added, "I'm very sorry for your loss." She turned to include Kim in her condolences.

"I'm sorry, too," Beth said.

Both Kim and Kyle nodded, and Lindsey realized they probably weren't used to talking about it. It had taken them a few days to get here. And now that they were in their home-town, it must be surreal to confront their father's shooting.

Kim shivered and Carrie frowned, looking full of motherly concern.

"Listen," she said. "I'm staying at Nancy Peyton's place, and she said you two could stay with me. She has enough room so long as you two don't mind bunk beds. Honestly, I haven't been able to face going back to the house yet."

Kyle put his hand on his mother's shoulder. "We'll do it together, Mom, when you're ready."

Carrie blew out a breath. For the first time in days, she had some color in her cheeks. Having her children here was a real boon for her. Lindsey was glad. She shouldn't have to bear all of this alone.

"Sorry to interrupt, but I need to go," Owen Pullman said. "I have an appointment I have to keep."

"No problem," Mimi Seitler said. She joined their group and handed a hot chocolate to Kim and another to Kyle. "Finish this up for me, will you?"

They both said thank you, looking grateful for the hot beverage.

"We're pretty much done," Mimi said. "Can I dismiss the troops, Carrie?"

"Absolutely," Carrie said. "And thanks for your help."

"Anytime." Mimi lifted the empty pot of chocolate and carried it to her car.

"If it's okay, we'll just finish up and lock up after we leave?" Carrie asked Owen. "We just have a few more boxes to move."

Owen scratched his bald head. "I don't see why not. Just latch the gate once you get all of your cars out of here."

"We will," Carrie said. "Okay, you two, head over to Nancy's. Kyle, I might need your help running an inventory of the boxes. There should be a couple of boxes of rare books, but I haven't had time to look for them."

"I'll be happy to help," he said. "We can make a sweet Excel file that will allow you to tabulate the value of each item."

Carrie raised her eyebrows. "Now that would be handy." She gave her kids each a kiss on the cheek and said, "I'll see you at Nancy's."

"Are you sure—" Kyle began, but Carrie cut him off.

"I'll just be a few minutes. Go before you freeze."

With one more hug, Kyle and Kim got into their car and headed over to Nancy's house.

"I'm going to thank everyone for coming," Carrie said. "Then we can lock up the new shed and I'll give you and Beth a ride home."

"Sounds good," Lindsey said. "Good job, President."

"Thanks." Carrie smiled.

Lindsey watched as Carrie gathered them all together. The group seemed pleased with what they had done. Even Bill had pitched in, and his usually fastidious attire sported dust streaks. It made him seem infinitely less insufferable.

Lindsey wandered down to the old shed. It was essentially a steel room about ten feet high and twenty feet deep and fourteen wide. She glanced up to examine the ceiling. It had been blown wide open. Several sheds on either side had sustained some damage as well, but this one had gotten the worst of it.

When she had spoken to Owen earlier, he had theorized that the hurricane-force winds had found a loose metal panel and ripped it open, dragging the ones around it with it.

But Lindsey remembered what Sully had told her and she had to agree. This didn't look nature-made.

"That storm was really something, wasn't it?"

Lindsey turned to find Edmund Sint standing beside her, surveying the damage.

"It sure was," she said. "I don't think I've ever been as happy as I was when the lights came back on."

"Yeah, I have to agree. Those were two of the longest days of my life."

"I suppose we should be glad the damage wasn't worse," she said. "Then again, if the storm didn't cause this . . ."

Edmund turned to study her. "You don't think the storm did this? Really?"

"Someone mentioned to me that it could actually have been a break-in," she said.

"For books?" he asked and then he laughed. "I love a good read as much as the next guy, but that's extreme."

He made a comical face and Lindsey had to laugh. He was right. Even if this had been done on purpose, surely the person hadn't been trying to break into the Friends' vault. No one even really knew what was in it. There was no inventory. Who would risk it in the middle of a storm, not knowing what they would be getting?

"You're right," she said. "That would be crazy."

Heathcliff pranced up on his big feet, and Edmund squatted down and made a snowball for him. He threw it way out into the drifts and Heathcliff took off after it. As the only light available was coming from the large bank of lights Owen used for security, Lindsey marveled that the puppy could find the snowballs he chased after.

"Edmund, are you ready?" Bill called to his nephew.

He did not acknowledge Lindsey, letting her know he still considered her responsible for his removal from office.

She sighed. Edmund put his hand on her shoulder. "He'll come around. You'll see."

"So long as he's still a member of the Friends and is talking to Carrie, I'm fine," she said. "I can handle a little misdirected anger."

"That must be why you're such a good librarian," Edmund said. He looped her free hand around his elbow and led her back to Carrie. "All of those unhappy taxpayers blaming you when the book they want isn't in must have given you a thick skin."

Lindsey smiled. He certainly understood the life of a public servant. Carrie and Beth met them halfway to their cars.

"I'm just going to check the last few boxes," Carrie said. "I want to make sure they're sealed up tight."

"I'll go with you," Lindsey offered.

"Me, too," said Beth, cradling her own cup of cocoa.

"Thanks for your help, Edmund," Carrie said. "You and Bill were great."

A horn honked and they all glanced up to see Bill sitting in his car, glaring at them. Mimi and the other volunteers returned his glower, but Bill didn't seem to notice.

Edmund sighed. "I'd better go."

The three women waved and trooped down to the new shed. It was dark, but Carrie had brought a flashlight. The boxes were stacked floor to ceiling, with a narrow aisle running down the middle to give access to the books at the back.

"We'll have to schedule a warm day in the spring to do that inventory," Beth said. "It's too cold in these sheds to do much in the winter."

"Maybe we'll get a nice day in the sixties soon," Carrie said. "I'd really like to find those rare books that were donated. It seems a shame that no one remembers what boxes they were in."

"Not even Bill?" Lindsey asked.

"No, he said he couldn't recall," Carrie said. "I didn't press since it was nice of him to come out and help."

Beth and Lindsey exchanged a look. Lindsey didn't voice her doubt aloud, but she couldn't help but feel that Bill probably wouldn't have told Carrie even if he knew. She suspected he could be passive-aggressive like that.

"So, how about those open boxes?" Lindsey asked.

"Right here," Carrie said. "Beth, will you hold the flashlight?"

She handed the flashlight to Beth, who aimed the beam at the top of the box. Lindsey held the lid closed while Carrie fumbled with the roll of box tape. She taped down the lid and they moved on to the next two, with Beth following them with the beam of light.

Once they were done, Carrie pocketed the tape and Beth handed back the flashlight.

"Okay, now where did I put the Master Lock?" Carrie asked as she shone the light across the floor and over the boxes. Lindsey and Beth began to look, too, but there was no sign of it.

"I must have left it on the latch outside," Carrie said. She stepped forward toward the large steel door, but it slammed shut with a clang.

"Whoa, the wind must be picking up," Beth said. "Let's get going before we all freeze to death."

Carrie turned the handle on the inside of the door, but it wouldn't budge. She handed the flashlight back to Lindsey and said, "Could you shine that on the handle?"

Lindsey did and watched as Carrie struggled with the door. The handle would move just a fraction of an inch but wouldn't open.

"I'm getting a bad feeling about this," Beth said.

"Don't panic," Lindsey said. "Here, let me try. You've

had your gloves off, Carrie; maybe your hands are just frozen."

Carrie stepped back and took the flashlight while Lindsey put her muscle into turning the handle on the door. She couldn't get it to unlatch either. She put her shoulder into it, but no luck. The door was stuck.

Lindsey turned to face the others. In the reflected beam of the flashlight, she could see they both looked wide-eyed and worried. She hated to confirm their fears, but there was no getting around it.

"We're locked in," she said.

CHAPTER

22

BRIAR CREEK
PUBLIC LIBRARY

"That can't be," Beth said. She handed Lindsey her cocoa and tried the door herself.

Lindsey watched her struggle, popping out some rather salty language for a children's librarian before she gave up and slumped against the door.

"This cannot be happening," Carrie said. "I don't like enclosed spaces. I don't even use the elevator at work when I can avoid it."

"Maybe if we all try it together, we can open it," Lindsey said.

Lindsey put down Beth's cocoa and the three of them shuffled around the boxes until they each found a spot against the door.

"On three," Lindsey said. "One, two, three!"

With an ear-jarring clang, they all rammed the door at once. It didn't budge.

"Again," Carrie said. She counted off and they did it again.

"I think I felt it move," Beth said. "Come on, one more time."

They tried several more times. In the end, they created quite a racket, but the door remained shut and locked.

Exhausted but warmer from the exertion, they each found a stack of boxes to lean against. To Lindsey, the flashlight beam seemed to be getting dimmer.

"I think we're going to need to conserve that light," she said.

Carrie looked stricken, but she nodded. Lindsey switched off the light and the shed went dark.

"So, any idea how we ended up locked in?" Beth asked.

Her voice had a disembodied quality, probably because Lindsey couldn't see her, that made it creepy coming out of nowhere. Lindsey kept waiting for her eyes to adjust to the darkness, allowing her to make out shapes but, no, it was just relentlessly black.

"I'd blame it on Batty Bilson, but she wasn't here tonight," Lindsey said.

"Unless, she arrived late," Carrie said. "Maybe she was watching from somewhere else and came when everyone else had left."

"Maybe," Lindsey said. She remembered the message on her phone this morning. Batty had said she'd be watching her. Lindsey shivered and not just from the cold. Although, now that she wasn't moving, she could feel the cold closing in on her extremities. Her nose, her fingers and her toes were beginning to stiffen and prickle with pain.

"So, who has a cell phone?" Beth asked brightly. "Mine is in the car."

"Mine, too," Lindsey said.

"Same for me," Carrie said.

Beth sighed.

Lindsey pulled down her glove and pulled up her sleeve. She felt her wrist. Yes, she was wearing her sports watch and it had an indigo light.

"I have a light on my watch," she said. "Hang on."

She had to remove her glove to press the button. When she did, a faint blue glow lit up the storage area.

"It's just after eight o'clock," she said. "It's not too late for someone to come by."

She could see hope flare in both Carrie and Beth's faces. She hoped she wasn't wrong.

A scratching noise sounded at the door and they all jumped. Someone was out there.

"Hello?" Lindsey shouted. "Is anyone out there?"

Beth went to cry out, but Lindsey held up her hand. They were all silent, straining to hear a voice or a footstep or anything that verified that someone had come to their rescue.

Then very softly, Lindsey heard a whimper, followed by a scratching sound, the sort made by claws against metal. Heathcliff!

"Heathcliff, is that you?" she cried.

The whimper turned into a yowl, and his puppy feet pounded frantically against the door.

"Turn on the light!" Lindsey said.

Beth reached over and flicked on the flashlight. Lindsey ran her hands along the bottom edge of the door. Maybe there was a way to pry it or jimmy it open. There was nothing.

She felt a burst of panic at the thought of Heathcliff out there in the cold. He was just a puppy. He couldn't handle being out there indefinitely. He would freeze to death! Lindsey couldn't bear it. Why had she brought him? What had she been thinking?

He continued to whimper and scratch against the door.

It was heartbreaking. Lindsey laid her hand flat against the metal, wishing she could reach through and pick up her boy.

"We have to scare him away," Carrie said. "For his own good."

Lindsey nodded, knowing she was right but not sure if she could do it. She didn't know the puppy's life story, but she suspected it wasn't one full of love and affection.

She felt sick to her stomach as she put on her tough voice. "Heathcliff, go home!"

The scratching stopped but the whimpering continued. Lindsey turned to face the other two women.

"I can't do this," she whispered.

"You have to," Beth said with a bolstering arm about her shoulders. "He might stay out there all night unless you scare him away. It's bad enough we might freeze to death, but he's out *there*. He stands a good chance of being found."

"It's the right thing," Carrie whispered.

"Heathcliff, go!" Lindsey yelled. "Go home, now. Get!"

The whimpering stopped and all was silent. Lindsey held her breath. The lump in her throat burned like a hot coal, but she knew if she cried, Heathcliff would never leave, and she just couldn't bear the thought of anything happening to him.

She stared at her watch; after five minutes, there was still no sound from outside. She hoped he had run away even as it broke her heart to send him.

Beth opened her arms and pulled Lindsey close. She held her tight, and Lindsey choked back the sobs that threatened to overwhelm her. After a moment, she reached out and pulled Carrie into the huddle as well.

The three of them stayed like that for a long time, not speaking. Finally, when the beam started to dim again, Beth shut off the flashlight.

"He'll be all right," Beth said.

Lindsey nodded, but then realizing that Beth couldn't see her in the dark, she said, "I hope so."

"How are you two feeling?" Carrie asked. "Do you have any numbness?"

"No," Lindsey said.

"My feet hurt," Beth said. "I think they are on their way to numb."

"That's not good," Carrie said. "Hypothermia is a sneaky bugger. We're dry and out of the wind, at least, but if either of you start to feel numb or tired, let me know."

"Okay," Lindsey and Beth agreed.

"Let's stay huddled up," Carrie said. "It'll help to combine our heat. Also, be sure to listen to each other speak; slurred speech is another indicator that hypothermia has set in."

"So we need to keep talking?" Beth asked.

"Yes," Carrie said.

They were all silent.

"I have nothing to say," Lindsey said. "Probably I would but now I feel pressured."

Carrie chuckled. "Isn't that always the way?"

They were silent again.

"I can teach you some of my story time finger plays," Beth offered. "How about *Ten Fat Sausages*?"

"That's going to make me hungry," Lindsey said.

"Yeah, maybe one without food," Carrie agreed.

"So, *One Potato, Two Potato* and *Five Fat Peas* are out," Beth said. "Okay, let's try *Here Is a Beehive*. Now make a fist but put your thumb inside."

It was dark, so she could have faked it, but Lindsey did as she was told, hoping it would take her mind off Heathcliff and the cold at least for a moment.

"Now repeat after me," Beth said. "Here is a beehive, but where are the bees?"

Lindsey and Carrie dutifully repeated the words.

"Hiding away where nobody sees," Beth continued and they repeated.

"Watch and you'll see them come out of the hive," Beth said. "Now as you count, release a finger until only your thumb is left."

"One, two, three, four, five . . . buzzzzz!"

Lindsey felt a thumb jab her in the cheek. "Hey, quit that."

"Sorry," Beth said, but Lindsey could hear her laughing. "I usually wear a little bee puppet on my thumb and it always flies into the kids and tickles them."

"Uh-huh." Lindsey grunted. She wasn't positive, but she thought she could hear Carrie laughing, too.

"Come on, let's do it again," Beth said.

So they did. Five more times to be exact. Then Beth got them moving a bit more with *Ten Puppies in the Bed* and *Five Little Monkeys Sitting in a Tree*.

Lindsey had a feeling that Beth had enough finger plays, poems and rhymes in her repertoire to keep them going all night. And she would have bet dollars to donuts that Beth hadn't considered this a life-saving skill back in library school.

Donuts. Why had she thought of donuts? Her stomach grumbled and she had to shake her head to clear it of the image of a ginormous raspberry jelly covered in powdered sugar. She felt a little drool pool in the corner of her mouth and wiped it away with her glove.

"How is everyone doing?" Carrie asked as they took a break. "Any numbness, nausea or disorientation?"

"I'm okay on the first two," Lindsey said, "But given that it's pitch-black in here, my internal compass is a bit wonky."

"Good point," Carrie said. "We'll let that one go unless you start to fall over."

"So, who wants to learn *Five Enormous Dinosaurs*?" Beth asked. "We get to roar," she added as if this was a huge selling point.

"I love you, Beth," Lindsey said with a chuckle. She told herself she wasn't saying it because this night in the shed might turn out really badly, but rather because it occurred to her that she didn't say it enough to her loved ones.

"I love you, too," Beth said. She took a deep breath and began the chant with Lindsey and Carrie repeating her.

They performed it three times, and Lindsey figured if

they ever got out of here, she would be officially certified to perform story times.

"Well, what next?" Beth asked as they paused to catch their breath.

"We could—" Carrie began but Lindsey hushed her.

"Shh, I hear something," she said.

There it was, the distinct sound of a man's voice and a dog's bark.

"There's someone out there!" Beth cried.

As one, they bolted for the door and began to bang on it with their fists. "Help!"

"We're in here!"

"Let us out! Please!"

There was no answer.

CHAPTER

23

BRIAR CREEK
PUBLIC LIBRARY

"Are we suffering from group delirium?" Beth asked Carrie. "I could have sworn I heard something."

The screech of metal sounded and they all jumped back from the door. A terrific bang sounded and the door popped open.

Backlit by the security lights of the storage facility, Sully stood in the doorway, holding a crowbar with Heathcliff at his side.

Heathcliff bolted for Lindsey and wrapped his paws about her leg as if he'd never let her go. She bent down and hefted him into her arms, letting him lick her face while she buried hers in his fur.

"Oh, buddy, you came back," she said. "And you brought help."

As if he understood, Heathcliff barked and licked and wiggled closer against her. Lindsey was afraid she might cry. She had been so worried about him and now he was here and he was okay.

Carrie and Beth hurried out of the shed, leaving Lindsey to follow with Heathcliff.

"How did you find us?" Lindsey asked Sully.

"Heathcliff," he said. "I was driving home from the pier and I saw him on the side of the road. I stopped to pick him up, but he wouldn't get in the truck. He kept barking and dashing down the road, so I followed him."

"And he led you here?" Carrie asked.

"Yep, he ran right to the shed," Sully said. "I had to park and follow him. I heard you banging, and I saw the lock on the door was fastened. I tried to yell to let you know I was there, but you're a noisy bunch."

"You should have heard our dinosaur roar," Lindsey said. The three women laughed at his bewildered look.

"Anyway, I knew something was wrong, so I went back to my truck to get my crowbar and managed to bust the lock off."

"Our hero," Beth said, and she gave him a one-armed hug.

"No, I'm just the muscle," Sully said. "He's your hero."

He reached over with his large hand and gently ruffled Heathcliff's ears. Heathcliff barked and licked his hand as if in agreement. Lindsey couldn't help but laugh.

"Well, let's go get you a nice big, juicy steak," she said to the puppy as she put him down on the ground. "Would you like that? Would you?"

Heathcliff danced on his feet and hurried over to Sully's truck. The door was still ajar and he jumped inside ready to go.

"Well, that settles that," Sully said. "I have a spare padlock in my truck." He fished a lock and a key out of the storage box in the back of his truck. He handed the key to Carrie and said, "I only have the one key."

"That's all right," she said as she pocketed it. "It's probably for the best."

The women watched as Sully closed the door and put the new lock on. They all headed back to the parked vehicles, where Heathcliff still sat in the truck, his tail thumping against the seat.

"Come on, Heathcliff, we're going home with Carrie," Lindsey said as she patted her leg in a gesture for him to come.

Heathcliff stayed where he was and kept wagging.

"It's all right," Sully said. "I'll give you a lift."

"And I'll take Beth home and meet you there," Carrie said.

Lindsey turned to see both Carrie and Beth make shooing motions at her with their hands. They were matchmaking *now*? Seriously?

She shook her head and climbed into Sully's truck, wondering if the cold had caused her friends to suffer some brain damage.

Carrie fired up her car, and she and Beth gave her a grin and a wave as they shot out of the parking lot. Yep, definitely brain damage.

Heathcliff made himself right at home between Lindsey and Sully on the bench seat in the vintage pickup truck.

Lindsey was just happy to feel the heat cranking out of the vent thawing out her toes and fingers.

Sully climbed in and drove them out of the lot, but then stopped to run back and close and lock the gates. She was so grateful she could have cried, because the thought of going back out in the cold was almost more than she could stand.

He climbed back in and rubbed Heathcliff's ears before he put the truck into drive. "This is some dog you've got."

"Yes, he is," Lindsey said, and she wrapped her arms around the puppy, grateful for his warmth. His tail thumped against the seat, and she wondered if he had been as terrified in the book drop as she had been locked in the shed.

"Well, you're never going to have to worry about being thrown away again," she whispered in his ear. "You have found your forever home—with me."

He thumped his tail harder, let out a bark and licked her chin.

"I take it you're keeping him?" Sully asked.

"Yes," she said. "If he'll have me."

"Are you kidding?" He laughed. "That dog is crazy about you."

"Good, because I feel the same way about him."

Sully turned and smiled at her. "Lucky dog."

Lindsey felt the bottom fall out of her stomach, so she turned and looked out the window in a feeble attempt to keep her cool.

It was late. The center of town was quiet. The drifts from the plows had been pushed back to the edges of the road, leaving six-foot tall mounds that lined the road like a wall of white. Lindsey wondered how long it would take for all of it to melt. She hoped it happened soon or she would be walking to work for the next few weeks.

Sully pulled up in front of her house. The car that Kim and Kyle had arrived in was parked out front. While Lindsey held the door for Heathcliff to leap out, Carrie pulled in behind her.

Kim and Kyle and Nancy all came outside. Concern was etched in the worried lines of their faces.

"Mom, what took you so long? We were starting to worry," Kim asked as she reached out to help her mother up the steps.

"Oh, well, we got locked in the shed," she said. "Pretty silly, right?"

"What?" Nancy asked. "Good grief, you could have caught your death. I have some stew in the Crock-Pot. Come in and eat, you, too, Sully."

"Yes, ma'am" he said.

Lindsey picked the meatiest chunks out of her stew and diced them up for Heathcliff. He was wagging so hard while eating that he was making a strong breeze with his tail.

Lindsey then attacked her own bowl. Nancy gave them heaping portions, with a chunk of fresh-baked bread. It was the best food Lindsey had ever eaten.

Neither she nor Carrie spoke while they ate, leaving Sully to tell the tale of how he'd found them. When they finished, Carrie explained that they had been taping up boxes when the door slammed shut.

"And locked?" Kyle asked. "Mom, I don't want to freak you out, but that was no accident. Someone locked you in there on purpose."

Carrie studied her son for a moment and then her daughter. Lindsey could tell she was trying to decide what they could handle. She gave a small nod and then said, "No, I don't think it was an accident."

Kim gasped. "You think someone tried to kill you?"

"No," Carrie said. "But scare us, yes."

"It worked," Lindsey said. "I think they were counting on someone coming back to check on us when we didn't arrive here and we would have been saved, but it all could have gone so very wrong."

She and Carrie both shuddered.

"We need to report this to the police," Sully said. "Chief Daniels will want to know."

"Can we call him in the morning?" Lindsey asked. "Right now I am too tired to think of anything but sleep."

She gathered her bowl and picked up Heathcliff's plate from the floor. Nancy took them from her and said, "No, no dishes for you. Go to bed."

Lindsey would have argued but a yawn stopped her.

"I'll walk you up," Sully said. He picked up Heathcliff in his arms, and the dog let out a big tongue-curling yawn of his own. He snuggled against Sully as they made their way up the stairs.

Two flights of steps had never seemed so long, and Lindsey felt as if her legs were made of lead by the time they reached the top.

Sully took her key and unlocked the door with one hand while still cradling the weary dog with the other. He pushed it open and followed her in. Lindsey switched on the main light, and Sully put Heathcliff down on the sofa. Then he made a cursory sweep of her apartment, checking all of the rooms and the windows. It made Lindsey feel oddly comforted, which she suspected was why he was doing it.

"All clear," he said. He paused in front of her and handed her keys back. He planted a swift kiss against her hair and said, "Sleep well. You're safe now."

He closed the door behind him, and Lindsey immediately missed his presence in her apartment.

"Lindsey!" he called from outside the door, making her jump. "Lock the door behind me."

"Oh, yeah, right," she said. She locked the dead bolt.

"Good night," he called, and she heard him move to the stairs.

"Good night," she answered. "And thanks."

In a few moments, she heard the front door open and shut, and she desperately wished she'd had the nerve to invite him to stay, even if he spent the night on her couch.

But, no, she was home and she was safe and there were other people in the house with her. She'd be fine. She heard a snore come from the direction of the couch and she smiled.

She picked up the sleeping puppy and moved him onto her bed. She was so tired she didn't even bother changing out of her clothes but climbed under the covers grateful for the warmth and softness that immediately enfolded her.

The next day, Lindsey sat staring at the computer monitor in her office. She felt restless today. Her hair was having static fits, so she'd combed it back from her face and styled it in one fat braid hanging down her back.

She had slept like the dead—probably not the best term to think of but accurate nonetheless. When she'd gotten up this morning, she couldn't help but review in her mind who might have been responsible for locking them in the shed, and had it been a warning or had the person really hoped to cause them harm?

The first person who came to mind was Batty Bilson. When Lindsey had left her apartment this morning, Chief Daniels had been at Nancy's questioning Carrie. Lindsey had added her two cents, but she doubted it would give him enough information to do anything.

She did an Internet search until she found the number she needed. She picked up her phone and made a quick call. She got lucky. Clyde Perkins had finished a job in town and was only a few minutes away.

Lindsey left her office and headed out to meet Clyde in the main lobby. At a quick glance, she saw that Ms. Cole was working the front circulation desk and Beth had a gaggle of kids in the children's area. Jessica was working the reference desk, helping a person with the copier.

Lindsey knew Clyde the minute he walked into the building. The tool belt around his middle made it pretty easy to deduce.

"Hi, Mr. Perkins." She greeted him and held out her hand. "I'm Lindsey Norris."

His hand was thick with calluses, but as if to compensate, his grip was gentle.

"Nice to meet you," he said. "Call me Clyde. Everyone does. If you call me Mr. Perkins, I'll be looking over my shoulder for my dad."

"And I'm Lindsey," she said. She supposed she shouldn't make a snap judgment, but she liked Clyde already. She couldn't really imagine him murdering anyone.

"So, what was it you needed done?" he asked.

"I need our book drop changed," she said. "Follow me and I'll show you."

She walked him over to the door that led into the book drop. She opened it and switched on the overhead light. The small room was chilly, as the metal door to the drop allowed the cold winter air into the room and there was no heating vent in there to combat the frigid temperature.

"This is our book drop," she said. She stepped around the thin mattress on the floor to let him see the six-foot by seven-foot room. "The mattress protects the books from damage when they come through this metal door."

Clyde nodded as he took in the little room and the metal slot. "And what is it you're needing done?"

"Well, last week someone put a puppy in the book drop," she said. She couldn't help the scorn that filled her voice. "He could have died from exposure or hunger. We only empty the drop a couple of times a day and we're closed on Sundays."

Clyde frowned. "That's just all-around wrong. That person should go to jail."

"I agree," Lindsey said. "But since I don't know who did it, I think my best defense is to fix the book drop so that it never happens again."

"How is the puppy?" he asked.

"He's doing fine," Lindsey said.

She couldn't help smiling when she thought of Heathcliff's morning antics in the snow. He really enjoyed bounding over the drifts, but he'd invariably land in the middle of one and it would take him a while to erupt out of it like lava out of a volcano.

"I took him to Dr. Rubinski and he got a clean bill of health."

"Good, Tom's the best." Clyde shook his head. "I have a basset hound named Yoyo, and I just, well, I love that dog. I'd be powerfully pissed, pardon my language, if anyone harmed him."

Lindsey nodded in agreement.

"Let me walk around and check it out from the front." He left the small cold room and Lindsey waited. The drop banged open a few moments later and she saw Clyde peeking in at her. Then it shut and he arrived back in the room.

"I can make it smaller," he said. "Big enough to return a couple of books at a time, but not so big that any wise guys will get the idea they can put anything but books in there."

"That would be excellent," Lindsey said. "Can you give me an estimate?"

"I'll have it to you by the end of the week," he said.

"Can I ask you something off the subject?" Lindsey asked. She knew it wasn't fair to ambush him like this, but she just wasn't sure how else she could work *Did you murder Markus Rushton?* into the conversation.

"Shoot," he said. He pulled his tape measure off his belt and began to measure the opening to the existing drop.

"You were recommended to me by Carrie Rushton," she said. She saw him go still at the name, and she hurried ahead so that he didn't cut her off. "You did some work for them?"

"Tiled a bathroom," he said. He began measuring again,

but Lindsey could see the tension in his shoulders. "Nice lady, Mrs. Rushton."

"She is," Lindsey said. "She's the president of our Friends of the Library."

Clyde said nothing, so she tried to sound casual as she continued, "Terrible tragedy to lose her husband like that."

He pulled a pad out of his back pocket and jotted down some numbers. "I suppose that depends upon whether you consider his loss an actual loss."

Lindsey held her breath for a moment. Was he going to say more? What could she say to encourage him? She decided to go for it.

"Do you consider it a loss?"

"Look, me and Mr. Rushton, we didn't get on, as anyone will tell you," he said. "Do I think he should have been shot? Hell, no. But do I think it's a real tragedy? Well, I'm sorry, but I don't. That man was lazy, selfish and mean. Mrs. Rushton is a real nice lady. She deserves better than him."

Lindsey nodded. She couldn't argue the point.

"Is that why you really called me out here? To find out if I'm a murderer?" he asked. He looked over his pad at her. His brown eyes were shrewd, and Lindsey felt a telling heat warm her cheeks.

CHAPTER
24

BRIAR CREEK
PUBLIC LIBRARY

"I really do need the book drop fixed," she said. It sounded lame even to her.

"Uh-huh," he said. Instead of anger, his voice was full of disappointment, which stung much worse than if he'd been angry. "I'll get that estimate to you."

"I'd appreciate that," she said.

He walked around her, but in the doorway, he stopped and turned around.

"For what it's worth, I was working a job out at the cottages, a kitchen remodel, at the time of Rushton's death."

"Oh, I didn't mean to—" she began but he cut her off.

"Yeah, you did."

Lindsey cringed. She was so busted. Her pained expression must have amused him, because he added, "It's all

215

right. Everyone knows me and Rushton were on the outs. The police asked me where I was, too."

"I'm sorry," Lindsey said.

Clyde shrugged as if it were no big deal, but she still felt bad that she had offended him. She watched him head toward his pickup truck. As he drove off, Beth appeared at her elbow.

"What was Clyde Perkins doing here?"

"I'm going to hire him to fix the book drop so that no puppies or any other critters can be shoved in it again."

"Good idea," Beth said.

"I also completely offended him by asking him about Markus Rushton's murder."

"You didn't!" Beth said.

"'Fraid so." Lindsey blew out a breath. "I was just following up on the incident that happened between him and Markus over the bathroom tile."

"How did he take it?" Beth asked.

"I think I hurt his feelings," Lindsey said.

"Seriously?"

"Yep."

"Wow, we need to work on your interrogation skills," Beth said. "You're supposed to get suspects to confess, not wind up feeling guilty that you've offended them."

"Or maybe I just need to mind my own business," Lindsey said with a sigh.

Beth smiled. "Nah, it's not in your nature."

"Clyde likes Dean Koontz, doesn't he?" she asked. "Maybe I can make sure he's first on the list for the next Koontz book to come out."

"I'm sure that would help," Beth said.

"Hey, what do you mean that's not in my nature?" Lindsey asked.

"Oh, there are so many examples to choose from," Beth said, tapping her chin with her forefinger.

Suddenly, Lindsey was not so sure she wanted to hear it. She led the way out of the book drop and closed the door behind them. She walked toward the break room, hoping there was some go juice in the communal coffeepot to get her through the long afternoon. Beth walked beside her, obviously having no intention of going back to the children's area as yet.

Lindsey glanced over at the enchanted island, hoping to see a patron or five needing Beth. There were none. Darn it!

Lindsey lifted the pot out of its holder and looked at the sludge in the bottom of the glass carafe. She poured the thick residue out and began to make a fresh pot.

"Let's see," Beth said. "How about when Tammy Jankowski wasn't going to graduate with us because they said she was a credit short?"

"What was wrong with that?" Lindsey asked.

"You stormed the registrar's office. You threatened to have their job if they didn't own up to their mistake."

"It's not my fault they didn't add up her class credits right," Lindsey said. "They were messing with her future. She had a job lined up, and if she didn't get her diploma on time, she would have been out of a job. They are darn lucky she didn't sue them."

"True, but my point is that you were not exactly minding your own business there."

"Point taken, but Tammy was so painfully shy, she needed someone to give her backup."

"Uh-huh, and then there was the time your boss put in that time clock, and your coworker, what was her name?"

"Gina," Lindsey said with a sigh.

"Gina was always late, so you would punch her card for her," Beth said.

"Hey, she always stayed late to make it up. If she hadn't, I wouldn't have done it for her, but she was a single mom and she needed a break," Lindsey said.

"Yes, but the point is that you are incapable of not helping a person in distress," Beth said. "Especially, if you think a wrong has been done. Look at how you helped me when I was being accused of murder."

Finally, the coffee was ready and Lindsey poured two cups and held one out to Beth.

"Maybe I need therapy," she said.

"Nah, I like you the way you are, flaws and all," Beth said with a wink. She left the break room and Lindsey pondered the beverage in her cup. Was it true? Was she incapable of not helping a person in distress? Or was she just a big buttinsky?

"Knock, knock," a voice called at the door.

Lindsey glanced up to see Edmund Sint standing there.

He was wearing a charcoal gray wool trench coat with his usual plaid cashmere scarf wrapped around his neck. He reminded Lindsey so much of her ex that she had to shake her head to dislodge the image of John from her mind.

"Hi, Edmund," she said. "How are you?"

"Bored to death and looking for a lunch date," he said. "I know it's spur of the moment, but can you get away?"

Lindsey glanced at the clock. It was lunchtime. She

needed to eat. She felt reluctant to go with Edmund, and she knew it was because he did remind her of her ex, which was unfair to him, but also because she knew she had feelings for Sully, and to encourage anyone else just seemed wrong.

"It's just lunch," Edmund said as if he was aware of her internal struggle. "You are allowed to eat, aren't you?"

Lindsey felt caught by his charming smile. He was right. She had to eat. It was only lunch. And besides, it wasn't as if Sully had even asked her out. To pine for him would be ridiculous.

"Sure, I am," she said. "I'll just go get my coat."

She hurried back to her office and took her coat off the rack by the door. She grabbed her purse out of her desk drawer and met Edmund by the door.

"My car is around the corner," he said.

He let her lead the way out of the library and down the walkway to the left. His car was waiting around the corner. It was a steel gray Jaguar with a wood dashboard and leather seats. Very nice.

"Lindsey!" a voice called form the parking lot. "Lindsey, wait!"

Edmund was holding the passenger door open for her, but she turned around and saw Carrie hurrying down the shoveled walk toward her. She had a file folder tucked under one arm, and her son, Kyle, was striding behind her with a grim expression on his face.

"Excuse me for one moment," Lindsey said to Edmund. He nodded as if he understood, and she hurried to meet her friend.

"Carrie, what is it? Is everything okay?"

Carrie was panting, so Kyle leaned around her and said, "No, it isn't. I went over the files for the Friends this morning, and I found some monumental discrepancies. I think someone has been stealing from the Friends of the Library."

CHAPTER

25

BRIAR CREEK
PUBLIC LIBRARY

66 "Hush, Kyle, we don't know anything for certain," Carrie said. She glanced over Lindsey's shoulder, and Lindsey turned and saw Edmund waiting for her by the car. "I'm sorry, Lindsey, it looks as if you had plans. This can wait."

"No, it's all right," Lindsey said. "It was just an off-the-cuff thing. I can reschedule. Go ahead to my office and I'll meet you there."

She turned and hurried back to Edmund.

"I'm so sorry," she began, but he cut her off.

"It's all right. I imagine being in charge of a place like this keeps your schedule constantly shifting and changing. We'll do it another time."

"Thank you," she said.

She hurried back to her office, where she found Kyle

and Carrie waiting for her. Carrie pulled some paperwork out of the folder while she hung up her coat.

"Kim, Kyle and I went out to the shed today to do an inventory," Carrie said.

"In this cold?" Lindsey asked.

"We felt the need to keep busy," Carrie said. She didn't elaborate but Lindsey suspected now that they were all together, the reality of Markus's death was hard to ignore.

"Anyway, Mimi came by with the inventory list of items in storage that I had requested, so it just seemed like a good time to get it done."

"Kim and I were happy to help," Kyle said.

Lindsey sat at her desk. "So, what did you discover?"

"It's what we didn't discover," Carrie said. "We went through every box, but the rare books that are on the list and supposed to be in the warehouse aren't."

"The list includes ten first-edition, signed classics from the William Culpepper collection," Kyle said. "They are said to be worth thousands."

"And they were put in storage like that?" Lindsey felt her archivist's soul shrivel at the thought of the heat of summer, the damp of spring and the cold of winter damaging the fragile books.

"As far as Mimi knows," Carrie said with a frown. "I did call Bill to see if they were kept elsewhere, but he hasn't returned my call."

"What about those boxes you had the night you became president?" Lindsey asked. Carrie looked confused, as if she didn't remember. Then her face cleared. "Oh, yeah, Warren gave me those. He said he didn't want to be entrusted with them anymore. At the time, I didn't think much of it."

"That sounds promising," Kyle said. "Like they're of value."

Lindsey glanced at the clock. "Let's go to the house. Maybe we can resolve this just by looking in those boxes."

Kyle hopped up immediately, but Carrie stayed in her seat, looking pale and nervous.

"I haven't been back since . . ." Her voice trailed off, and she cleared her throat. "That is, shouldn't we wait until Kim can come with us?"

"She's learning to knit with Nancy," Kyle said. "Besides, you know how sensitive she is. We should probably check it out before she goes inside."

Carrie nodded. She took a deep breath and stiffened her spine.

"All right. The police called and told me they were done. I suppose we might as well go and get it over with."

Kyle drove them in Carrie's car, which was good, because with each passing mile, she became even more tense.

He parked in the drive in front of the house. Someone had plowed the drive, but the walkway was matted from the many footprints of the police and the investigators coming and going. They picked their way to the door, avoiding the spots where ice had formed. Carrie took her keys from her son and unlocked the door.

She pushed the door open and they stepped into the foyer. Lindsey flashed back to the last time she had stood here. The house had been warm, the lights were on and Sully had been beside her. Not this time. The house was cold and dark and, frankly, creepy.

Carrie snapped on a light and led the way up the stairs. When she got to the top, she let out a gasp and stepped back. She would have fallen down the steps if Kyle hadn't braced her with a hand at her back.

He looked over her shoulder and then turned to Lindsey and said, "Call the police."

Lindsey peeked around them both and saw what had startled Carrie. The Rushton house had been thoroughly ransacked. No police investigation could have caused this much damage.

In a quick glance, Lindsey took in the scattered papers and open drawers and cabinets. Even the closet she and Sully had put the boxes of books in had been left with its door hanging open and its contents strewn on the floor. Lindsey quickly glanced down and noted that the spot where the boxes had been was empty.

The police arrived within twenty minutes. Not wanting to disturb anything, the three of them waited outside and met Emma and Chief Daniels when they pulled up behind Carrie's car. Chief Daniels's face was grim as Carrie reported what they had seen.

They watched the two officers disappear into the house and Carrie sighed. "I'm beginning to feel as if the drama will never end."

Kyle put his arm around his mom's shoulders and gave her a one-armed hug. Lindsey was glad Carrie had him to support her. As if it wasn't bad enough that her husband had been killed in that house, now it appeared that everything she owned had been looted.

The neighbor in the house on the left came out to see them. Her coat was unbuttoned and she wore gloves but no hat or scarf, so she must have been in a rush to get to them.

She was somewhere in the midst of middle age, with her short hair more gray than brown, and she was sturdy, as if built to withstand what the years had dished out at her.

She hugged both Carrie and Kyle and shook Lindsey's hand. Lindsey had seen her before in the library. Her name was Marcia, and she was a big fan of cozy mysteries and frequently checked out the latest food-related mysteries by Cleo Coyle and Krista Davis.

"What's going on?" she asked Carrie. "Why are you standing out here? You'll catch your death."

"Someone's been in my house," Carrie said. Her voice quavered a bit. "They trashed it."

"Oh, no," Marcia said. "When?"

Kyle and Carrie shrugged. "This is the first time we've been back."

"Have you seen anyone around the house?" Lindsey asked.

"No," Marcia said. "Although . . ."

"What?" Carrie asked. "Anything you noticed might be important."

"Well, it wasn't me. It was Frank," she said. She turned to Lindsey and added, "Frank's my husband. I want to say it was the day before yesterday, but you know it could have been yesterday. This snow storm has really made me lose track of all time. Anyway, Frank was looking out the window and he asked me if you had gotten a new car."

"Me?" Carrie asked.

"That's how I reacted," Marcia said. "I said, 'Oh, sure, her husband was just killed, but, yeah, she's going car shopping.'"

"Why would he think that?" Lindsey asked.

"He said he saw a strange car parked near your house. He said it was a blue sedan."

Carrie and Lindsey exchanged a look. "Did he happen to mention anything else about it?"

"No, just that it was a woman driver, she had long brown hair like yours, and when he waved, the woman waved back. He just assumed it was you."

Carrie and Lindsey exchanged a glance, and Lindsey said, "If she was wearing a heavy coat, it would be hard to see how tiny she is."

"Who?" Kyle and Marcia asked at the same time.

"Marjorie Bilson," Lindsey said. "We have to tell the police."

"But why would Marjorie break into my house?" Carrie asked. "It makes no sense."

"The boxes of books are missing," Lindsey said. "It has to have something to do with that. Maybe she's trying to get you in trouble with the Friends so that they'll reinstate Bill. It's hard to say what goes on in her head."

"We don't know what else is missing yet," Kyle said. "The burglar could have taken more than just the books, making this a straight-up robbery. Everyone in town knows what happened to Dad and that we haven't been in the house. It could have been anyone."

"True," Carrie said. "We'll have to wait until the police let us inside again. Oh, Lindsey, you have to get back to work, don't you?"

Lindsey glanced at the time on her cell phone. She'd been gone almost an hour. "Yes, I'd better get back."

"Kyle can take you," Carrie said.

He looked at his mother with concern, and Marcia said, "It's okay, I'll wait with her."

"Are you sure?" Lindsey asked. "I can walk."

"Don't be silly," Carrie said. "I'll be fine."

Kyle opened the passenger-side door for Lindsey and they headed back to the library. Occupied with their own thoughts, neither of them spoke for a few minutes and then Kyle said, "I don't feel like I ever really knew my father. Now I'll never get the chance."

"I'm sorry," Lindsey said. She wasn't sure what else she could say.

Kyle shook his head. "Don't be. Honestly, he was never really a part of Kim's or my life. He sort of orbited around the three of us but never really participated in the family. Mom did everything from coaching Little League to chaperoning all of our field trips. When I picture my father in my mind, all I see is him in his recliner yelling at us to keep it down because he couldn't hear his program."

Lindsey blew out a breath. She studied the handsome young man beside her and felt sorry—for his father. By being so wrapped up in his own whatever, he had missed knowing this really bright and interesting young man. She couldn't help but think that was terribly sad.

"I suppose it's cold comfort, but you've been given an excellent life lesson by your dad," she said. "You and your sister won't be like that. You won't miss out on the things that matter most."

Kyle parked the car in front of the library and turned to smile at her. "Now I know why my mom likes you so much. You know just what to say."

Lindsey laughed and said, "If only that were true." She

climbed out of the car and added, "Thanks for the ride. Tell your mom to call me if there's anything I can do or if she just wants to talk."

"Will do," Kyle said. With a wave, he headed back down Main Street toward his boyhood home.

Lindsey turned and walked into the library. When the doors slid open, she found Ms. Cole standing at the circulation desk with her arms crossed over her formidable front, glowering at the door.

"Mr. Tupper never took long lunches," she said. Her lips puckered up tight, and Lindsey had to resist the urge to tell the lemon to take an antacid and calm down.

"It started as lunch," Lindsey said. "It turned into a police investigation."

Knowing the lemon would want to know more, Lindsey purposefully strode past her and went into her office, where she shut the door.

Five minutes passed and there was a knock. Without waiting for an invite, Beth opened the door just a crack and peeked in with one eye.

"What happened?" she asked. "Rumors are flying all over the library."

Lindsey waved her in. Beth came in and took the seat across from her. It was only then that Lindsey realized Beth was dressed as a dog, with floppy ears and a long tail, and her nose was painted black.

"Bingo was his name-oh?" she asked.

"Yeah, it never gets old," Beth said. She bobbed her head and her ears flapped against her face.

Lindsey was quite sure that for Beth, it never would. The woman was a walking encyclopedia of finger plays, poems, stretches, songs, rhymes and picture books. The residents of Briar Creek had no idea how lucky they were to have such an advocate for children and reading.

"Now dish," Beth ordered. "I have my afternoon crawlers coming in shortly."

"Carrie and her kids went to the storage unit today and did inventory," she said. "They found some discrepancies."

"How so?" Beth asked.

"Several rare books worth thousands are missing," Lindsey said. "We went out to Carrie's house to see if the missing books were in the boxes we brought to her house on the night her husband was killed, but her house has been ransacked and those boxes are missing."

"No!" Beth's eyes went wide.

"Yes, and Batty Bilson was spotted by a neighbor at the house the day before."

"Do you think she broke in?" Beth asked. "Why would she want those books? She's not even a reader, is she? I mean she only joined the Friends to be near Bill."

"The only thing I can figure is that she stole those books to make it look like Carrie was irresponsible with them in some crazy scheme to make Carrie look bad and get Bill reinstated."

"That's mental," Beth said.

"Yeah, well, we're not dealing with the most rational person in town now, are we?"

"But to break into someone's house," Beth said. "That's serious stuff. And if she is that crazy, then we have to assume that she's the one who shot Markus."

"I know," Lindsey said. "And if that's the case, the murder may be solved."

"What do you think will happen?" Beth asked.

"I think the police have to consider her suspect number one, don't you?"

"Hello, ladies, I couldn't help but overhear," a high-pitched voice said from the door. "Who are we talking about?"

Lindsey felt her heart thump in her chest as she found herself staring into the crazy eyes of Marjorie Bilson.

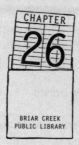

CHAPTER

26

BRIAR CREEK
PUBLIC LIBRARY

"Can I help you?" Lindsey asked. She was pleased to hear that her voice was almost normal.

Marjorie slipped around the edge of the door. The bright pink hat she was wearing had a fluffy pom-pom about the size of her head on top. It was pulled low over her brow as if she were using it to hide behind. Her coat was unbuttoned, but she still wore her scarf and mittens, also in an eye-watering shade of pink.

Lindsey could see Beth sit up straighter, as if bracing herself for the onslaught of crazy. She sat up straighter, too.

Marjorie looked at her out of the corner of her eye and said, "I was just wondering if you had decided to reinstate Bill yet."

"It's not really up to me," Lindsey said. "I work with the Friends, but I'm not a member. It would be a conflict of interest for me to get involved with the leadership of the group."

"That didn't stop you from getting Bill kicked out," Marjorie said through gritted teeth. She was staring at a spot on the wall over Lindsey's shoulder, which was completely unnerving.

Lindsey took a deep breath. "I didn't have anything to do with that."

Marjorie's eyes got wide and focused on Lindsey for the first time, and she snapped, "Liar!"

Beth jumped up from her chair, looking ready to rumble. Lindsey rose from her chair, too, and circled the desk. She'd had it with Marjorie and her weird phone calls, almost getting run over by her in her car and most probably being locked in the shed to freeze by her, too. The fact that she had probably ransacked Carrie's house was just the capper.

"Marjorie, let's have a chat," she said. She gestured for the woman to have Beth's vacated seat. "Beth was just leaving. Let's take this opportunity to clear the air, shall we?"

Marjorie gave her a suspicious look. Lindsey took that to mean she was crazy but perhaps not stupid. Lindsey took Beth's elbow and led her to the door. As she pushed her through, she whispered, "Call the police."

Beth gave her a quick nod and hurried off.

Lindsey left the door open just a crack, in case Marjorie went batty on her, and then took her seat behind her desk.

"Now, I understand that you are unhappy with me," Lindsey said. "What can I do to make things better?"

"Make Bill the president again," Marjorie said.

"The Friends have to make that decision," Lindsey said.

She had a feeling this conversation was going to be as repetitive as a hamster's run on a wheel, and they'd probably get about as far.

"You control the Friends," Marjorie said. "They will do whatever you tell them to. That's why they voted him out to begin with."

"I never told anyone to vote him out," Lindsey said.

"Then why were you at the meeting that night?" she asked. Her gaze fleetingly met Lindsey's before moving to fixate on something behind her head.

"I was at the meeting to bear witness to the fairness of the proceedings," Lindsey said. She did not add that she'd been there mostly to keep Bill from having a hissy fit, because she didn't really think it would help her case with Marjorie even if it was the truth.

"Fair?" Marjorie's voice became shrill, and Lindsey glanced out her office window, hoping to see a police car arriving. Nothing yet.

"Would you like a mint?" she asked. She pulled a canister of mints from her desk drawer and offered it to Marjorie. "They're butter mints; they melt in your mouth."

Marjorie frowned at her, her expression distrustful. "Why are you being nice to me?"

"I'm nice to everyone," Lindsey said.

"Not Bill," Marjorie retorted. She took off one mitten and then opened the canister. Snatching a fistful of mints, she shoved them in her coat pocket as if afraid Lindsey was going to grab the candy back.

She looked like a scared little kid, and Lindsey felt a pang of sympathy for her. Marjorie couldn't help it if she

233

was a few cards short of a full deck . Maybe she just needed some understanding.

"I'm sorry that the Friends vote has been so upsetting for you," Lindsey said. "But you can't go around threatening people and trying to run them over with your car because you don't like the way things turned out."

Marjorie stuffed a mint in her mouth and chewed furiously.

"That sort of behavior doesn't help anything," Lindsey said. She spoke calmly, hoping that maybe she was getting through to Marjorie.

"You know what I think?" Marjorie asked. She swallowed her candy, and her eyes went wide, so wide that Lindsey could see white all around the irises.

"No, Marjorie, what do you think?"

Marjorie jumped from her seat and pointed a bony finger at Lindsey. Then she bellowed in a voice so loud and deep that it sounded like it came from the bowels of hell.

"I think you killed Markus Rushton, that's what I think."

At that moment, the door swung wide and in walked Chief Daniels.

"You had a torrid affair with Markus Rushton," Marjorie continued, still pointing at Lindsey. "You were madly in love with him, but he ended it, and you were devastated, so you shot him and killed him."

The chief looked at Lindsey, who gave him a bemused smile and a finger wave. "Hi."

The chief glanced between them and then shook his head as if to clear it of confusion. Then he looked at Marjorie and said, "Marjorie, I'm going to need you to come to the station."

"Why?" she asked. "She's the one you should be arresting. She's a murderess!"

Chief Daniels stepped forward, and Marjorie started shifting her weight from foot to foot as if gauging how she could run around him and get out the door.

Chief Daniels was not a little man, however, and the odds were unlikely that she'd make it even if her reflexes were faster than his. The man just took up too much space.

"I need to talk to you about what's been happening over the past few days."

"What about her?" Marjorie pointed at Lindsey. "Don't you need to question her?"

Chief Daniels turned his back to Marjorie and looked at Lindsey. He opened his eyes wide, and she figured he was trying to tell her to go with it.

"I've got Officer Plewicki coming to pick up Ms. Norris here."

"So, you know she killed Markus Rushton," Marjorie said. She looked impressed with the chief.

Lindsey opened her mouth to protest, but the chief gave her a look that clearly said *shut up*, so she did. It wasn't easy.

"We have several people we need to question in regards to the murder," he said. "And, of course, I need your statement."

"Oh!" Marjorie's little body went aquiver. "Of course I'll give my statement. I have all kinds of information about everyone, you know."

"That's what I'm counting on," he said.

Lindsey watched as he led Marjorie out of her office and through the library. She exhaled and realized she'd been holding her breath for the past several minutes. There was something in those eyes of Marjorie's that made her skin crawl.

And she wondered, did Marjorie's crazy accusation hold some truth to it? Like maybe Marjorie'd had the affair with Rushton, maybe she was the killer?

Beth appeared at her side with Ann Marie.

"What was that all about?"

"Marjorie seems to think I had a torrid affair with Markus Rushton and killed him because he dumped me," Lindsey said.

"Wow," Ann Marie said. "I wouldn't be too concerned if I were you. She once told me that my boys were the obvious by-product of an alien-on-human experiment gone wrong."

Both Lindsey and Beth looked at her. Ann Marie's boys were known for TPing their teachers' houses and teaching Beth's mechanical parrot dirty words, and last year they hijacked a float in the annual Fourth of July parade so they could sing "The Star-Spangled Banner" with armpit fart accompaniment into the microphone, among other things.

"Well, I'm not saying she's wrong about everything," Ann Marie said and then grinned.

Lindsey chuckled, happy to release the knot of tension that had torqued her from the moment Batty had walked into her office.

The front door to the library slid open and Officer Emma Plewicki walked in. She glanced around the room and headed toward Lindsey.

She was dressed in her usual uniform of dark blue pants and pale shirt. She had on her government-issued fleece-lined coat and a matching hat with earflaps; only someone as pretty as Emma could make that hat look fashionable.

"Hi, Emma," Lindsey said. "Thanks for responding so quickly. You wouldn't believe the crazy talk Marjorie was spewing. She was really beginning to make me nervous."

Emma nodded, then cleared her throat and glanced quickly down at the floor before glancing up to meet Lindsey's gaze with hers. "Ms. Norris, I'm going to need you to come to the station with me."

CHAPTER

27

BRIAR CREEK
PUBLIC LIBRARY

"What?" Lindsey, Ann Marie and Beth asked together. Officer Plewicki leveled them with her best you're-parked-in-a-red-zone-and-I'm-giving-you-a-whopper-of-a-ticket stare. Then she doubled over. Her shoulders were shaking and Lindsey was sure she was having a fit. Then a snort escaped through her nose and Lindsey realized she was laughing.

"Oh, that was just mean," Lindsey said, but she couldn't help but smile, especially as her heart had resumed beating again.

"I got you," Emma said. "I got you good."

Beth and Ann Marie both sagged with relief, and Beth exchanged knuckles with Emma. "Well played, girlfriend."

"Can I hire you to scare my boys with that?" Ann Marie asked and Emma grinned.

"All kidding aside, I really do need you to come to the station," Emma said. "The chief thinks it will encourage Marjorie to talk if she sees you coming in."

"Do I have to wear cuffs?" Lindsey asked.

"No, but if you put up a fight, I'll taze you," Emma said and Lindsey blanched. Then Emma busted up again and said, "I am on a roll today."

Lindsey glanced at the clock. She was beginning to think she was never going to get any work done.

"How long will you need me?"

"Not long," Emma said. "It's just a walk-on part. In through the front door, past the interrogation rooms and out the back door."

"All right, I can do that," Lindsey said. She looked at Beth and Ann Marie. "Back in fifteen."

"Don't get tazed," Beth said with a wave.

As they passed Ms. Cole, the lemon puckered up at the sight of Lindsey leaving. "I was not aware that we were closed already."

"We're not." Lindsey sighed. "I'll be back shortly."

"Mr. Tupper never had police officers escorting him from the building."

Perhaps after the stressful events of the day, she had just reached her breaking point, but for once Lindsey simply could not listen to the effusive worship of her predecessor.

"That's because Mr. Tupper was as boring as day-old bread!" she snapped.

Ms. Cole stood there with her mouth hanging open like the cover of a book with a broken binding, and Lindsey turned and followed Emma out the door with just the tiniest bit of self-satisfied swagger in her step.

* * *

"Those were Italian," Lindsey said.

Heathcliff looked at her from under his bushy eyebrows. Then he lay his head down on his paws, looking pitiful.

Lindsey sighed and tossed the brown flats into the trash. There wasn't a shoemaker alive who could mend the shredded leather.

"Come here," she said. Heathcliff bolted for her and she knelt down and caught him as he wiggled up against her. "I shouldn't have left them out where you could chew them. It was my fault."

He licked her chin as if grateful for her forgiveness with a promise not to do it again. Lindsey didn't doubt his intentions, but she went through her apartment, moving anything that might prove too tempting for his itchy puppy teeth.

She took him out for a walk afterward, and while he was cavorting in the snow in the small front yard, a car pulled up. It was Edmund Sint.

"Don't tell me you actually have an honest to goodness day off," he said.

"It happens twice a week," Lindsey said. "Like clockwork."

"So, how is the wonder dog?" he asked.

"Heathcliff, a wonder dog?" Lindsey repeated as she walked over to stand beside his car.

"Well, he's the talk of the town since he rescued you ladies from that locked shed," he said.

"Oh, yes, that was definitely his shining moment, unlike

this morning's incident with my shoes." Lindsey glanced back at the puppy frolicking in the snow bank.

"Shoes?" Edmund asked.

"Better tasting than Milk-Bones, apparently," she said.

"Well, you have to give him a pass since he saved you from hypothermia," he said. He bent down and clapped his hands and Heathcliff came bounding over.

He sniffed Edmund's gloves and then his shoes. They must not have been on his tasty list, because he trotted over to Lindsey and sat on her feet.

"Was it something I said?" Edmund asked.

"Probably just not his taste in footwear," Lindsey said.

Edmund laughed. "I can live with that."

"Well, I don't think he'll have to be on alert anymore. I doubt if there'll be any more dangerous incidents like the shed now that Marjorie Bilson has been arrested for murder."

"She has?" Edmund asked. "Was she the one who killed Rushton, then?"

"Yes. I got the call this morning," Lindsey said. "Marjorie has been terrorizing Carrie Rushton since she took over for the Friends. The police think she may have let her feelings for your uncle cause her to shoot Markus Rushton in the mistaken belief that if Carrie was arrested for murdering her husband, then Bill would be president again."

"But that's mental," Edmund said.

"Precisely," Lindsey said.

"I mean why wouldn't she just shoot Carrie if she didn't want her to be president?"

"Well, she's not exactly operating at full capacity,"

Lindsey said. "It's hard to imagine what her reasoning might have been. Honestly, it's just all-around sad."

"Well, since you have the day off and there are no murderers lurking about, why don't we have that lunch we had planned on?"

Lindsey tipped her head and looked at Edmund. He was handsome and charming and so very much like her ex that he was comfortingly familiar. But she didn't feel that rush of attraction or interest that she felt when Sully was around. Of course, Sully had yet to invite her to lunch, and she had no idea if he ever would.

"You know, that sounds nice," she said. It wasn't a date. It was just lunch. Besides she'd get to look at the Sint estate, and given that it was the most opulent residence in Briar Creek, she couldn't help but be curious.

Edmund consulted his watch. "We could go now."

Lindsey clipped Heathcliff's leash to his collar. "I'll just take him in and freshen up. Back in a few minutes?"

"Excellent," he said.

Lindsey hurried through the front door and found Nancy in the foyer.

"Is that Edmund Sint?"

"It is," Lindsey said.

"What's he want?"

"He's invited me to lunch at his place," Lindsey said. She went to go up the stairs, but Nancy put her hand on her arm.

"And you're going?" she asked.

"Yes," Lindsey said. She turned to go up the stairs again but Nancy tightened her grip.

"What about Sully?"

Lindsey turned around. "What about him?"

"Well, everyone knows you two like each other. I just assumed . . ."

"Sully hasn't asked me out," Lindsey said. "Edmund has."

"But . . ."

"No buts," Lindsey said. "If Sully wants me, he knows where to find me."

"Sully's nicer," Nancy said.

"Agreed." Lindsey turned and began to go up the stairs, but Nancy slipped Heathcliff's leash out of her hands. "I'll dog sit. He's good company."

"Are you sure?" Lindsey asked. "He has shoe issues, you know."

"Not to worry," Nancy said. "I'm making peanut butter cookies today. They're his favorite."

As if to voice his agreement, Heathcliff barked and wagged.

"Well, thank you, I won't be late. It's just lunch."

"Have fun," Nancy said. "But not too much."

Lindsey smiled as she headed up the stairs. It was obvious who Nancy's favorite was. She had just reached the second-floor landing when Nancy yelled, "Sully's funnier!"

"Agreed," she called down.

At the third-floor landing, she heard Nancy shout, "Sully's more charming!"

"Agreed," she answered, hanging over the banister to be heard.

She was opening her door, when she heard Nancy cry, "Sully's hotter!"

Lindsey felt her face get warm, and she did not bother answering. Instead, she slipped inside her apartment, pretending she hadn't heard Nancy, and closed her door with a click.

Five minutes later, she dashed down the stairs with her hair brushed and fresh mascara on. She had traded her comfy sweatshirt for a royal blue turtleneck sweater over black jeans and felt perfectly respectable for a casual lunch.

Nancy was in her doorway with Heathcliff sitting at her feet. Lindsey stopped to pet her pup and kiss his head.

"Be good," she whispered in his ear. "No chewing."

He thumped his tail and she felt reassured that he would behave.

"Back in two hours," she said. "Tops."

"Sully's—" Nancy began, but Lindsey cut her off.

"I get it," she said. "And I feel the same way, but he hasn't asked me out. So there we are."

Nancy pursed her lips. "Men are stupid."

"Agreed!" Lindsey said. She stepped close and gave Nancy a quick hug. "Not too many cookies. He might get sick."

Nancy waved her out the door, and Lindsey hurried down the shoveled walk to Edmund's car. He held open the door and she slid onto the warm leather seat. He hurried around the car and they started off.

As they turned onto the street, Lindsey felt her eyes widen as they passed Sully's beat-up pickup truck. For just a second, her eyes met Sully's and the world narrowed to just the two of them. Then Edmund hit the gas, and they sped on, leaving Sully behind.

CHAPTER

28

BRIAR CREEK
PUBLIC LIBRARY

Lindsey's mouth went dry. What had Sully been doing there, looking as if he was about to turn into Nancy's drive? Had he been coming to see her?

Oh, no. What could he possibly think of her in Edmund's car? Wait. Why did she care? The man hadn't asked her out. Yes, she liked him, but really, other than a heated moment during the blizzard, what did she have to go on that he liked her?

". . . and then I put on a bird suit and jumped off of the roof, but no matter how hard I flapped, I could not fly."

"Huh?" Lindsey shook her head and focused on Edmund.

"I just wondered if you were listening," he said. "You seemed a million miles away."

"So, you didn't put on a bird suit?" she asked.

"No, I did however mention that Simpson, our domestic staff person, makes a fabulous lobster bisque if that works for you."

"It sounds delicious," she said.

She shook her head. She refused to dwell on Sully or what he thought. This was lunch. No big deal. She blamed Nancy. It was her fault for pointing out how Sully outshined anyone within his vicinity. Very annoying.

The Sint estate sat on an isolated ten-acre section of the bay. Built in the 1800s with railroad money, it had been in the Sint family since Cornelius Sint had it built for his bride Margaret Astor. The winding, gravel drive was framed on both sides by giant copper beech trees. Despite their present lack of leaves, they still had the look of benevolent sentries, monitoring the comings and goings of the estate.

The driveway made a loop around a large and currently dry fountain. Edmund stopped in front of the house. This was the closest Lindsey had ever been to the estate, and she glanced up at the magnificent Roman Renaissance Revival–style mansion, which towered over them in all of its stone glory.

Edmund led her up a few long steps and unlocked one of the two double doors. He pushed open the door and Lindsey felt her breath catch. With the snap of a light switch, a chandelier sparkled overhead. A wide staircase swept up the wall to the right to the floors above. The ornate tile floor drew her forward, and she saw several sets of tall carved doors, which opened into a variety of opulent rooms. She caught glimpses of rich carpets, ornate furniture and masterpieces hanging on the walls.

"It's exquisite," she said.

"Isn't it?" he asked. "Come, let me show you to the parlor and I'll tell Simpson we're here. He's our man Friday and does the cooking and keeps track of what needs doing and when. He's been with Uncle Bill forever."

A fire crackled in the cozy blue room that Edmund showed her. Lindsey let him take her coat and purse and stood by the fire to ward off the day's chill. She wondered if Bill was here and, if so, how he would feel about seeing her here. This had been such a spontaneous plan, she was sure Edmund hadn't forewarned him.

It would be a good opportunity to clear the air. She suspected, however, that Bill was going to be hard to convince that she'd had nothing to do with the Friends' vote. Blaming her seemed to be the balm he was using soothe his bruised ego, and she didn't think he'd give it up willingly.

She held out her hands and let the heat from the fire wash over them. It was only January, but she was good and done with the snow. As far as she was concerned, they could move right into spring.

She glanced up and examined the painting over the fireplace. It was an Impressionistic piece; no, not an actual Monet, but definitely someone of note from that era.

She wondered which of the Sints had been the art collector. She'd only glanced into a few of the rooms they had passed, but she'd seen enough to know that collecting art had been someone's hobby. Given that the pieces were on display and not stored away in some vault, she had to assume that whoever collected didn't just do it for the investment but because they loved art and they loved to have it around them.

She turned her back to the fire and let the heat wash over

her. When she was pretty sure her bones were melting, she moved away, but the chilly air quickly enfolded her in its shivery embrace, and she tried to find the perfect distance from the fire to be warm, but not hot. Four feet seemed ideal.

She studied the room, admiring the powder blue drapes that framed the large windows, which boasted a view of an intricate stone garden below that gave way to a sweeping lawn, now covered in snow, which ended at a private beach on the bay. The Thumb Islands dotted the horizon, and Lindsey could see the town of Briar Creek nestled on the far end of the bay. She could just make out the pier, and she thought instantly of Sully, which made her feel guilty, which was ridiculous. There was nothing to feel guilty about, she assured herself, but somehow she couldn't seem to help it.

"All set," Edmund said. "Simpson is setting another plate for lunch, which should be ready in twenty minutes. While we wait, why don't I give you a tour?"

"That would be fantastic," Lindsey said.

"This is the blue parlor, named for the obvious," he said. He gestured to the ornate furniture upholstered in shades of blue velvet, which rested on a gorgeous Aubusson carpet in shades of navy and gold. "This was my grandmother's favorite room. She liked to sit by the fire and enjoy the view out the window while she worked on her needle-point."

"That sounds like a well-spent afternoon," Lindsey said.

"She made those pillows," Edmund said. "I can still remember her working on them when I was a child."

Lindsey glanced at the throw pillows on the velvet settee in the corner. They had peacocks stitched in minute detail done in brilliant jewel-toned silk thread.

"They're lovely," she said.

"Everything in this house is," Edmund said, and he glanced around appreciatively. "I never understood why my father, well, no matter."

Lindsey glanced at him curiously. "Did you grow up here?"

"No," he said. There was a trace of bitterness in his voice. "My father was disinherited."

Lindsey raised her eyebrows. She waited for him to continue, but he said no more.

"Come on," he said. "There are twenty-eight rooms in all. Let's get going or we'll miss lunch."

Lindsey followed him out of the blue parlor and into a study, a concert hall and a sunroom. The opulence reminded her of the mansions in Newport, Rhode Island. This had probably been a summer getaway for the Sints. Having been brought up in academia and now being a public servant, Lindsey couldn't really wrap her brain around having so much money to spend on a home. It did, however, explain why Bill was such a pompous ass.

They made quick work of the upstairs, touring the vacant bedrooms and peeking into the large marble bathrooms. Lindsey's favorite room by far was the solarium built on the southeast corner of the mansion. It was filled with all sorts of exotic plants and boasted glass walls and a glass ceiling that she imagined was amazing when the stars were out at night.

A bell chimed in the distance, and Edmund led her back to the main hall. "I believe that is Simpson, letting us know that lunch is served."

Walking down the stairs, with her hand running down

the banister, Lindsey felt like she should be in a satin ball gown with a tiara on her head. The thought made her smile.

Edmund caught her expression and grinned at her. "It gets under your skin, doesn't it? The house?"

"It's the stuff of dreams," she said.

"Dreams can come true," he countered. At the bottom of the stairs, he offered her his elbow and Lindsey put her hand on the crook of his arm. He escorted her into a small sunny dining room that looked out over the snow-covered stone garden. Lindsey wished she could see it in the spring. She imagined it was lovely.

There were only two places set, and Edmund helped her into her chair before taking his.

"Bill isn't joining us?" she asked.

Edmund frowned. "He's taking longer than I thought to come around. I'm sorry."

"No, it's all right," Lindsey said. Although, in all honesty, she felt like he was really being a bit of a whiner. "His feelings were hurt. I'm sure it just takes time to get over these things."

"That's very understanding of you," Edmund said. "Especially given that he's always had everything handed to him and has never had to work a day in his life. One could argue that he is bit spoiled."

Simpson came into the room through a swinging door. He had a tray loaded with two salads and a basket of warm French bread. The salad was leafy greens with raspberries and walnuts and a zesty vinaigrette drizzled on top of it.

"Will there be anything else?" he asked.

Edmund glanced at Lindsey and she said, "No, thank you. It looks wonderful."

Simpson gave her a nod and she noticed that a small smile played upon his lips. He wore a blue chef's coat, buttoned up to the throat, and his gray hair was slicked back from his broad forehead, making his features seem sharper than they were.

Recognition suddenly hit Lindsey. She knew Simpson from the library, except everyone there called him by his first name, Harvey. He was partial to spy novels like Ludlum's Jason Bourne series and Le Carré's George Smiley.

She would have liked to have asked him if he'd read any new spy novels lately—the cold snowy days had put her in the mood for a nice espionage thriller—but Edmund dismissed him with a curt nod before she could ask.

Lindsey reached for her glass and clumsily dropped her napkin. Harvey quickly stooped to retrieve it. When he handed it back to her, his gaze met hers and he whispered, "Sully is better read."

Not him, too. Lindsey took her napkin from him and gave him a quelling look. She was beginning to think there was a conspiracy afoot.

"What was that?" Edmund asked him.

"If she would prefer, there is also red," Harvey lied without even fluttering an eyelash as he indicated the bottle of white wine on the table with a wave of his hand.

Lindsey wondered if he learned that from his spy novels or if it was just a survival skill for hired help.

"White is fine," Edmund said and looked at Lindsey. "Yes?"

Harvey disappeared behind the swinging door with a soft swoosh.

Edmund poured them each a glass of French Sauterne,

a dry white wine served cold. Lindsey took a small sip, enjoying its light, delicate flavor.

They spent the rest of the meal talking about Lindsey's time at the Beinecke Rare Book and Manuscript Library at Yale. Lindsey had been an archivist there upon graduating with her library science degree. She had always been fascinated by the preservation aspects of library science. To her delight, she had been lucky enough to work primarily with illuminated manuscripts from the Medieval and Renaissance periods.

Surprisingly, or perhaps not, given the house he lived in, Edmund asked very intelligent questions about the business of rare books. How they were appraised, what constituted a rare book and where one would go to buy rare books if one wanted to invest in them. It was a delightful conversation, and Lindsey felt the part of her that had been an archivist glory in discussing something so dear to her heart.

She had loved her work and still missed it, but budget cuts has forced a reduction in staff, and she had fallen on the last-hired-and-first-fired sword.

They had finished the main course and Harvey had just brought in cream puffs and espresso when the door banged open and there stood Bill, looking almost as deranged as Marjorie Bilson on a bad day.

"What is *she* doing here?" he cried.

"Hello, Bill," Lindsey said. She decided to pretend he wasn't being rude and see if that would calm him down.

He glowered at her and turned to Edmund. "Well?"

"Lindsey is my guest for lunch," he said. "We were hoping you would join us."

"Not likely." Bill scoffed. "I will not be dining with the enemy anytime soon."

This was getting ridiculous.

"Bill, I am not your enemy," she said. "Honestly, I didn't have anything to do with how the Friends voted."

"Huh!" Bill snorted. "She hasn't been near my library, has she?"

"Well, I . . ." Edmund was obviously at a loss in the face of his uncle's ire.

"You let her in there?" he cried. "In my precious sanctuary?"

"I gave her a tour and we just peeked in the door," Edmund said. "I had no idea it would upset you so."

"Did you touch anything?" Bill asked. "Where's your bag? Did she bring a bag?"

"Mr. Sint, may I offer you a refreshment?" Harvey appeared and stood behind Lindsey.

She wondered if this was normally his way or if he was offering her moral support. Either way, she appreciated his calm demeanor in the face of Bill's hysterics.

"Did I ask for a refreshment?" Bill snapped.

"Now, Uncle," Edmund said in a placating manner.

"Don't patronize me," Bill snapped. "I know all about you, little miss library director. You were an archivist at Yale, you love rare books, but you got fired, didn't you? What happened? Were you helping yourself to the goods?"

"What? No!" she protested.

"Even your law professor boyfriend dumped you," Bill continued. He narrowed his eyes in a speculative gaze. "What happened? Was he afraid you were going to go to jail and tarnish his reputation so he dropped you like a bad habit?"

"No! It's none of your business what happened between me and my former fiancé," Lindsey said. "How did you find out about him anyway?"

"I have my sources," Bill said.

"Well, your sources are wrong; I dumped him, after he cheated . . . Well, it really doesn't matter," she said. "The fact is, I was let go from my job due to budget cuts, not fired."

"There," Edmund said. "See? It's all perfectly reasonable. I think you owe Ms. Norris an apology."

"Like hell," Bill snapped. He turned on his heel and strode from the room. "I am going to inventory my library and make sure every single title is exactly where it is supposed to be."

He charged from the room. Edmund and Lindsey exchanged a worried look and followed after him. The man appeared to be having a nervous breakdown. For Lindsey's part, she was particularly irked. He was all but accusing her of theft. She had to tamp down the urge to kick him in the seat of the pants.

They found Bill climbing his rolling ladder. He had begun his inventory on the top shelf and was checking the title of each book. Part of Lindsey was impressed that he knew them all and another part of her was alarmed for the same reason.

"Uncle Bill, come down," Edmund said. "This is ridiculous. Lindsey didn't even step into this room. She's a librarian, for Pete's sake; she's not going to steal your books."

Bill was muttering under his breath, reading the titles as he worked his way across the shelves.

"Bill, if you're accusing me of theft, I'd like you to come down here and do it to my face," said Lindsey.

She could feel herself getting fairly steamed over the whole thing. She had a pretty long fuse, but when her temper blew, it generally took the doors and windows out with it.

She looked at Edmund, who appeared to be getting equally agitated.

He reached over and shook the rolling ladder. "Uncle Bill, come down here now!"

Bill had to clutch the side of the ladder to keep from falling, and Lindsey let out a gasp. With as much dignity as was possible, Bill straightened himself up and glanced at the shelf in front of him. He then reached out and grabbed a dark, brown leather-bound book. He climbed down the ladder with the book in his hand.

"Well, this is curious," Bill said. Gone was his anger and instead his tone sounded bewildered. He tipped his head and looked at Lindsey and then Edmund. All of his panic and hysteria seemed to have evaporated as he studied the book in his hand.

"How so?" Lindsey asked.

"This book isn't mine," he said. "It doesn't belong in my collection."

CHAPTER

29

BRIAR CREEK
PUBLIC LIBRARY

"Obviously, you're mistaken," Edmund said. He went to take the book out of Bill's hands, but Bill moved it out of reach.

"No, I'm not," he said. "I know every single title in this room."

"Where would it have come from?" Lindsey asked. "Maybe you just forgot it."

"I would expect as one archivist to another," he said, his tone quite condescending, "that you of all people would appreciate my knowledge of my own collection."

"May I see the book?" Lindsey asked. "Maybe there's a reasonable explanation."

"No!" Edmund stepped forward and snatched the book out of his uncle's hand.

"Now really, there's no call to be grabby," Bill said. "Bindings are fragile, you know."

"Sorry, but enough is enough, this is just ridiculous," Edmund said. He tucked the book under his arm. "I'll take this book for now and we can discuss it when I get back. Lindsey, I'm sorry but I think it best if we finish our luncheon another day since Uncle Bill is obviously not feeling at his best."

Bill had turned back to the shelves, and Edmund twirled his index finger at his temple and pointed to him. Lindsey nodded. Her presence had definitely made Bill agitated.

She turned and headed toward the door, where Harvey, rather Simpson, stood with her coat and her handbag.

"Thank you," she said.

"No trouble, Miss Lindsey," he said. He then disappeared and returned with Edmund's coat and gloves.

"That will be all, Simpson," Edmund said as he shrugged into his coat. "As you can see, Uncle Bill is quite upset about Ms. Norris's presence. We should all clear out and give him some space. You may take the rest of the day off."

"Very good, sir," Harvey said and left for the kitchen.

While Edmund had a low murmured conversation with his uncle, Lindsey pulled on her coat and moved over by the window to scrounge through her purse for her phone. She wondered who she could call for a ride because she felt Edmund should probably stay here with Bill given the circumstances.

She would have called Beth, but like Lindsey, she didn't have a car. Sully? Awkward. She hit the contacts button and found Nancy's number. She turned away from the men and pressed the button. She wanted to be tactful after all.

"Well, now here's another one!" Bill cried out. "What is going on? I would never shelve Jean-Jacques Rousseau with Oscar Wilde."

"Rousseau?" Lindsey asked. She dropped her phone in her bag and hurried to Bill's side, her call forgotten.

"Yes, look at this," Bill said. He spun around and held it out to her. "It really is an exquisite edition. Look at the embossed fleur-de-lis on the cover."

Lindsey reached out and took the book. "Bill, why do you have this?"

"I don't know," he said and raised his hands as if mystified by the whole thing.

"This was on the inventory list of items that went missing from the Friends' storage shed," she said. "I am sure of it. It fits the description exactly."

"But why would it be here?" Bill asked.

"You didn't offer to keep it for the Friends?" she asked.

"No," Bill said with a shake of his head.

"Then how did it get here?" She and Bill glanced at one another, and then they both looked at Edmund.

Bill's eyebrow went up as he studied his nephew. "Care to explain yourself, Edmund?"

"Surely, you don't think that I—" Edmund broke off as if shocked at the accusation.

"Yes, I do think it's you," Bill said. "Do you think I haven't noticed your sticky-fingered tendencies? I didn't want to believe it of my own brother's son, but the evidence has become overwhelming."

"What evidence?" Edmund protested.

"My grandfather's wooden golf clubs," Bill said. "I know you were planning to sell them."

"I was not. I was merely taking them to be repaired."

"There was nothing wrong with them. How about my grand aunt's Havilland?"

"China? What would I do with some dusty old yellow rose China?"

"A twelve-piece place setting does not go missing from the attic without help."

The two men were nose-to-nose now, and both had grown red in the face with veins throbbing in their necks.

"What makes you think all of this is yours?" Edmund exploded. His shout reverberated around the library, making the crystal knickknacks and porcelain statuettes wobble within their glass case.

"I inherited it all, that's why it is mine," Bill said. He looked as if he was struggling to keep his voice in a quieter decibel than he would have liked.

Lindsey felt like she was caught in the middle of a family squabble with no hope of escaping. Even if she wanted to leave them to it, she had to find out what the Friends' books were doing here, and she had to get them back.

Still, she felt as if she was intruding. "Should I wait outside?"

"You inherited it all," Edmund repeated in a singsong mocking voice. "Why? Because you were the favorite, the Goody Two-shoes, Ivy League–graduating son, while my father was the black sheep, who lived in a commune and was all peace, love and no earthly possessions. So instead of a mansion, I grew up in a hut, eating organic vegetables while my parents smoked pot and sang 'Kumbaya' every night with their idiot friends."

Bill looked at his nephew with sadness in his eyes. "Our

parents were afraid that if they left anything to Eddie, your father, that he would just sell it. That's why they left it all to me."

"It should be mine," Edmund said.

His voice was not the affable one Lindsey had come to know and like, but instead, he sounded petulant and whiny and very, very bitter.

"You are my only heir," Bill said. "It will all be yours one day."

"Yeah, but here's the thing: I'm tired of waiting," Edmund said.

"What is that supposed to mean?" Bill looked affronted.

Lindsey thought he might want to go for scared instead, because judging by the hair standing up on the back of her neck, Marjorie Bilson wasn't the only Briar Creek resident who was touched in the head; so was Edmund.

She started inching her way to the door, hoping that Harvey was still in the vicinity and could show her the way out. She got just to the doorway when Edmund lunged for her, grabbed her arm and yanked her back into the room.

"I'm sorry, it looks like another change of plans," he said.

"You know, it sounds like you two have a lot to work through," Lindsey said. "So, I'll just . . ."

Edmund put the book he'd been holding down. He opened the top drawer of a small vanity table and pulled out a small, but nonetheless lethal-looking handgun.

"I said there's been a change of plan," Edmund said. "It does not include you leaving."

"What is the meaning of this?" Bill asked.

"The meaning is that you die and I inherit," Edmund said. "Isn't it wonderful?"

That shut Bill up. Lindsey glanced down at her handbag and saw the blue glow from her phone. She hadn't disconnected it when she'd dropped it. If Nancy had picked up, she might be able to hear them.

"You stole the rare books from the Friends," she said.

Edmund sighed. "So what?"

"Why? Why would you do that?" Bill asked.

"Duh, for the money," Edmund said. "I happened to be reading your e-mail and saw the one Warren sent you about their value. Except the stupid oaf said they were in the storage shed, which they weren't."

"You broke into the storage shed and then you ransacked the Rushton's house," Lindsey said.

"You have a keen sense of the obvious," Edmund said. Gone was any vestige of charm; instead, he was positively creepy and mean. "Unfortunately, Batty Bilson saw me in the Rushton house. I had to promise to get you to date her, Uncle. She will be devastated at your demise, but it should make things easier for me."

"You told Marjorie that I would date her? You stole the Friends' books? And you hid them here, in *my library*?" Bill asked. He sounded more offended by that than the theft.

"Yeah, it turns out Poe's 'Purloined Letter' was not exactly accurate. Hiding things in plain sight is not always the best spot."

"You killed Markus Rushton," Lindsey said. She wasn't sure what made her say it. She had no evidence. She had no reason to think that it was him except that he was holding a gun and it didn't look unnatural for him to do so.

"Rifle shot through the window," Edmund confirmed.

"Oh, dear Lord," Bill gasped and clutched his chest. "Murder? You committed murder."

"Apparently, I was not the only one with the idea to steal the rare books and sell them," Edmund said. "The night you were jettisoned from office, I stole your key and went out to the storage shed. I figured I'd better get the goods before you were out of office and lost your key. Well, whom did I meet out there but Markus Rushton. He'd heard about the rare books from his wife and planned to take them before she was voted into office, so the blame would land squarely on you, Uncle. Quite a conniving fellow, that Rushton. Of course, we couldn't find them, so we figured we'd have to go back. Neither of us knew at the time that Warren had handed off the books to Mrs. Rushton instead of putting them in storage."

"But why kill him?" Lindsey asked.

"He knew too much, and I had no intention of sharing my profit," Edmund said. He stated it as if it should be obvious. "I went back to his house with him to work out a deal for when we got the books, but instead I just cut him out of the equation. With the Friends meeting in full swing, Carrie wasn't there to hear the gunshot. It was perfect."

"The day we were shoveling snow in front of the library, after the storm . . ." Lindsey's voice trailed off.

"Yeah, I had just come from breaking into the shed; a small explosive device ripped it wide open. Sadly, I found nothing. I was so sure someone must have put the books in there by then, but no. You never even suspected, did you?" He made a silly, mocking face at her, and Lindsey wanted to smack him.

"I can't believe it," Bill said. "My own flesh and blood."

"Yes, but not for long," Edmund said. He glanced at his watch. "I have to say it was really accommodating of you two to have your little tiff in front of Simpson. This is going to be great. We'll drive out to the storage area and make it look like you've had a fight over the books, a tragic fight where you both end up dead. Poetic, don't you think?"

"So, you were the one who locked us in the storage shed?" Lindsey asked. Dread filled her at the thought of being locked in again.

"Oh, heck, no," Edmund said. "That really was Batty Bilson. She is going to mourn you, Uncle. But I expect she'll have time to get over you while doing time for killing Markus Rushton."

"You won't get away with this," Bill said.

"Oh, please," Edmund said. "Spare me the histrionics."

"He's right," Lindsey said. "Too many people know that I had lunch with you today."

Edmund tipped his head and studied her. "Yes, but I fell ill and Bill offered to take you home. I can't imagine why you went to the storage shed."

Lindsey felt her heart thump in her chest.

"You know, I do hate to kill you," he said. "I'm quite fond of you, but you weren't as much help as I had hoped with finding a buyer for the rare books. So, moving on, shall we?"

Edmund gestured with the gun, and Lindsey and Bill moved forward, down the hall and out of the mansion to the waiting car that would drive them to their deaths.

CHAPTER

30

BRIAR CREEK
PUBLIC LIBRARY

Bill drove. Lindsey sat in the passenger seat. What had seemed like such a luxurious car on the ride over now seemed more like an opulent coffin.

She peeked into her handbag. The blue glow of her phone was no more. She had no idea if anyone had heard them or not. When they got to the storage facility, Edmund ordered Lindsey to go and open the gate.

"Don't try to run off," he said. "I'm an excellent marksman. Thanks for those lessons when I was a kid, Uncle Bill."

Lindsey glanced at Bill. He looked like he was about to choke. The bitter winter air hurt her lungs when she took too deep of a breath. The hurt felt good. It reminded her that she was still alive.

She hefted the large metal swing gate and pulled it

open, shuffling her feet as she cupped the end of the gate in her gloved hands. When it was propped open, she went back to the car. The idea of running tempted her, but she knew Edmund meant what he said. He would shoot her, then he would make it look like Bill had done it and then kill Bill. The only chance she and Bill had was to stay together. Maybe they'd get lucky. Maybe Edmund would make a slip. Maybe they could overpower him.

When she climbed back into the car, Bill gave her a wry look. "You should have run."

"I'm not like that," she said.

"I was wrong about you," he said. "I'm sorry."

"Yes, yes, very touching," Edmund said from the back. "Move it forward, Uncle; I'm on a tight schedule."

"You know, there is more to me than being the keeper of the family estate," Bill said to Lindsey. "Did you know I study Kung Fu?"

"I didn't," Lindsey said. "That's actually quite cool."

"Thank you," he said. "And I want someone to know that I have been very discouraging of Ms. Bilson. She reminds me of a little sparrow the way she hops around. Not terribly restful."

Lindsey smiled. "I thought the same thing when I met her."

"Blah, blah, blah," Edmund said. "Is there a point to this drivel?"

"Yes, in fact. I wanted to warn Lindsey that I am a huge fan of action-adventure films and advise her that she might want to fasten her seat belt."

Lindsey saw the manic look in Bill's eye and hurriedly buckled herself in.

"Why would she want to do that?"

"Because of this!" Bill yelled, and he slammed his foot onto the gas.

The Jaguar's rear wheels scrambled for purchase, hit a patch of fresh dirt that had been laid down and lurched forward, picking up speed just as the car hit one of the speed bumps as hard as a fist through glass.

Edmund, who did not have his seat belt on, smacked his head on the roof and let out a violent string of curses, but when he would have righted himself, Bill let out a maniacal laugh of his own and cut the wheel sharply to the left, sending Edmund into the door, face first.

"Oh, my nose!" Edmund dropped his gun and clutched his face as blood spurted forth. "Why you . . ."

But anticipating his move, Bill cut the wheel again in the other direction and Edmund was sent careening into the other door.

Lindsey bent over and reached under the seat trying to find the gun. It was just out of her reach.

"Slam on the brakes!" she yelled.

Bill did and the gun slid into Lindsey's fingers. It was cold and hard and gave her the heebie-jeebies. What if she shot someone by mistake?

Edmund's head appeared between theirs. "Drop it or I shoot him."

Lindsey glanced over her shoulder. He had another gun to Bill's temple. She opened her hand and dropped the gun.

"Get out," Edmund said. "And don't try anything."

Both Lindsey and Bill eased out of their doors. She glanced at him over the roof. "Nice driving."

He shrugged. "A man has dreams."

Edmund had wadded up his plaid scarf and was holding it up to his nose. He waggled the gun at them, indicating that they should walk.

If there was anyone in the storage facility, surely Bill's driving would have brought them forward. The place was as quiet as a cemetery. Lindsey regretted the imagery immediately.

"Walk," he said. "And keep your hands up, so I can see them."

Bill and Lindsey walked side by side. The Friends' new shed was halfway down and around a corner toward the back. As they turned the corner, they were each grabbed and yanked in separate directions.

Lindsey would have cried out, but a hand was clamped over her mouth and a voice said, "Shh. You're safe."

Edmund came around the corner, and Officer Plewicki surged out from an open shed, knocked him to the ground, took his gun and cuffed him all in the time it took Lindsey to inhale.

She turned to see who held her. It was Sully, and she sagged against him with relief. He wrapped his arms about her and held her close. Lindsey could feel herself starting to shake as the hysterics began, but she buried her face against his wool coat and kept breathing until it passed.

"Pretty smart to call Nancy and leave your phone on," Sully said.

"It was an accident," she said.

Chief Daniels joined them, with Bill at his side.

"You had your phone on?" Bill asked her. She nodded and he said, "Well, that was smarter than my driving."

"Your driving was brilliant," Lindsey said. Then she

smiled. Who'd have thought that under his immaculate attire Bill had the heart of a hero?

"That was something," Chief Daniels said and clapped him on the shoulder. "Tell me, have you ever considered a career in law enforcement?"

The rest of the afternoon was spent at the police station. When they arrived, Nancy was there with Heathcliff. As Lindsey wrapped her arms around his wiggly dog body, she realized one of her biggest regrets had she been killed would have been never seeing her dog again.

Sully hunkered down next to her and scratched his head. "He's not the only one who is happy to see you in one piece."

"Thanks," she said.

"So, Edmund turned out to be not all that," he said.

He was glancing at her out of the corner of his eye, and she knew he was trying to gauge her reaction. Well, she had a reaction for him.

"At least Edmund actually asked me out," she said. She rose to her feet and looked down at him. "I like you, Mike Sullivan, there's no question about that. I like that you're well read and funny, when you choose to talk. I like how gentle you are with your big man hands when you pet my dog, and I like the dimples that bracket your grin, which is a stunner. But damn it, I am not going to chase you. If you want to ask me out, you're just going to have to strap on a pair and get it done."

Sully's mouth slid open in surprise and then turned into a grin that outshone the sun.

"Lindsey, we need you back here." Emma entered the main room from the back of the station.

"Not now!" Nancy said. "Can't you see she's busy?"

"Oh, God, did I say all of that out loud?" Lindsey asked, horrified. "Near-death experience, please forget what I just said."

She spun on her heel and hurried around the counter after Emma.

"Not so fast," Sully said. The entire station went quiet as everyone turned toward him. "Lindsey Norris, I like you, too. I like that you're smart and funny and can remember what everyone in town likes to read. I like that you ride a ridiculous bike to work in terrible weather, and I like that your eyes change color with your moods, like the sea reflects the sky. I like that you adopted a puppy who needed you, and I like the way the wind tangles up your hair when you let it loose, and I do like it loose."

Lindsey was riveted, her gaze locked onto Sully's while her breath stalled in her lungs. She could feel everyone watching them, and the heat in her cheeks reached the scorching level of DEFCON five.

"So, will you go out with me?" he asked.

"Yes," she said. It came out breathier than she would have liked, but he seemed fine with that.

"Friday at seven?" he asked.

Unable to speak, she just nodded.

"Are we done now?" Emma asked, but she was grinning.

"Yes, I think so," Lindsey said. With a small wave, she left the main room, with Heathcliff on her heels, and headed back to the interview rooms. As she turned the corner, she saw Nancy give Sully a knuckle bump.

CHAPTER

31

BRIAR CREEK
PUBLIC LIBRARY

66 I found Heathcliff and Catharine's love to be very
unrealistic," Violet said.

It was crafternoon Thursday, and in honor of Lindsey's
new puppy, they had read *Wuthering Heights*.

"Did you?" Nancy asked. "I thought it was powerful,
especially when Catharine declares, 'I am Heathcliff.'"

"But then she marries Linton," Lindsey said. "I found
that very sad, especially for Heathcliff."

"But did they truly love one another or was it more of an
addiction?" Violet asked.

"It seemed to me that they were all disappointed in love
and then intent upon destroying those unfortunate enough
to love them," Beth said. "Very selfish people, really."

"A lot like Edmund Sint and Markus Rushton, if you
ask me," Nancy said.

"How is Carrie doing?" Violet asked.

"Better now that she and the kids can plan Markus's funeral and start to heal," Lindsey said. "Bill Sint was so upset by his nephew's actions that he has even offered to help her keep her house."

"You know, this tragedy has really shined a light on Bill," Nancy said. "Who knew he had so many layers?"

"I suppose it takes a crisis, like how we locals really banded together to get through the storm, to see what a person is made of," Lindsey said.

She, for one, was very glad Bill had turned out to have more going on beneath the starched shirts and perfectly creased pants. He had undoubtedly saved her life.

"How's that scarf coming?" Nancy asked her.

"See for yourself," Lindsey said.

As she pulled her hook through the last stitch on the edging, she couldn't help but feel quite pleased with herself. Five feet long by six inches wide, her mohair-cashmere scarf was finished.

It was a frothy confection, and with its sea foam green color, it looked as if it could have been snatched from an unsuspecting mermaid and washed ashore during a storm.

"Oh, now that turned out just darling," Violet declared.

"You can wear it on your date with Sully," Beth teased her.

Lindsey felt her face get hot. "Aren't we supposed to be discussing *Wuthering Heights*?"

"Not without me," Charlene said as she dashed into the room with Mary right behind her.

They took the last two seats and immediately pulled out their projects. Charlene had a ways to go to be finished with her ripple afghan, but Mary had finished her tea cozy and was now working on a red doggie sweater for Heathcliff.

Violet had brought the food today, and it was a calorie-inducing spread of homemade sticky buns, fruit salad, hot tea and a deli platter. Lindsey folded up her scarf and tucked it into her bag, then she filled up a plate and settled back in her chair. The fire crackled in the room, keeping the January chill at bay. She would have been happy to stay here all day.

"I think Lindsey is just trying to avoid talking about her date with Sully," Nancy said with a twinkle in her eye.

"Tomorrow, isn't it?" Mary asked.

Lindsey took a bite of sticky bun and indicated that she couldn't talk with her mouth full.

"Where is he taking her?" Charlene asked Mary.

Lindsey would have protested this discussion of her personal life, but her mouth was still full.

"I don't know," Mary said. "He's being very close lipped about the whole thing. It's very annoying."

Lindsey swallowed and said, "Did you know that Emily Brontë originally published under the name Ellis Bell and was believed to be a man?"

"There she goes, changing the subject," Beth said with a tsk.

"The subject is supposed to be *Wuthering Heights*, not my personal life," Lindsey said.

"Can we at least talk about what you're going to wear?" Violet asked. "It is a first date, so it's somewhat critical."

"I'll wear my scarf," Lindsey said. "Happy?"

"If that's all you're planning on wearing, I know Sully will be, happy, that is," Mary said.

Lindsey felt her face grow hot. "No, that's not what I meant, oh, you!"

The women were laughing now, and Lindsey couldn't help but laugh, too. She supposed it was a big deal, her first real date since her breakup almost a year ago. She had no idea where Sully was planning to take her, but it didn't matter. She was happy just to spend time with him.

In fact, after escaping Edmund with her life, she was happy just to be here with her friends, sharing good food and a good book, and looking forward to seeing her puppy later. It made her realize that it really was the little things that made life worth living. Okay, that and a hot date.

The Briar Creek Library
Guide to Crafternoons

What is a crafternoon? Well, in Briar Creek it is a meeting between close friends where they discuss a good book, work on a craft and share some tasty food. Here are some ideas for having your own crafternoon.

Start with a good story. Lindsey recommends revisiting the classic *Wuthering Heights* and has included a handy discussion guide in the back of this book.

Share a craft, such as crocheting, where participants can work on their own project at their own pace. See the following pages for the pattern Lindsey used to make the crocheted scarf for her first date with Sully.

Don't forget to bring some scrumptious food, and if you're including pets in your crafternoon, you may want to pack them a snack as well. Recipes for Nancy's peanut but-

ter cookies for people and one for pooches follow the crochet pattern.

Finally, the most important part of crafternoons is to
relax and have fun with people you enjoy!

Readers Guide for
Wuthering Heights
by Emily Brontë

Emily Brontë's only novel, *Wuthering Heights*, is a passionate tale, considered to be one of the greatest literary works of all time. It was published in 1847 under the pen name Ellis Bell with only two hundred and fifty copies printed.

1. *Wuthering Heights* is considered to be one of the greatest love stories ever written. Would you consider it a romance? Must all romances have a happy ending?

2. Catherine loves Heathcliff and Edgar, but her feelings for these men are very different. What is real love? Which of these two men should she have married and why?

3. Vengeance is a powerful motivator in the novel. In fact, it is what drives much of Heathcliff's actions. How is revenge related to love? Are Heathcliff's actions justified? Is Heathcliff a hero or a villain?

4. The setting of the novel is Yorkshire, England. Catherine loves the moors of this landscape. What does this tell us about her character? What do the moors represent in the novel?

5. Social class and class distinction play a pivotal part in the novel. How does the social position of each character affect his/her actions? If Heathcliff and Catherine's places in society were switched, how different would the novel be?

LINDSEY'S CROCHET SCARF

Crochet Hook K (6.5 mm)
100 g baby mohair
100 g cotton cashmere

Work the two yarns together.

ch = chain
sl st = slip stitch
sc = single crochet

ch 2 sp = chain 2 space
dc = double crochet

Beginning row: Ch 18, sc in sixth ch from hook (ch 3, skip 2 ch, sc in third ch). Repeat across until last 2 ch, ch 2, dc in first ch of foundation chain.

Row 1: Ch 5, turn, sc in first ch 3 loop (ch 3, sc in next ch 3 loop). Repeat 3 times, ch 2, dc in first ch of ch 5 loop.

Repeat: Row 1 until scarf is 50 inches long.

Border: Sc all around the scarf to give it a nice edge.

Fringe: If desired, cut 13-inch pieces of both yarns for fringe on each end. Fold the yarn lengths in half and use the crochet hook to pull the folded end through the sc border until a one-inch loop is visible. Then use the hook again to pull the ends of the yarn lengths through the loop, pull tight, making a knot. Trim lengths to make them even.

Recipes

NANCY'S PEANUT BUTTER COOKIES

1 cup unsalted butter
1 cup crunchy peanut butter
1 cup white sugar
1 cup packed brown sugar
2 eggs
2 ½ cups all-purpose flour
1 teaspoon baking powder
1 ½ teaspoons baking soda
½ teaspoon salt

Cream together butter, peanut butter and sugars. Beat in eggs.

In a separate bowl, sift together flour, baking powder, baking soda and salt. Stir into batter. Put batter in refrigerator for 1 hour.

Roll into 1-inch balls and put on baking sheets. Flatten each ball with a fork, making a crisscross pattern. Bake in a preheated 375-degree oven for about 10 minutes or until cookies begin to brown. Do not overbake.

NANCY'S PEANUT BUTTER DOG BISCUITS

3 cups whole-wheat flour
1 cup quick-cooking rolled oats
1 ¼ cups warm water
½ cup natural peanut butter
2 tablespoons vegetable oil

Preheat oven to 350 degrees. In a large bowl, whisk together flour and oats. Stir in water, peanut butter and oil. Knead dough on a lightly floured surface, mixing in more flour as needed until dough is smooth and no longer sticky. Roll out dough to ¼-inch thick. Cut into desired shapes with cookie cutters and place ¾ of an inch apart on an ungreased cookie sheet. Bake 20 minutes. Turn oven off, leaving biscuits in oven until completely cool.

Turn the page for a preview of Jenn McKinlay's
next Library Lover's Mystery . . .

BOOK, LINE, AND SINKER

Coming soon from Berkley Prime Crime!

"**D**aisy Buchanan is an insipid, shallow, soulless woman," Violet La Rue declared. "Jay should have found someone else."

"But he loves her," Nancy Peyton argued.

"Why?" Violet asked. She shuddered. "The woman is a horror."

"She was charming and sophisticated. She was old money," Lindsey Norris said. "She was everything that the new money, like Jay Gatsby, aspired to be."

It was lunchtime on Thursday at the Briar Creek Public Library, where the crafternoon group met every week to work on a craft, eat yummy food and talk about their latest read. Per usual, Violet and Nancy were the first to arrive.

Lindsey was the director of the Briar Creek library, and

this group had been one of her ideas to boost the popularity of the library in town.

"Tom Buchanan was a bully. He thinks of Daisy as a possession not a wife," Nancy said. "She should have run off with Jay Gatsby."

"Yeah, I'm pretty sure I've dated him; well, men just like him at any rate," Beth Stanley said as she waddled into the room.

Beth was the children's librarian, and today she was dressed as a giant green caterpillar, the puffy underbelly of which seriously impeded her ability to walk. Dangling from one arm, she held a large basket of plastic fruit and foodstuffs.

Lindsey lowered the sampler she was attempting to cross-stitch and studied Beth.

"Don't tell me, let me guess," she said. "You read Eric Carle's *The Very Hungry Caterpillar.*"

"What?" asked Mary Murphy as she stepped over the tail end of Beth's costume to enter the room. "I thought we were reading F. Scott Fitzgerald's *The Great Gatsby.*"

"We are," Nancy said. "Beth read the caterpillar book to her story time crowd."

"Oh, phew, you had me worried there," Mary said as she plopped into the chair beside Lindsey.

"Well, you might want to take a gander at some of the picture books," Nancy said. Her look was sly. "You know, if you and Ian ever decide to have some babies."

Mary tossed back her long dark curls and sent Nancy a grin. "My husband is all the baby I can handle at the moment, thank you very much. Although, things seem to be progressing nicely between Lindsey and Sully, so perhaps you'll have some luck there."

"Ouch!" Lindsey jammed her thumb into her mouth before she bled all over her sampler.

"Interesting," Nancy said, giving Lindsey a piercing look.

"Food's here," Charlene La Rue announced as she stepped into the room bearing a tray of mini bagel sandwiches and a carafe of lemonade.

Like her mother, Charlene was a tall, beautiful black woman with warm brown eyes and a smile that lit the room. But while Violet had been a stage actress, Charlene was a local news anchor. Lindsey always marveled that she was able to balance her public life, be an exemplary wife and mother and still make time for their crafternoon Thursdays.

Nancy turned her attention away from Lindsey and tucked her cross-stitch needle into the corner of her canvas cloth. She leaned forward to help herself to the mini bagel sandwiches Charlene was setting out on the table.

"How is Sully?" Violet asked. "I haven't seen him in ages."

Violet and Nancy were not only best friends, they were also tag-team buddies in the information-seeking game. Where one left off, the other stepped in.

"Did you know that *The Great Gatsby* is considered to be one of the great American novels?" Lindsey asked.

"There she goes, changing the subject," Beth said.

She shimmied out of her caterpillar costume and hung it up on the coat rack. The static from the costume made her short spiky black hair stand up on end, and she ran her fingers through it in a futile attempt to tame it. She grabbed her project bag from where she'd tucked it into her fruit basket and took the last remaining seat in the room.

"I am not," Lindsey said. "I'm just keeping us on task. We're supposed to work on a craft while we discuss our latest book, which is . . ."

"*The Great Gatsby*," the rest of the ladies said together.

"We know," Charlene said. "It's just that you've been dating Sully for a few months now, so we're curious. Can we assume it's going well?"

Lindsey glanced at Mary for backup, thinking that since she was Sully's sister, surely she wouldn't want to hear about his love life, but no. She nodded at Lindsey encouragingly. Lindsey just shook her head. Her crafternoon buddies were incorrigible.

"Hey, that's not your Granny's cross-stitch," Beth declared, looking at the cross-stitch hoop in Lindsey's lap. "I love that."

"Well, we did say we were doing 'subversive' cross-stitch," Lindsey said. She glanced at her sampler, which when she was done would read *Books Are My Homies*, with a border of books on bookshelves going around it. She planned to hang it in her office, if she ever stopped stabbing herself in the thumb and bleeding on the darn thing.

"You need a thimble," Violet said. "You're a hazard with that needle."

"I have an extra." Mary reached into her bag and handed one to Lindsey.

"So, what do yours say?" Lindsey asked the group.

"Mine says, 'Bake your own damn cookies!'" Nancy said.

Lindsey laughed. Nancy was not just her crafternoon

buddy, but also her landlord. After sixty-odd years of living in Briar Creek, Nancy had come to be known for her cookie-baking skills, which occasionally annoyed her as she had also become the go-to gal for cookie exchanges.

Violet held up her cross-stitch, and in her best stage voice, she read, "To be or not to be. That is not the question. The question is, what time is lunch?"

Nancy snorted and gave Violet a high-five.

"I went with an old restaurant standby," Mary said. "Kiss my grits."

Mary and her husband, Ian, owned the Blue Anchor Café, the only restaurant in town, which just happened to serve the best clam chowder in New England.

"Love it," Beth said. "Hang it by the cash register."

"Mine is going in our master bathroom," Charlene said. She held up a pretty cross-stitch with a half-finished border of red swirls. It read, *Cap on. Seat down. Or else.*

Mary cracked up and said, "If I pay you, will you make me one just like it?"

Lastly, Beth held up hers. It, too, had a pretty pink border and in the middle, it read, *#@&$!!*

"Oh, no you didn't!" Charlene said with a delighted giggle.

"Yes, I did," Beth said. "I wanted to drop in some really rough language, but I thought this was pithier and more imaginative."

"I think Fitzgerald would approve," Nancy said. "I do love his way with words. My favorite line was when Nick Carraway meets Gatsby for the first time and thinks: 'He smiled understandingly—much more than understandingly. It was one of those rare smiles with a quality of eternal reassurance in it, that you may come across four or five times in life.'"

"That makes me want to date Jay Gatsby," Beth joked.

"Which brings us to the biggest question in the book: Do you think Daisy was guilty of driving the car that struck Myrtle, and Jay took the blame or no?" Mary asked.

A knock on the door frame interrupted and prevented anyone from answering. Lindsey turned in her seat to see Charlie Peyton, her downstairs neighbor who was also Nancy's nephew, standing in the doorway.

"Hello, ladies," he said. "Sorry to interrupt."

"Hi, Charlie," they all greeted him.

"Is everything all right?" Nancy asked.

"Well." He put a hand on the back of his neck. "It's Heathcliff."

"What's wrong?" Lindsey asked as she rose from her seat.

"Oh, he's fine but . . ." Charlie began but was interrupted when a black fur ball raced through his legs and launched himself at Lindsey.

Lindsey fell back into her chair with an *oomph* as her dog, Heathcliff, began to lick every part of her face he could reach.

"Hey, there fella." She laughed and scratched his head. He wagged in delight and then jumped off her lap to greet the rest of the crafternooners.

"I'm sorry, Lindsey," Charlie said. "But I got a call for a job interview, and I didn't want to leave him alone in the house, you know, with his chewing issues and all."

"No, it's fine," she said. She glanced at her watch. She used her lunch hour for crafternoons and her time wasn't up yet. "I have enough time to take him for a walk on the beach before I bring him home."

"I can take him home," Nancy said. "I have no plans for this afternoon. But, Charlie, what job interview do you have? Are you not working for Sully anymore?"

Charlie worked for Mike Sullivan, known to everyone as Sully, who owned a tour-boat company that gave tourists rides around the storied Thumb Islands off the shore of Briar Creek. He was the same Sully who Lindsey had been dating for the past several months.

"No, I'll still help out Sully," Charlie said. "But this is a once-in-a-lifetime opportunity."

"Sort of like that tour your band went on last winter?" Nancy asked. "You know the one that was supposed to make you famous but ended up breaking up the band?"

"Life on the road is tough," Charlie said. "And, no, this is way more solid than that."

His flipped back his long stringy hair, and Lindsey saw that he had increased the gauges in his earlobes to their next level, giving him even bigger holes. Charlie was very into body art.

"What's the job, then?" Violet asked, looking as dubious as Nancy.

"Treasure hunting," Charlie said. "I've been hired to help find Captain Kidd's treasure."

What is the only word in the English
language that ends in -*mt*?

BOOKS CAN BE
DECEIVING

-A Library Lover's Mystery-

JENN MCKINLAY

Answering tricky reference questions like this one
is more than enough excitement for recently single
librarian Lindsey Norris. That is, until someone in
her cozy new hometown of Briar Creek, Connecticut, commits murder, and the most pressing question is whodunit . . .

"A sparkling setting, lovely characters, books, knitting,
and chowder . . . What more could any reader ask?"

—Lorna Barrett, *New York Times* bestselling author

facebook.com/TheCrimeSceneBooks
penguin.com
jennmckinlay.com